AN UNHOLY
UNION

PETER RALPH

ISBN: 978-0-6480514-5-9

Typesetting and layout by WorkingType Design

BOOK 1

LUKE 1978

Chapter 1

Englewood wasn't a suburb where the residents strolled around enjoying the night air, but it held no fears for me. As I trudged along South Ellis Avenue through heavy snow, a blue and white pulled up beside me, and one of Chicago's finest rolled down his window and shone a flashlight in my eyes. "What ye doin', lad?"

I squinted, put my hand to my eyes, and caught a glimpse of a ruddy face and a huge gray mustache. "Is that you, Officer O'Flaherty?"

"Aye. I didnae recognize ye, Luke, me lad. Each time I see ye, you've grown a foot. What are ye now, six-one?"

"I dunno."

The big cop sniffed.

"Ye didnae answer me. What ye doin'?" O'Flaherty said, before turning to his partner. "Ya wouldnae believe it, eh? He's just turned thirteen. Have a look at them shoulders. He could pass for eighteen. I know his da, Harry Cramer. A good man, so he is."

"I'm on my way home."

"Yeah, but what ye been doing? I hear ye've been running with them Taipans. Is that true, lad? I hope not because I don't want to be the one who takes yer da to the morgue to identify yer body, or sits in court and watches ye get put away for life for killin' someone. He don't deserve that, so. Ye may not know it, but he sacrificed his life to bring ye up after yer ma took off with that vacuum-cleaner salesman."

"Just hangin' around with the guys. I don't run with no gangs," I lied, the steam from my breath seeming to freeze in front of me.

"Yeah, yeah," O'Flaherty sighed. "Look at ye. Curly black hair, sculpted cheekbones, and an aquiline nose. The face of a girl on the body of a man. If it's not yer fists that get you into trouble, it'll be yer pecker."

"Can I go, Officer O'Flaherty?" I asked, rubbing my hands together. "It's freezing."

"Yeah, piss off now," O'Flaherty said and hit the accelerator.

I watched until I could no longer see the tail lights of the blue and white, then headed for the mob's headquarters in The Latin Club on Maryland Avenue.

O'Flaherty hadn't had to tell me about the old man's sacrifices. I knew the poor bastard toiled under hot and oppressive conditions, for Chicago Iron & Steel, to put a roof over our heads and food on the table. He was a staunch unionist and always ranting about the unfairness of the fat-cat bosses. *We're living in a two-bedroom hovel in Chatham eating yesterday's bread, and the bosses are driving Lincolns and drinking champagne. I dunno what I'm gonna do for a job, but I sure as hell ain't gonna be a unionist steelworker!* I thought but I never said anything.

As early as I could remember, I wasn't a fan of teachers and classes, but by the time I got to Chicago's Werner High School, I flat-out hated them. I was only interested in making money and soon found I could earn as much as the old man by making deliveries for the mob. I had made my last delivery only minutes before O'Flaherty interrogated me. I didn't know who Columbus and Washington were, but I could recite Al Capone's life story right up until the day he died from syphilis. I also knew everything there was to know about Chicago's worst serial killer, John Wayne Gacy. I could understand Capone. I couldn't understand Gacy and hoped someone would put a bullet in his head.

Two years later, the odds were strongly in favor of O'Flaherty's predictions coming true. I was drinking heavily, partying, and going out with girls years older than me. I rarely attended school and often came home with a bloodied and swollen face, but more frequently with bruised fists and grazed knuckles. In the rare instances that I lost a fight, I invariably won the rematch.

The Taipans got their cash from breaking into shops, stealing cars, shoplifting, providing protection, accosting and robbing old folks on the street, and running errands for the mob. There wasn't much I wouldn't do, but much to the chagrin of the other gang members, I drew the line at mugging and stealing from the elderly. The violence was gratis and usually arose because of territorial disputes with other gangs. My closest buddy, Joe Ratsch, better known as Ratsy, was only five-foot four. His ribs showed through his T-shirt, but he had been born with a chip on his shoulder and an uncontrollable violent streak. He was a fiercely loyal friend and had the two main qualities the mob looked for in those who made deliveries – he was street smart and fast. It didn't take long before we were promoted to making collections which paid double the rate of just making deliveries.

The old man watched in frustration as I went from bad to worse. In despair, he threatened to pull me out of school and get me a job at the steelworks. Then, in my last year at school, an amazing transformation took place. The boy who hated school suddenly started arriving on time and never missing a day. Her name was Kiara Gonzalez, and she was the new girl at Werner High – a petite, stunning brunette, with olive skin, a button nose, and a dazzling smile that melted my heart the minute I laid eyes on her.

Like me, Kiara came from a broken home, but her circumstances were worse. Her father, a bully and a violent drunk, had regularly bashed her mother. Kiara, her two siblings, and their mother had fled Puerto Rico in the middle of the night for cold and windy Chicago with virtually only the clothes on their backs. In some ways, we were opposites. Kiara loved school and excelled academically, and, while my attendance improved, my results didn't. Were it not for Kiara, I wouldn't have attended at all. Soon we were inseparable, drawn even closer by the similarity of our backgrounds. I had no interest in college, and when the old man again suggested getting a job at the steelworks, I nearly puked. "Jeez, I don't want to work in some stinking, hot factory. I want to be outdoors."

"There are no surf beaches in Chicago," the old man sarcastically replied. "What do you have in mind?"

"Vaughan Constructions is always looking for workers. I'll get a job with them."

"You want to be a construction laborer?" He sighed. "Your back will be shot to pieces by the time you're thirty. No one will employ you then. It's a dead-end job, and do you really want to work outdoors when it's snowing in Chicago?"

Dead-end job, I thought. *What do you think working in a steel mill is?* "I won't be a laborer, but, if I am, it won't be for long."

"What, you're gonna start as CEO?" The old man laughed. "They'll start you off getting the lunches, sweeping out site offices, and getting rid of the trash. You'd be better off working for a small homebuilder. At least, you'd learn something, and we both know learning's not your strong suit."

"Oh, I'll learn. I'll learn how to build skyscrapers, not piddling little suburban shacks."

"You have big ideas, son, but it's a hard world out there, and no one does nothing for nothing. At least, if it doesn't work out, I can get you a job at the steelworks."

"I'll never work in that hellhole. Never!"

At the end of the year, Kiara started college, and I got a job with Vaughan Constructions pouring foundations on its Wells Fargo Office Tower site. After being told that it was compulsory to join the Builders Laborers Union, I met the union representative on my first day and signed up. The supervisors were quick to utilize my strength, and the work was physically demanding and tough. Despite the union's presence, the wages were lousy, but I wasn't worried; I was supplementing my income by continuing to run errands for the mob at night. I was surprised to frequently see wise guys from the club on site talking to the union representatives and bosses. I had no idea what they were doing and kept my head down. If they recognized me, they didn't let on.

While I had shown no interest in school, I was like a sponge on site, soaking up everything I could. In the rare times I was in the site office, I'd try to steal a look at the plans and drawings, particularly for the concreting and formwork which I was becoming more familiar with every day. Three months into the job, one of the senior supervisors pulled me aside. "You're a bloody fool lifting beams and steel reinforcing. No one's gonna look after you when you get hurt. What are you trying to prove? That you're the strongest guy on site?"

I enjoyed showing off my strength and didn't like what I was hearing. "I'm just doin' my job. I'm not gonna get hurt, but if I do, the union will make sure I'm looked after."

"Jesus, kid, you're so wet behind the ears they're dripping. Haven't you seen those musclebound thugs dressed in black? They work for the mob. The mob controls the union, and they couldn't give a shit about you. They control the bosses, the contractors, subcontractors, the pension funds, and they get a cut from everyone. If you get injured, do you really think they're gonna help you?"

"I don't plan on getting injured."

"I hope you don't," the supervisor said, "because if you do, you'll find the mob also controls health and safety and the workers' compensation insurer. Here's the rub. The bosses pay them to make problems with injured workers go away, and if you get hurt, they're not gonna rock the boat to help you. Tell me, what do you want to do with your life? I might be able to point you in the right direction."

"I want to build buildings like this."

"You want to be a project manager?" The supervisor laughed. "Jesus, don't you know you have to have a college education? You'd be better off aspiring to be a supervisor. I earn a good living, and the company pays my health benefits."

"I don't want to be a project manager. I want to learn everything there is to know about building skyscrapers. I want to be Vaughan."

The supervisor grinned and slowly shook his head. "Vaughan Constructions has been around for seventy years. You don't just become Vaughan overnight, and you need a lot more than just knowing how to build. You need money, and you need contacts - contacts in government, the councils, the mob, and the unions for starters. Lower your sights, or you're going to end up being very disillusioned."

"I'll settle for learning how to build. Once I know how, the rest will be easy."

"You have big aspirations. If you're not going to go to college, you better enroll in night school."

"I'll learn on the job."

"Kid, they'll have you laboring on foundations, formwork, and concrete for years. You're young, and you've shown them how strong you are. They're gonna make sure they use every ounce of your strength. You're not gonna learn anything. If you want to learn how to build, go to Vegas."

"Why?" I asked, scratching my head.

"They build high-rises faster than anywhere else in the world," the wizened supervisor replied. "They work six days a week, sometimes twelve hours a day, and Sundays, if necessary. They're always looking for labor, and you can learn a lot in a compressed time frame. You can also make a heap of money."

"Thanks for the advice, but I'll find a way here. I like Chicago."

With Kiara and the job, I had less time for the Taipans. I gradually drifted away but never lost contact with Ratsy, and we continued to run errands for the mob. The money was good, and there were never any hassles. That was, until the afternoon I delivered a sealed brown paper bag to a druggie living in an apartment on Yale Avenue. It was one of the times that I had been told to make sure I received an envelope before handing over the bag. Fifty bucks for less than an hour's work was easy money, and I deposited the envelope at the club and headed home well satisfied. That night, I left home at seven o'clock to take Kiara to the movies. I was about fifty yards along the street when two wise guys from the club jumped out of a black limousine and threw me into the back. "What's this about?" I shouted.

"The boss doesn't like getting shafted," one of the wise guys replied.

"I don't know what you're talking about."

"Tell it to the boss," the other thug said.

"Where are we going?"

"The club. Now shut up."

Chapter 2

I was bundled out of the car and shoved up a set of stairs at the rear of the club and into a windowless office on the second floor. I had never met the man sitting behind the desk, Vince Sordi, but I knew who he was. I'd seen or knew the other six men hovering around by first name. Sitting immediately in front of Sordi was the pimply-faced druggie who pointed at me and shouted, "That's him. I gave him the money. He stole your money."

"I don't know what he's talking about," I said, addressing Sordi. "I gave Bruno the envelope. I never opened it. I never looked inside."

"Liar!" the druggie screamed. "Liar!"

"Shut up, Lenny," Sordi growled. "Kid, there was meant to be five gorillas in the envelope, but, instead, it was filled with newspaper cut to the size of bills. If ya have my money, I'm gonna give ya the chance to fess up and hand it back. Yar young and naive so, if ya give it back, I'll let ya walk."

"I never took your money, Mr. Sordi. I'm not stupid."

"Lying bastard," Lenny sniffled, dribble running down his chin.

"What am I to do?" Sordi said, getting up and rolling up his sleeves to reveal a pair of meaty forearms. "One of ya is lying, but which one?"

As Sordi was talking, two other men entered the room, and one whispered something to Sordi. A grim smile crossed the mob boss's face, and he reached behind the desk and picked up a baseball bat. "Lenny, Lenny," he continued, "ya really are a dumbass, aren't ya? Ya know what my boys found in yar trash bin? Cut-up newspapers. Ya tried to scam me and then pin it on the kid."

Lenny tried to stand, and slime ran from his bloodshot yellow eyes, but two of the wise guys shoved him back in the chair. "I-I was short. I need-needed time. I-I-I'll get-get you your money."

"Too late, Lenny. If I let ya go, all the bums in Chicago will think they have a free pass to steal from me. That ain't ever gonna happen,"

Sordi said, swinging the baseball bat back and forth. "Gag him and tie him to the chair."

As Sordi came from behind the desk, Lenny writhed against the bindings, and his head jiggled as if on a swivel. Then I smelled shit and saw urine running down his leg. One of the wise guys grabbed me and pushed me up against the wall behind Sordi. The first blow killed Lenny, the second splattered blood and brains all over the room, and the third completely destroyed his face. Sordi slowly rolled down his sleeves and grabbed my arm. "Hey, ya have balls, kid, yar not even trembling. I just wanna let ya know that everything I said to ya was bullshit. I don't care how young ya are – if ya'd stolen from me, ya'd be where Lenny is now. Does that tell ya anything?"

"To be honest, Mr. Sordi."

Sordi laughed. "That's not what I meant. Nah, ya don't have to be honest, but ya do have to be honest with me. I would've killed ya because it's all these schmucks understand. Let's step out into the corridor, and I'll tell ya why."

"Sure," I said, as Sordi pushed me out of the office.

"If I'd let ya go, they would have thought old Vince was getting soft, and then it would've only been a matter of time before one of them tried to take my place. Fact is, they know what they can expect if they cross me. They think I'm a lunatic, and that's why they live in fear of me. That's why I'm the boss. I learned it from watching a world title fight. Yar too young to remember, but no one gave Ali a chance when he fought Liston. Then Ali fronted up at the press conference – his eyes were rolling; he was screaming, all but frothing at the mouth; and he wanted to fight Liston there and then. Liston couldn't conceal the fear in his eyes when he looked at Ali carrying on like he'd just been released from the loony bin. It was an act, but Ali knew the value of fear. There is no other motivator like fear - not carrots, not sugar, not money, not diamonds. Ya know the only reason those bums in there will never turn on me? Fear. Don't ever forget it."

"Yes, Mr. Sordi."

"Good," Sordi said, grabbing my cheek and pressing $200 into my hand. "That's for ya time, kid. I've heard only good things about ya on the Wells Fargo site. I'm glad I didn't have to whack ya. I'm gonna be keeping me eye on ya. Now get outta here."

As I went down the stairs, I heard Sordi say, "Get rid of that bum's body and the baseball bat. Oh, and pick me up a new bat. That made me hungry. I'm gonna have something to eat."

It was the first killing I had witnessed, but it wouldn't be the last. I felt nothing for Lenny. The druggie's lies may well have gotten me killed. I might not have trembled or wet my pants, but I was scared and confused. The old supervisor had told me that the mob controlled Vaughan and the Wells Fargo site, but I hadn't believed him. Did the mob really control the union? The thought of Sordi keeping an eye on me was unnerving, but there was nothing I could do about it.

Six months later, two events changed my life. The mayor appointed a new superintendent to head up the Chicago P.D., and he immediately cracked down on organized crime. The mob's messengers were no longer a protected species. The police who'd been getting freebies at the mob's brothels and taking bribes were replaced with clean cops. I'd never opened a bag or envelope, but I was no fool and knew they contained heroin, cocaine, ice, or some other drug. Now the cops were prosecuting the messengers for drug running, and more than a dozen had been tried and sent to prison. Ratsy and I weren't all that concerned at first. We knew every alley and shortcut in Chicago, and we were confident we could outrun and outsmart the cops.

The first cracks in my confidence came when Ratsy told me that he had jumped a steel, mesh fence at the end of an alley, only to find the police waiting on the other side. If there hadn't been a down pipe affixed to the side of the adjoining old eight-story building, Ratsy would have almost certainly been caught. He had scaled the down pipe to the roof and made good his escape by leaping across the sixteen-foot alley to another building. On the plus side, the mob more than doubled its payments, and Ratsy and I were in great demand. I enjoyed the cash, but the thought of doing three years in Chicago's notorious Falconhenge Prison was always in the back of my mind, something I'd never worried about before.

The second event was more personal. At just seventeen, Kiara was pregnant. When she told me, she was apprehensive about what my attitude might be. She need not have worried. I was overjoyed and immediately proposed. However, the old man didn't like the idea of his son marrying a Latino and, worse, a Catholic. "Tell the berry picker to abort the greaser," he shouted at me. "Get rid of it, or get out."

I knew that with my job at Vaughan, the small nest egg I had saved, and the errands that I ran for the mob, I had enough to support my family. However, just as the old supervisor had warned, all I was doing at Vaughan was heavy work and learning nothing. Worse, if the police caught me delivering drugs, who would look after Kiara and our baby when I was in prison? The solution was a fresh start, but I didn't know whether Kiara would go for it.

Kiara told me that her mother was no more supportive than my father. "Stupid damn puta fucking that gringo pendejo," she'd screamed. "I can't afford to support your bastardo."

When I suggested that I buy an old car, and we elope to Las Vegas, Kiara jumped at the idea, even though it would be another ten weeks before she turned eighteen, allowing us to marry.

Chapter 3

The only person I let know what I was doing was Ratsy, and we agreed to stay in touch, no matter what the future held.

Four days later, Nevada greeted Kiara and me with shimmering roads and a hundred-degree day – something we'd soon discover was the norm. We rented a cheap motel room on the Strip, and I went to an employment agency looking for a job. The agency quickly found me a laborer's position on the outskirts of Vegas where a huge warehouse was being built. They also promised that they'd find me work on the strip in six months when construction of The Tuscan Casino commenced.

I wasn't surprised when the warehouse site boss told me that I had to join the Laborers Local 620. I was desperate for a job and wasn't about to argue about union dues of $20 a month. Two days later, I heard a similar conversation, but this time the job seeker, who was in his early forties, screamed about Nevada being a *right-to-work* state, and that a job couldn't be withheld from him because he wouldn't join the union.

The site boss didn't bat an eyelid when he said, "You're not qualified or suitable for the position on offer," and the disgruntled applicant was frog-marched off the site. I didn't know what right-to-work meant, and I wasn't rushing to find out. I had a job, and the know-it-all was out the gate on his ass.

The warehouse was little more than a gigantic steel shed on a concrete slab with an office at the front. My job was to help pour the slab, erect the steelwork, and attach the cladding. I didn't learn much, but the money was good, and I worked ten hours a day and some Saturdays.

We rented a three-bedroom air-conditioned house just outside of Vegas. We liked the heat, dryness, and excitement of the desert city. We went to the occasional show on the Strip but were careful with our spending, not wanting to be caught short when it came time to provide for our baby. Standing at the front of The Parisienne where

Brad Spencer was playing, I put my arm around Kiara and promised, "One day we'll be seated at the best table in the place."

I developed a muscular sun-bronzed body, and my hard work didn't go unnoticed. As the warehouse neared completion, the subcontractor who had tiled the offices and amenities offered me a job. I declined, saying that I didn't know how to tile and that I'd already been promised work on The Tuscan. "We'll teach you, kid," the tiler said. "You're bright, and you're a hard worker. It won't take long. Besides, you're just gonna be exploited for your strength on The Tuscan. You'll be pouring concrete and lifting steel all day. Why not learn a trade instead? We have the contract on The Arc de Triomphe and can guarantee you six-day workweeks for eighteen months. You'll make more with us than you will pouring concrete. Think about it."

"I don't need to." I grinned. "When do I start?"

The Arc de Triomphe, with its four thousand rooms and thirty floors, was going to be the grandest casino on the Strip. The projected build time, from the day the first clump of soil was turned to completion, was only two years. When I started, the shell for the fifth floor had been completed, the trades had already started their fit-outs on the lower floors, and the cranes were lifting steel and other materials onto the sixth floor. It didn't take long for me to become a competent tiler. I spent the few spare moments I had talking to the electricians, plumbers, air-conditioning mechanics, carpenters, and elevator installers. I never stopped asking questions and was the antithesis of the boy at school who had never raised his hand.

Two months later, our son was born at the Las Vegas Private Maternity Hospital. He was the spitting image of me with black, curly hair, dark blue eyes, and pronounced cheekbones. The only visible feature he'd inherited from Kiara was her olive skin. I wanted to name him after myself, but Kiara told me that the only person who had ever shown her any kindness as a young girl was her uncle Carlos. She loved her uncle, and I wasn't about to object. Except for some sleepless nights, I was living the American dream. I was earning good money while learning something new every day, and Kiara was happily looking after Carlos.

Better still, my hard work and thirst for knowledge hadn't gone unnoticed. When I was offered a job with the ducting contractor on The Arc de Triomphe, it wasn't just the money that attracted me, but the opportunity to continue my education. There was one catch though. "You're in the Laborers Local 620, aren't you?" the boss asked.

"Yeah," I replied, "it's only $20 a month."

"Straight into the pockets of organized crime. Look, Nevada's a right-to-work state, so you can't be forced to join a union. Most of our guys aren't unionists, but some are in The Sheet Metal Employees Union. It's a good union that has the best interests of its members at heart, and fortunately, it hasn't been infiltrated by the mob. It's reasonable, not militant, and its secretary knows that, if we're not profitable, his members won't have jobs. You don't need a union when you work for us. We'll look after you. If you must be in one, you should switch to The Sheet Metal Employees Union."

I grimaced. I now knew what the right-to-work laws were, and the fact that I didn't need a union left me in no doubt about what my boss wanted me to do. The union had done nothing for me, but I wasn't concerned. I hoped I'd never need its help, but if the bosses under-paid me, or the insurers denied a workers' compensation claim, it would be there for me. It was the same as insuring your car. You paid the premium, hoped you'd never have to make a claim, and only did if something went wrong. "I think I'll stay where I am."

"Have it your way." The boss frowned.

Just like with the formwork and tiling, I didn't take long to become a proficient ductwork installer, and to understand how the heating and cooling systems on huge buildings functioned. I kept my head down, worked hard, and was favored with extra hours whenever they were available. My only disappointment was that, after ten months, I'd learned all there was to learn, and the work started to become boring. As if reading my mind, my boss took me aside and said, "We have an office block in Montreal that's running behind schedule, and we're facing a claim for liquidated damages. We're sending a team up there for two weeks. We'd like you to go. You'll work fourteen days straight, but you'll be well rewarded. What do you say?"

I paused, and before I could respond, my boss said, "Does the cat have your tongue?"

"No. I'd like to go, but I can't without my wife and son. They need me. I'm sorry."

"It's only two weeks. Surely, they can survive that long without you. You'll make a heap of money. There are a lot of other guys who'd kill for this opportunity. We have to meet the completion deadline and know you can help. If you agree, you'll fly out this Saturday."

Again, I paused. "I don't have a passport. I've never been outside the country."

"Oh, shit! That finishes that. We can pull some strings, but there's no way you're gonna get a passport in time. Do yourself a favor, Luke. Get yourself a passport, and get one for your wife and kid. We might have been desperate enough to send them with you, but as it is, none of you could've gone."

I didn't know it, but this advice would prove to be very opportune.

I continued to pick the brains of the other tradesmen and was always on the lookout for new jobs that would improve my knowledge and skills. However, the money I was earning as a ductwork installer and air-conditioning mechanic was so lucrative that it made a change unappealing. After three years in Vegas, I had a nice little nest egg at the bank and was thinking of putting down a deposit on a house. That was, until the strike.

Chapter 4

The dispute came out of the blue. One of the crane drivers came to work in the morning still suffering from a heavy night's drinking and was instantly dismissed. In response, the Laborers Local 620 called a snap strike, and workers dropped their tools and picketed the site. I gave it no thought and kept working until one of my fellow unionists reminded me that I should be supporting the crane driver. When I found out what had occurred, I couldn't understand why they were striking. The crane driver was hammered when he came to work. He was a danger to himself and other workers on the site. *Of course, he should have been fired! Why should I lose out because of him? I'm not going on strike*, I thought.

It was only when my boss told me to drop my tools that I realized I had no choice. "The union's withdrawn its labor, Luke," my boss explained, "and you're a member. We can't thumb our nose at the union."

"Are you telling me that, if I weren't a member, I could keep working?"

"That's right."

"I'll resign. I don't want to stop working."

"It's not that easy. Right now, you're a paid-up member of the Local 620. Resigning might not be as easy as you think. I think you'll find you have to do it in writing and mail it to the union's offices."

"Jesus!" I shouted, picking up my tools. "I'll complete the forms and hand-deliver them this afternoon. I want to work tomorrow."

"Good luck. I hope you don't have any problems," my boss said. "The idiot crane driver's not gonna get his job back so they'll still be picketing in the morning. Be careful. The union will have paid thugs at the entrance egging the men on. When you cross the line, they're gonna be very aggressive. Ignore them. Don't let 'em provoke you."

"I can look after myself."

As I left, there were hundreds of workers milling around the front of the site. Some cheered when they saw me, but I pushed through the throng. I had one thing in mind, and that was to get to the Local 620's office and resign.

The following morning, I parked about half a mile from the site and off the main drag. I didn't want the strikers trashing my car. The picket had grown, and workers with the guts to attempt crossing the line were being harassed, jostled, and called scabs, rats, and vermin. *Nevada might have been one of the first states to adopt the right-to-work laws, but no one must have told the unions*, I thought. As I surveyed the seething crowd, I saw a group of heavyset men wearing T-shirts with their arms interlocked, completely blocking access to the entrance. I didn't recognize any of them but hoped to slip past the line virtually unnoticed. It wasn't going to happen.

I fell in behind a big man in his late thirties who was trying to push his way through the picket. "Fucking scabs," one man yelled, and the jostling and shoving intensified. Shouts of "low bastards" and "dogs" followed when the big man broke through the linked arms and entered the site. Another yard and I'd be there, but then I felt the spit hit the back of my head.

Infuriated, I turned to see a brawny, heavily tattooed thug wearing a navy-blue T-shirt, holding a galvanized steel pipe in his right hand, and grinning at me. I instinctively grabbed his right arm and threw a vicious left hook to his jaw. I had never hit anyone that hard before, and vibrations rippled up my arm as teeth and blood splattered everywhere. The thug raised his free arm, and then his eyes glazed over as he crashed to the ground. There was perhaps five seconds' silence before the now raging strikers came at me, but with two quick steps, I entered the site, leaving the hissing and booing behind me.

I was working on the twentieth floor when I heard the wail of sirens but gave it no thought until I was confronted by my boss. "I thought I told you to ignore the picketers," he said.

"I did until one of them lobbed a glob of spit on my head. What was I meant to do? Turn the other cheek?"

"Yes. Did he hurt you? You should have ignored him. If you had, you wouldn't be in trouble."

"Trouble? What trouble?"

"Didn't you hear the ambulance sirens? The guy who you hit is still unconscious. His jaw is broken in three places, and he may not regain consciousness. He –"

"He provoked it," I interrupted. "He was just a troublemaker. I hadn't seen him before today. I doubt he even works here."

My boss sighed and shook his head. "He doesn't. He works for the people who control the union, and they were making a show of supporting the crane driver. The guy you put in the hospital was one of their enforcers, and unluckily for you, his brother is a made man. You know what that means? They're not gonna let you get away with it."

"What can they do?" I said with false bravado, my mind drifting back to what Sordi had done to the druggie.

"Beat you up. Break your legs. Maybe have you killed. They might even go after your family. They're gonna be waiting for you when you finish work. You've gotta get your family and get out of Nevada today."

As soon as I heard made man, I knew I was in trouble, and there was no sense blustering. "How am I gonna do that? According to you, I won't make it home."

"You're a good kid, and we're gonna help you. There's an ambulance on its way. The picketers won't try to stop it, and they probably won't check it when it leaves. You're gonna be in the back when it does."

"Where am I gonna go?"

"I'd go to Mexico, Canada, maybe even Europe. You need to get away until the heat dies down. You're unlucky that the guy who you hit is connected, but in time, it'll die down. In six months, you'll be forgotten, and it'll be safe to return. I wouldn't come back to Vegas though."

"I can't just up and leave. What about our furniture? Our appliances? Blankets, towels, cutlery, crockery?"

"Jesus! You're not listening. They're all replaceable. You're not. You've gotta get out but not via McCarran. They'll be watching. Here's what you do. Hotfoot it south - not to LA, though, because they might be watching there as well. Phoenix, Dallas, Houston, New Orleans. I don't want to know. Don't use your credit card for anything. Pay cash for everything. I don't think they're gonna be chasing you all over the country, but it won't hurt to play it safe. Oh, and wherever you decide to go, stay away from the big cities. Do you have enough money?"

There goes our down payment. "Yeah, I'll clean out my bank account before we leave."

"They won't be looking for you until after you don't show up this afternoon. You'll have at least five hours' start. Make the most of it," my boss said, as we heard the wailing of an ambulance siren. "There's your ride. Good luck."

"Thanks," I said, shaking his hand, while hoping Kiara wouldn't be too upset with the unscheduled move. "Can I use one of the site office phones before I go?"

"Make it quick. Oh, and Luke, the cops have been bought and paid for. Whatever you do, don't seek their help."

"Yeah, I guessed that. It was the same in Chicago."

As the ambulance left the site, I looked out the tinted windows. The strikers were raging and far angrier than they'd been earlier. I doubted that anyone else would be crossing the picket line.

Closing the bank account took longer than expected as the bank officers were worried about me carrying so much cash. After I left the bank, I went to the nearest service station, filled up, and bought a road map which I studied for five minutes. By the time I arrived home, Kiara was waiting at the front door, her face filled with apprehension. "I'm packed," she said, "I hope you can fit all the stuff I have in the hallway in the trunk. Hurry, Luke."

"Don't panic, honey," I said, putting my arms around her. "God, you're trembling. It's not that bad."

"You slugged some Mafia goombah, and now you're telling me it's not that bad? Let's load the car and get out of here."

"He's not Mafioso. He's a thug. That's all. If his brother weren't connected, they wouldn't be paying any attention to me. Don't worry. I'll never let anything happen to you and Carlos. Besides, they think I'm still on site. We have a few hours up our sleeves. By the time they realize I'm gone, we'll be hundreds of miles away."

"How can you be so calm? Where are we going?"

"Honey, everything's under control. Trust me. We'll head to Albuquerque, and on the way, you can think of a place you'd like to go. Mexico, Canada, England, France, anywhere. We won't be gone long. Think of it as a well-earned holiday."

"I think you're enjoying this, Luke Cramer," Kiara said, her frown turning into a half smile. "You did say we'd live an exciting life."

"Ah, the smile I fell in love with. I'll take the holiday comment back. This will be the honeymoon we never had."

Chapter 5

Nine hours later, we checked into a small motel on the outskirts of Albuquerque. I was hyped up and not in the least tired but knew that Kiara and Carlos needed to rest. "We'll be on a plane tomorrow night," I said, "which will be a first for me."

"Me too," Kiara said. "I'm scared. Are you sure those men won't be waiting at the airport?"

I'm not that important. Had I stayed, they probably would've beaten me up. If I hadn't seen what happened to that druggie, I wouldn't be running. They might be watching Los Angeles International Airport, but I doubt it. It's not like I slugged Gambino's brother. They'll be happy saying they ran me out of town, I thought. "Honey, they can't check out every airport in the country, and Albuquerque will be the last place they'll be looking – if they are looking. Get a good night's sleep. We'll find a travel agency in the morning. After we have the tickets, I'll sell the car, and we'll be on our way. Have you decided where you want to go?

"As far away as possible. Let's wait and see what the travel agent says."

The travel agencies in the Yellow Pages that could afford large advertisements all guaranteed the cheapest fares. The motel manager gave us directions to the nearest agency which was only a few miles down the road. There was a strip of shops, but one stood out because its windows were covered with gaudy sign writing, advertising everything from weekends in Hawaii to cruises in Alaska. Inside was no better, and brochures covered three walls. As we entered the shop, we were greeted by a man with a welcoming smile who introduced himself as Julio and told us that he was the owner and at our service. Kiara told him we were taking a vacation and asked whether we could see some brochures. "Certainly," Julio gushed, pointing to a small table surrounded by chairs. "Make yourself at home. Call me if you need any help."

Ten minutes later, the table was covered in brochures, and Carlos was pointing and saying, "Plane, Mom, big plane."

I picked up a brochure for travel to Canada and said, "The only thing I don't like is the cold. Vancouver looks like it might be okay though. I like the idea of Mexico better. What do you think, hon?"

"Too close. I want us to get as far away as we can. What about Australia? Have a look at this brochure on the Gold Coast. It looks fantastic - warm to hot climate, tropical, great beaches, and it's a holiday destination."

"Australia? You're kidding. It's the ass end of the world. I wanna get away, but I wanna be close enough to come home whenever I want."

"It's a twenty-four-hour flight. Isn't that close enough? Besides, you'll be safe down there. You won't have to be continually looking over your shoulder."

I called Julio over after Kiara had made up our minds. "We want to be on a flight to the Gold Coast, Australia tonight."

"The cheapest flight is via Los Angeles and Sydney with United and Qantas," Julio said.

Kiara's face dropped, and she asked, "Do we have to go through Los Angeles?"

"Señora, you are not going to Los Angeles. You are stopping over at LAX. You are in transit. You'll change planes, but you won't have to pick up your luggage. You'll clear customs in Sydney and take a domestic flight to Coolangatta Airport."

"It'll be fine, honey," I said, "don't worry."

"You didn't answer my question," Kiara persisted.

"You could go through Houston and Auckland and disembark in Sydney with United and Air New Zealand. It'll add three hours to your trip and will cost an extra $100 a seat."

Kiara looked over at me, her expression leaving me in no doubt as to what she wanted to do. "We'll go with United and Air New Zealand."

"Three tickets to the Gold Coast," Julio said, pulling out his calculator. "When are you returning?"

"Two tickets," I said. "I'll hold my son, and can you leave the return date open?"

"You can't do that. You must buy a ticket for your son too. It's an international flight. It's the law."

"Perhaps I should see what your competitors will do."

"Please feel free to use my phone," Julio said. "They will tell you the same. We have no choice. I'm sorry."

I made two calls, and the agents confirmed Julio's advice. "What a racket," I said. "Make it three tickets."

"What about accommodation? You don't want to be running around the Gold Coast looking for somewhere to stay. I can put you into a nice, inexpensive low-rise two-bedroom, fully furnished unit for your first two nights. I can let you have it for $50 a night."

"Okay," I said, pulling out my very fat wallet. "What do we owe you?"

I could tell Julio knew we were running from something. His eyes asked, How many young guys carry that much cash? I could also tell that he knew we had never traveled before and that he thought we were naive which our questions definitely proved. However, I also sensed that he didn't want to get on the wrong side of me. "I feel sorry for you," he said. "I'll throw in a third night for nothing." Even I knew you got nothing for nothing, and that he was probably going to screw the property manager.

That night we boarded a flight bound for Houston at Albuquerque's airport. Before boarding I made one call – to Ratsy. I hadn't seen him for more than two years but always knew he was nearby. Now I was traveling halfway around the world and felt an acute sense of loss. I was going to miss him, but at least it was only for three months, and we'd most likely settle in Chicago when we returned.

Thirty hours and four flights later, QF 127 touched down at Coolangatta Airport late in the afternoon. Carlos was grumpy, Kiara was exhausted, and I was excited. It was a sunny eighty-five degrees, and there wasn't a cloud in the sky. The tourist airport was small but busy, and it was forty minutes before we had our luggage and were on a bus to our Surfers Paradise accommodation. I didn't know it, but Coolangatta was the most southerly part of the twenty-five-mile coast, and Surfers Paradise was close to the most northerly. Kiara rested her head on my shoulder while I held Carlos, my eyes darting from side to side. On the right, I saw the high-rise tourist motels and the thumping waves that had made the coast a mecca for surfers around the world. On the other side, dense, lush greenery and tropical trees stretched into the hills as far as the eye could see. As beautiful as it was, my real focus was on the cranes and the plethora of buildings under construction. *I've been delivered into God's country*, I thought.

Chapter 6

The Casa De Oro was an old, yellow, sixty-unit, double-story motel that looked like it had seen better days. As the bus pulled in, Kiara laughed and said, "It translates into House of Gold." We picked up the keys from a woman in the office and climbed the stairs to our unit. The furniture, beds, and carpets were like everything else – old and worn – but on the plus side, it was clean, and there was fresh milk in the fridge. Kiara put Carlos down just after 6:30 P.M. and told me that she had to get some sleep or she'd collapse. It was hot and sticky, but when I tried to turn on the air conditioner, it didn't work.

"Leave it," Kiara said. "I'm so tired I could sleep through anything."

A few hours later, just before turning in, I decided to have a cooling shower, but all I got was clunking pipes and a trickle of water. I wished that I could get my hands on Julio.

The following morning, I was down in the office at eight o'clock with a list of complaints. We might only be staying for three nights, but I wasn't going to put up with a unit where the power and plumbing weren't functioning. The man behind the counter had rapidly receding oily brown hair, was wearing a sweat-stained white T-shirt, and was smoking. "Yeah, yeah," he said, with a big yawn. "When I can get someone, I'll send him up. It ain't easy, you know. Bloody handymen, they're so unreliable."

"That's not my problem," I replied. "We can't even boil water. The air conditioner doesn't work. We can't take a shower. I want to talk to your boss. This –"

"Look, Yank, I've heard it all before," he said, lighting up another cigarette. "I'm the property manager, and for your information, that means I'm the boss. There is no one higher up, and the unit owners couldn't give a shit about you. They're just hanging out for an offer that will see this place torn down and replaced with a forty-story skyscraper."

"It's not right."

"No, but for $50 a night, you have to suck it up. I'll get someone as soon as I can, but I can't promise when."

"Jesus. I could fix it myself, but why should I?"

"Whoa, hold that thought," the property manager said. "Can you fix the plumbing, electrical, and air conditioning?"

"Easy," I said, "but I'll need tools and parts."

"I have the tools. Why don't you come into the kitchen? Joe Molloy's the name," he said, extending his hand. "I might have an offer that'll interest you. Let's have a beer and talk about it."

You're drinking at this time of the morning? I thought, as I shook his limp hand. "It's too early for me, and why would I want to fix this place when I'm on vacation?"

"Hear me out, kid. I get a headache listening to complaints like yours every day. You're not the only one venting. This might be mutually beneficial. I'm guessing you don't have much money because, if you did, you wouldn't be staying in a shithole like this. You can't work because if they catch you, they'll put you on a plane, and you'll be back in the U.S. before you can scratch yourself. Your green card has nothing on our labor and immigration laws, believe me. However, there's a way around them that can help us both. You do the building maintenance, and I let you stay here for as long as you want for nothing. How does that sound?"

Terrific, but with a few changes. "I dunno. I could end up working all hours fixing this place, all for the price of a room. It doesn't sound like much of a deal to me."

Molloy took another can of beer from the fridge. "Are you sure you won't have one?"

"I told you, it's too early."

"Yeah, yeah, I heard you the first time. I know you have no money, so why don't you put a proposition to me?"

"Sure. I do a maximum of two hours a day from nine to eleven excluding Sundays, and then the rest of the day is mine. Oh, and it would be most unwise of you to try to kick me out after I've finished the work," I said, my face only inches from his.

"You have nerve threatening me, Yank," he replied, trying to hide the concern in his eyes.

"You heard my offer. Take it or leave it, and if you take it, the first unit I'm fixing is mine."

"I'll take it, but you better be as good as you say you are. I'm fed up with the whining," Molloy said apprehensively.

I smiled. *Sordi was right. Fear was a powerful motivator.*

The next few weeks I attended to complaints that hadn't been looked at for months. The work was easy; the only difficulty was getting materials. I would tell Molloy what materials to buy to fix the problem permanently, but he would respond, "Can't we use something cheaper? It doesn't have to be permanent. Jesus, who knows when they're going to bulldoze this place?"

"But I'll have to fix it again in two weeks. It doesn't make sense."

"Not to you it doesn't, but put yourselves in the place of the owners. They don't want to spend a cent on maintenance, and when their checks are reduced by the cost of repairs, who do you think they blame?"

"I don't understand. The people who own my unit aren't getting a cent in rent. They're carrying the maintenance costs for the whole complex, but they don't know it."

"Kid, the rent is pooled and then divided among the owners. The people who own your unit are getting a check every month. The owners can understand lousy occupancy rates. After all, they know what a shithole this place is. What they can't understand is anyone outlaying good money to maintain it. Now do you understand?"

Yeah, and it saves you having to answer the hard questions. I'm the perfect solution for you. I'm keeping the tenants and owners off your back. "Sure."

The temperature on the coast fluctuated between seventy-five and ninety degrees, and the sky seemed to be permanently blue and cloudless. The Queensland Tourism Authority's slogan was "beautiful one day, perfect the next", and we agreed. The main street in Surfers Paradise, Cavill Avenue, was bustling with families enjoying themselves. It was short and dominated by restaurants, coffee shops, fast-food places, and gift shops. It led to a magnificent, sandy, surf beach where the water was warm and alluring but also with a dangerous undertow. We never took our eyes off Carlos as he ran into the shallows and squealed with delight as the waves chased him back to the beach. I picked him up and was drying him when I started to laugh. "What's funny?" Kiara asked.

"My dad once told me there were no surf beaches in Chicago. If only he could see me now."

"It's a pity the tall buildings shade the beach."

"The developers have no choice," I said. "People want to walk out the back gate and be on the beach. I'm amazed by the number of buildings under construction along the coast. They should call it Builders Paradise."

"You love watching high-rises getting built, don't you?"

"Yeah, one day in the not too distant future, I'm gonna be building them. I like to see what the builders are doing. The Japanese are building a luxury hotel on the Southport Spit. It's only four miles north and tracks the coast. I'd like to look at it. Carlos will sleep in his stroller Do you feel like a walk?"

"A spit? What's a spit?"

"Molloy told me that it's a narrow, sandy peninsula that juts out into the sea. According to him, mainly sand and sand dunes, but developers have been paying huge prices to get a foothold. There's a Sea World theme park there - dolphins, sea lions, water ski shows, and that type of stuff."

"Carlos would love to see the dolphins. So would I." Kiara giggled.

Seventy-five minutes later, we reached the start of the Spit. A slightly inclined bitumen road led to a small shopping center and a partially constructed upmarket hotel adjacent to a large roundabout. Concrete mixers were lined up in front of the hotel, and some of the drivers were standing around smoking and chatting while they waited. I walked around the roundabout to get as close to the hotel as I could.

On the other side of the roundabout, a white Mercedes pulled up in front of the shopping center, and a chauffeur held the door open while a woman holding a baby climbed out. I was focusing on the construction site when I saw a driverless concrete mixer start to roll down the slight hill. As it gathered momentum, I knew exactly where it was going to finish, and I shouted at the woman and her driver, but the noise from the site drowned out my warning.

Then I was running as fast as I could in a race against the huge truck that was rapidly gathering speed. The last thing I remembered before someone turned the lights out was snatching the baby to my chest and shoving the woman out of the way with all my strength.

Book 2

MONTGOMERY BEAUREPAIRE

Chapter 7

It all happened in a split second. One minute Luke was standing next to Kiara, the next he was sprinting across the roundabout with a huge truck bearing down on him. With every roll of its wheels, the truck increased velocity, and Kiara screamed at him to stop. She was still screaming when it slammed into the Mercedes, and he was hurled into the air like an insect. By the time she reached him, workers from the site and shoppers were scurrying to help. "I've never seen anything so brave," one bystander said. "Did you see the way he was still clutching the baby as he hit the ground? He looks like he's in a bad way."

"Luke, oh Luke," Kiara cried, bending down next to him.

A woman on her hands and knees screamed, "Felicity, Felicity, where's my baby Felicity? Edward, Edward, where's Felicity?"

A shop assistant knelt next to her. "Your baby's safe, lady. No harm came to her. Your driver's in a bad way though. Don't try to get up. The ambulance will be here soon."

"Is there a doctor or nurse around here?" someone shouted.

"I'm a vet," a bearded man said as he pushed his way through the growing crowd. "Give me some room."

"Help the driver first," someone said pointing to a large gray-suited man lying on his back and staring blankly up at the onlookers. The vet took his pulse, closed the man's eyes, and then looked up and shook his head.

"My husband," Kiara yelled, "please help my husband!"

As the vet grasped Luke's wrist, the distant wail of sirens could be heard. "His pulse is strong, but he's taken a severe knock to the head."

"Will he be all right?" Kiara sobbed.

As the wailing of police and ambulance sirens filled the air, Kiara didn't hear the vet mutter, "I don't know. I hope so."

The paramedics checked Luke's vital signs and then gently secured him on a stretcher. The ambulance driver comforted Kiara while folding up Carlos's stroller and putting it in the front of the ambulance. A few minutes later, the ambulance was racing toward The Gold Coast Mercy Hospital.

Kiara tried to keep her composure, but the doctors, while sympathetic, wouldn't answer her questions. As she sat fretting in the hospital's waiting room, she heard a man with a refined, distinctly English voice, demanding to know the condition of his wife and daughter. Unfortunately, she couldn't make out the response. Then she heard him say, "Where is the young man? Is he all right?" Again, Kiara couldn't hear the reply, but she did hear the man say, "Spare no expense. I want him looked after. Put him in the best private room." And then Kiara distinctly heard one of the doctors say, "His wife and son are in the waiting room. Her name is Kiara Cramer."

A few minutes later, a tall man wearing an immaculate, blue pinstriped suit and highly polished, black shoes strode into the waiting room. His dark hair was starting to gray at the temples, and his eyes were filled with concern. "Mrs. Cramer," he said, "my name is Montgomery Beaurepaire. Your husband saved my wife's and daughter's lives. He's a very brave man."

Kiara took one look at him and broke down sobbing uncontrollably. Beaurepaire sat down and put his arm around her. "You've been through an awful lot. They're operating on Luke now. The good news is that he's going to be okay. The injuries to his head are superficial. There's no brain damage. The bad news is that his leg is broken, and he'll be in a cast for six weeks."

"Thank God," Kiara said, crossing herself and bursting into a fresh flood of tears.

"I wanna go home," Carlos squawked.

"Your little boy is tired and stressed," Beaurepaire said. "He's had a big day too. I think I should take you home. Luke's not going to be talking for hours, and I'll be here when he wakes up."

Kiara resisted at first, only agreeing after a doctor assured her that Luke was no longer in any danger. The same doctor informed Beaurepaire that they had sedated his wife and dressed her abrasions but were going to keep her for observation overnight. "Who's looking after your baby?" Kiara asked.

"Her nanny. Don't be concerned. She's being well cared for. Come on, let's get you home."

Kiara didn't know that the large black car parked in the no-standing area in front of the hospital was a Bentley, but she could tell it was expensive. Beaurepaire held the back door open for her and Carlos, putting the stroller in the trunk. He was gushing in his gratitude, but Kiara was uncomfortable. She didn't know many people like Montgomery Beaurepaire – on reflection, she didn't know anyone like Montgomery Beaurepaire. When they arrived at the Casa De Oro, he parked and looked around disdainfully, saying, "I'll carry the stroller."

As he followed her up the stairs, he added, "This won't do, Kiara. Luke's going to be in a wheelchair or on crutches. He's not going to be able to get up these stairs. I have a nice little holiday place at The Meridien where he'll be able to use the elevators. He'll find it far more comfortable. Why don't I help you pack, and I'll take you there?"

Again, Kiara resisted, but she soon realized that Beaurepaire was a man who rarely heard or listened to the word no. An hour later, they drove into The Meridien's underground parking garage, and Beaurepaire carried the suitcases to a bank of elevators and swiped his security card. The doors to the elevator marked penthouse opened and whooshed them to the thirtieth floor. Kiara silently gasped. The luxuriously furnished apartment took the complete floor, overlooked the ocean, and gave unimpeded views of the hinterland and the city. What had Beaurepaire called it? *A nice little holiday place.* "I can't tell you much about the kitchen other than that I've had the fridge restocked," he said, handing Kiara a security card. "This opens the doors, and you'll need it for the elevator and garage. Here, let me show you how the lights, phone, and television work. Then I must get back to the hospital. If you need anything, and I mean anything, call the concierge. Oh, there'll be a car and driver available to take you to the hospital. I'll call you when Luke awakens."

"Thank you, Mr. Beaurepaire."

Carlos had wandered into the living room and was sound asleep on the sofa.

"My pleasure. My friends call me Monty, and I think we're going to become good friends. You're exhausted. You need to get some sleep.

Luke's in good hands. Try not to worry. Here's my business card," he said, jotting on the back of it. "I've left you my private number. Don't hesitate to use it."

"Can I ask a favour?"

"For you, anything."

"Luke is hiding from some gangsters in Las Vegas. I'm worried about what the media are going to report and whether they're going to name him. I know you probably can't stop them reporting the incident, but I'm wondering if you can keep his name out of the newspapers and television."

"Consider it done," Beaurepaire replied, "and rest assured Luke's name won't be mentioned. Is there anything else?"

"Thank you. No."

He was obviously accustomed to getting his own way and after he left, Kiara picked up his business card, which read, *Montgomery Beaurepaire, CEO, Hall Samuel, Investment Bankers, The Venetian Tower, 27ᵗʰ Floor, Creek Street, Brisbane.*

When Luke awoke, he was drowsy and in a room of which he had no recollection. A slim, well-dressed man was sitting in a chair next to the bed. "Where-where am I?" he asked. "Where are my wife and son?"

"Don't you remember what happened?" the man asked. "You're in the hospital. You're a hero."

"The concrete truck. I remember it careening down the road toward a Mercedes. There was a woman, a driver, and a baby," Luke said, trying to sit up. "What happened?"

"Don't try to move. You have a broken leg and some lacerations and took a heavy knock to the head when you hit the ground. It's a clean break, and as long as you're not looking for a career as a basketball player, you'll soon be as good as new. They're going to keep you here for a few days for observation."

"Are you a doctor? Where are my wife and son?"

"Kiara waited to make sure that you were out of danger, but Carlos was getting grumpy and needed sleep. Don't worry, they're being looked aft-"

"Who are you?" Luke interrupted.

"My name's Montgomery Beaurepaire. I'm the lady's husband and the baby girl's father. You saved their lives. I will be indebted to you for the rest of my life. No amount of thanks is adequate."

"How-how are they, an-and what happened to the driver?" Luke asked, fighting back a yawn.

"Thanks to you, Felicity is unmarked. My wife Veronica is being treated for shock and cuts and abrasions to her head, legs, and arms. A small price to pay for her life. Poor Edward didn't make it," Beaurepaire said. "It's tragic and so sad. He's been with me for years."

"I didn't get there fast enough."

"You couldn't have done more. You're lucky to be alive. Don't beat yourself up."

As Luke fought to stay awake, his face clouded over. "I don't have any medical insurance. How am I going to pay?"

"It's all been taken care of. There's nothing for you to worry about. I've moved Kiara and Carlos into a holiday place I have on the coast. They and you will be more comfortable there. Oh, and your secret is safe. The media don't know your name or who you are, and even if they find out, I've ensured nothing will be reported."

Luke raised his hand to protest. Then fatigue took over, and he fell asleep.

"Thank you, Luke," Beaurepaire said, resting a manicured hand on his shoulder. "My life would have been over had it not been for your bravery."

Chapter 8

The following morning the anesthetic had worn off, and Luke's head had cleared. Beaurepaire was still sitting in the same chair but wearing a charcoal gray suit. "Have you been sitting there all night?" Luke joked.

"How are you feeling? You look a little better than you did last night."

"I'm okay. I think I heard the doctor say I'm going to be in a cast for six weeks. That's a pain in the ass because my visa expires before then. I dunno how I'm gonna sit on the plane," Luke said, the muscles in his arms rippling as he propped himself up on the pillows.

"Forget about the visa. I can arrange for you to stay here as long as you want," Beaurepaire said, in a tone that indicated that the matter was settled.

"Thanks, but I'm running short of funds. I have to get back."

"No, you aren't, and no, you don't. You and your family are my guests."

"Mister, I know you're grateful, but picking up the medical bills is more than enough. You don't have to do anything else."

"Please call me Monty. Do you believe in fate, Luke? I do. Fate brought you into my life. If it hadn't, I'd be a broken man right now. Let me help you. You never know where it might lead."

Luke sighed. "Okay. Have it your way."

"Good. Kiara and Carlos are getting acquainted with my apartment. The building has elevators. You'll find it easier to get around there while you're recuperating."

After Monty left, Luke channel surfed, hoping to watch some American sports. There was nothing, but as he flicked through the channels, he heard a pompous voice, not unlike Monty's, say, "In a murder trial, without the police finding a body, I would guarantee any client lucky enough to be represented by me, either a hung jury or a not guilty verdict." Luke quickly flicked back to hear the moderator say, "You're an éminent queen's counsel. Don't you have a conscience? Aren't you concerned that you might be putting a murderer back on the streets?"

"Not my concern," the portly QC replied. "If the police were doing their job, they would produce the body."

Another panelist wearing a police uniform said, "There have been many cases in Australia where murder convictions have been obtained despite the lack of a body. How can you be so sure that you'd get an acquittal?"

"You're not listening. I didn't say an acquittal, I said a hung jury. The convictions you're referencing were obtained because of inadequate representation. If I were appearing for the accused, short of a confession, it's inconceivable that the prosecution could obtain a conviction without a body. On reflection, make that impossible. I don't have to prove my client is innocent. I just have to stop the prosecution from proving he's guilty. Without a body, any attorney worth his salt should be able to do that."

"Inadequate representation?" the policeman butted in. "You've just defamed countless defense lawyers. You could find yourself in trouble."

"I don't think so." The QC smirked. "I don't think those incompetents are going to want to take me on in court - no body, no conviction. It's Law 101."

The moderator shook his head and stared at the pompous QC. Luke wasn't sure why, but he was intrigued by the exchange. He turned the television off and immediately fell asleep.

Three days later, Kiara helped him out of the hospital while their driver held the rear door of the new minivan open. Luke threw his crutches in and then, using the overhead handles, hauled himself into a seat. Monty had thought of everything. Kiara had warned Luke what to expect when he saw the apartment but even being forewarned did not prepare him for its opulence. "He bought the minivan just to make it easy for you, Luke, and the driver is on call for us. He must be incredibly wealthy."

"Yeah, he's obviously not short of a buck. He's a nice guy. He went out of his way to visit me every day in the hospital. It's a hundred-mile round trip from Brisbane. He's been talking to me about fate, destiny, and forks in the road. I dunno what he's thinking. I just say 'yeah' and 'no' and hope I get 'em right." Luke laughed. "With luck, they'll take the cast off in five weeks."

"Can you imagine living in a place like this?"

"More than that. I'll own buildings like this one day. You just wait and see."

Chapter 9

In the ensuing weeks, Luke and Monty Beaurepaire got to know each other. The Englishman was a good listener, and Luke told him why he'd left Las Vegas in a hurry. Beaurepaire, a savvy businessman had been sent out to Australia from his employer's head office in London five years earlier. He had made a huge success of the Brisbane operation and had been handsomely rewarded with shares and options. He and Veronica had despaired of ever having their own children and had gone through four cycles of IVF before giving up. Then, within six months of finishing, Veronica fell pregnant naturally, and along came Felicity. It had been a difficult and traumatic Caesarian, and they had been warned against trying to have more children. "My life would have ended that day had it not been for you, Luke. All the riches in the world couldn't replace Felicity and Veronica."

"Yeah, that's what you keep telling me. Don't you think you've done enough for us? We can't continue to live in luxury at your expense. We have to get back to the States."

"How do you know those bad guys won't still be looking for you? Wouldn't it be safer to stay in Australia? Isn't the climate in Queensland far better than Vegas or Chicago? This state is booming, and if you play your cards right, you could make a fortune."

"I thought it was almost impossible for a foreigner to work in Australia."

"Yes, it is, but different rules apply to those with money. I'd be honored to sponsor you, and if you like, you could apply for citizenship in a few years. It's a great country abounding with opportunities. Kiara loves it."

"You're not only a financier, you're also a salesman. I'd like to start my own business. I know I can build more efficiently than the builders on the coast."

"Hold on." Monty laughed. "It'll be years before you build a high-rise, if ever. You have to crawl before you can walk. You don't know anything about Queensland building regulations. I can get you a job with one of the builders we're financing, and you'll need to spend a year at night school so you can get registered. After that, I'll happily support you in your own building business but forget about high-rises. There's plenty of money to be made building houses, shops, factories, and warehouses. If you're successful, who knows, one day you might end up building skyscrapers on the coast. Luke, every person's destiny is determined by the life choices they make. You're at the crossroads now. One road could see you getting beaten up or worse and working in a job you hate without the chance of advancement. The other could see you earning a fortune while working in paradise. It's an easy decision."

When Luke bounced the idea of staying in Queensland off Kiara, she was all for it. Beaurepaire had done a great sales job on her, not that she needed much convincing. After two weeks of swimming and intense physiotherapy, Luke started his new job with Progressive Builders on a thirty-story apartment block on Pacific Close overlooking the ocean and the beach. Monty had used his influence to get him a position assisting the project manager. The site was a closed shop which meant that, if workers didn't have a union ticket, they didn't get a job, but because Luke was management, he didn't have to join. Meetings between the boss and the union representatives were always in private, but Luke had accidentally interrupted a meeting just as a union man was slipping a fat brown envelope into his pocket. He gave it no thought, but in only a few short years, fat brown envelopes would bring down the Queensland government.

Luke thrived in his new job. No longer did he have to slink around trying to steal a glimpse at the drawings. He was working on them every day and organizing the trades to maximize efficiency. Three times a week he went to night school with a group of young men not much older than himself. The boy who hated school had morphed into the young man who couldn't learn enough and always had a book in his hand.

The smartest guy in class, Max Tilson, was only two years older than Luke and also worked for Progressive Builders on another site.

They quickly became friends, and Luke found a fresh source of learning and information. The only thing he didn't like about Max was his ambition to become a project manager. He couldn't understand why anyone as smart as Max would want to work for someone else.

Monty was happy for Luke to remain in The Meridien, but he wanted to be independent. As soon as he started work, he rented a semi-luxurious, three-bedroom house in Paradise Point overlooking the Coomera River, something he couldn't have dreamed of affording in Vegas. To celebrate he bought a little fox terrier pup, Roxy, for Carlos. At the end of the year, his boss promised him a raise and promotion to project manager within twelve months, but Luke wasn't interested.

When Luke called Ratsy and told him he was staying in Queensland, his friend was disappointed. "I might not ever see you again," he said.

"That's not going to happen, Ratsy. When I have some money, we'll be going back for holidays. I might even build a stash and use it to start a business in Chicago. You could be my partner."

"I dunno anything about building, but thanks for the offer."

"What are you doing for a buck?"

"I'm helping the mob."

"You're still running errands?"

"I didn't say that. I've progressed. You could say I'm on call."

"Do you get paid well?"

"I have my own apartment and drive the latest model Caddy. I'm doin' okay."

"Don't tell me you're a made man."

"Nah, but I could've been."

"Tell me. What do you do?"

"You don't want to know."

"Have it your way, Ratsy. I don't want to lose contact with you, buddy. Let's agree to talk every month."

"I'd like that, Luke."

Chapter 10

In late 1990 – with the help of Monty's blue-chip lawyers, Carr & Carr – CramerBuild Pty. Ltd. was incorporated. With a little more assistance from his new, powerful friend, getting registered as a builder was a mere formality. Soon Luke was scanning the daily newspapers and government tenders looking for jobs that he could quote. Most of the jobs he wanted to quote on were far too big.

"You don't have the money. You don't have credit with suppliers. You don't have a team with the expertise to build shopping centers and low-rise office complexes. You have to take baby steps when starting out," Monty said.

"Yeah, yeah, that's what you always say. I know how to build and organize labor. You said you'd arrange the finance."

"And I shall." Monty laughed. "I also need to make sure you can repay me. I can stand the loss, but I know what it would do to you."

"That's hardly a vote of confidence."

"On the contrary, it is. I'm happy to back you, but I don't want you to overreach. You have a few contacts, and I know you can put a team together. Here, look at this," Monty said, handing Luke a folder. "It's the tender documents for a warehouse on Ferry Road, Southport. The owner's a client of ours, but he may finance it elsewhere. It's a little too small for us. Prepare a quote, and once it's finished, I'll go over it with you."

"Jeez, it's not much of a job," Luke complained.

"It's a start."

Luke was surprised by Beaurepaire's building knowledge as the financier went over his quote for $750,000, making amendments with a red pen. "You've priced it to perfection, Luke. There's nothing in the quote for contingencies, and you've underquoted the cost of labor. I've added $130,000 before NFR."

"NFR?"

"No fucking reason," Beaurepaire said.

Luke tried not to laugh but failed. Monty's voice was so polished that the use of the f-bomb completely lost its impact.

"It's to cover everything and anything we might have missed. Let's add $70,000 for NFR, which rounds the quote up to $950,000."

"Yeah, but is it competitive? It's no good quoting high and losing out."

"Luke, Luke, you have so much still to learn. Yes, you know how to build, but if you're going to make money, you must also understand the numbers. We finance buildings like this, and we're not going to provide funds where the value of the security is inflated. I know that the cost per square yard at $950,000 is competitive. When you've spent a year quoting, you'll know the same."

"Okay, is there anything else I should know?"

A knowing smile came to Monty's lips. "Plenty, but you'll learn more from your mistakes than my telling you. One thing you must do when submitting quotes is to make them conditional on receiving progress payments every week. You'll claim as much as you can, and the owners and their financiers will try to pay you as little as possible. It's a game where you'll soon become adept. If you don't, you won't be building for very long."

During the twenty-two weeks that it took to complete the warehouse, there was rarely a break in the energy-sapping hot and humid weather. Luke found the conditions even more uncomfortable than Las Vegas, and this motivated him to drive himself and his men relentlessly. Queenslanders loved their beer, and at the end of each day, he made sure there were a couple of cold cans of XXXX, the state's home brand, for each man. He also issued a wrestling challenge to anyone game enough to take him on. Some of the contests lasted more than ten minutes and were against huge men who outweighed him by fifty pounds, but Luke was never beaten. The men thought they were fun, but every win Luke had made them a little warier about ever confronting him. When he cracked the whip, the men responded, but at the end of the day, the cold beers made them think that he wasn't such a bad guy. The balance of fear and respect was exactly what he was seeking. After clearing a profit of nearly $150,000 on Ferry Road, he was on his way.

Monty and Veronica Beaurepaire regularly threw lavish dinners at their Hamilton mansion, and the Cramers were always invited. Monty had subtly suggested to Luke that, if he wanted to reach the top, he should drop the "gonnas," "wannas," and "dunnos" and try to improve his literacy. The guests were a potpourri of politicians, doctors, lawyers, architects, and engineers who were leaders in their respective fields. Luke was uncomfortable in their presence, but Kiara shone and would participate passionately whenever the subjects of Aboriginal rights, the homeless, and child abuse were raised. While Luke's participation was almost nonexistent, he listened and learned a great deal. One night a doctor and two lawyers were debating the merits of DNA evidence. "It's just getting started," the doctor said. "In twenty years' time, they'll be using DNA to solve crimes that are occurring right now."

"That's providing the police keep the evidence," one of the lawyers said.

"And it hasn't been contaminated," the other chimed in. "I'd be surprised if I couldn't create reasonable doubt after twenty years."

The doctor ignored their comments and followed up with, "It's a damn shame that so many murder victims were cremated. Their murderers will never face justice." He paused and added, "Not on Earth, anyway."

"I'm not with you."

"Simple," the doctor replied, "at eighteen hundred degrees Fahrenheit, everything is destroyed. There's no DNA. Hence my conclusion that those cases will never be solved."

Luke knew that there had recently been a case in England where DNA evidence had been used, and that some in the medical profession and police enforcement were claiming that it was a panacea. It was interesting but hardly likely to ever affect him, and he gave it little more thought.

After Luke finished the Ferry Street warehouse, winning new jobs became a little easier. Potential clients had something to look at, and

CramerBuild gradually developed a reputation for building on time and on budget. In the first three years, it mainly built factories and warehouses, but at the start of the fourth year, it won a contract to build a small shopping center.

CramerBuild was successful and growing. It had thirty employees and more than sixty subcontractors. Luke was a hard but fair boss who looked after his workers when they were hurt or ill, and perhaps this was the reason he hadn't experienced industrial-relations problems. The other reason was that CramerBuild was too small for the union to worry about, but that changed with the commencement of the Opal Shopping Center.

A heavyset, flabby delegate from the Builders Laborers and Miners Union, better known as the BLMU, approached Luke on site and told him that the union didn't want to cause any trouble – it just wanted to help him. If he supported it, it would support him. The last thing he wanted was a union, but he listened politely and maintained his composure. The delegate's attitude quickly changed when Luke said, "My workers are already well looked after and don't need a union."

In the blink of an eye, the delegate went from charming to threatening, saying, "You realize we can cause you a lot of trouble."

"All you'll do is hurt those who you're meant to be helping and protecting. You're not going to hurt me," he said, fixing his steely blue eyes on the delegate, knowing that every worker was watching. "Besides, you have enough trouble with MultiStruct without worrying about a small-timer like me."

"MultiStruct's not your concern. I want to talk to the men during the lunchbreak," the delegate demanded.

"Want what you like," Luke said, now standing so close to the man he could smell the alcohol on his breath. "Now get off my site."

"I'll be back. You better get used to seeing me. Make up your mind. You can do it the hard way, or you can do it the easy way, but this is gonna be a union site."

"You can walk off the site, or I can throw you off," Luke said, confronting the man. "Make up your mind. You have fifteen seconds."

As the man backed away, he lost his footing and stumbled. When he looked up, Luke yelled, "Five seconds."

At knockoff time, when the men were enjoying their beers, Luke spoke to them in small groups, giving them the message that if they chose to join the union, it would cost them their bonuses and benefits. George Simpson, a huge supervisor in his early thirties who had all but defeated Luke in a hard-fought wrestle, said, "Don't worry. I've never had a boss who shared profits with his workers until now, and no one's gonna join the union as long as I'm on site. Two-bit bloody hoodlums."

Chapter 11

The stock market smashed MultiStruct Ltd.'s share price as the BLMU's three-week strike at its Creek Street site almost brought work on its forty-story Federal Insurance Office Tower to a complete halt. Financiers, bankers, and shareholders were desperate to end the strike. The union demanded a closed shop, health and safety officers of its choice, and insisted that its flag fly above the site. A small percentage of workers labeled as scabs continued to work while those on strike struggled to survive without their wages and vented their rage on the company and the scabs.

After twenty-four days without the company caving in, the union decided to increase the ante. Construction sites all over Brisbane closed, and thousands of BLMU members congregated in Creek Street, bringing the city to a standstill. That night the strike was the major news story carried by the media.

Luke sat glued to the television watching mounted policemen try to clear the street. Thugs like those in Las Vegas, this time wearing BLMU T-shirts, punched the horses' heads, spit on the policemen, and dragged one off his horse, viciously kicking him while he was on the ground. Only a few workers tried to cross the line and were punched, kicked, spit on, called scabs, and warned that their families would pay for their treachery. Anarchy was the order of the day.

Luke seethed as he watched and resolved that no union would ever control his sites. Politicians from all sides and the chief police commissioner condemned the union leaders and strikers. A spokesman for MultiStruct claimed that the union was acting illegally and declared the company would not back down. In response, Col Decker, the BLMU's boss, accused the company's management of acting deceitfully and not being concerned about his members' safety. He also added a new demand – full payment for all workers for the duration of the strike before they would consider returning to work.

The following day the crowds were even larger, but now there were hundreds of heavily armed police carrying shields providing a clear way for the few workers with the courage to run the gauntlet. Many of the non-unionists stayed home rather than running the risk that their families might be harmed. The company got an order from the Federal Court, declaring the strike illegal and ordering that the workers return.

Decker tore the order to pieces to the chants and cheering of thousands of workers and warned that, if the court or police tried to enforce it, the unions would close the state down. A spokesman for the Wharf Workers' Union said that its members stood ready to support their brothers in the BLMU and, if necessary, they would close every port in the land. The company moved from litigation to mediation in a vain attempt to resolve the dispute.

Luke watched the company's CEO talk about compromise, both sides' needing to give something, and his genuine desire to end the strike. Luke was young but streetwise, and he knew he had just listened to the weasel words of surrender. The union was going to get everything it wanted. The late news carried an interview with Col Decker saying that he recognized and applauded MultiStruct's bona fide attempts to reach an agreement. Negotiations were tough but nearing fruition, and he looked forward to his members, the hardest-working building workers in the world, being back on site before the end of the week.

On the plus side, perhaps because the MultiStruct strike was so drawn out, no one from the BLMU returned to the Opal Shopping Center site.

Some suppliers were still reluctant to supply CramerBuild without a bank guarantee or large deposit. Webster Glass, the glazing supplier to the Opal Shopping Center, insisted on payment on delivery, and Luke arranged to meet Frank Webster, the company's CEO and founder, to see whether he could change his mind.

As Luke pulled up at Webster Glass's gatehouse, he stared in surprise at the expansive warehouse and factory complex. The double-story cream brick offices in front of the warehouse spoke of yesteryear. Despite this, they were clean and tidy, and the reception-ist informed Luke that Mr. Webster was expecting him. She led him to an office at the very end of the corridor, knocked gently, and said, "Mr. Cramer is here for his two o'clock appointment, Mr. Webster."

Luke heard a gruff voice say, "Well, show him in, girly. Don't keep him waiting."

The gray-haired, slightly stooped-over man standing behind the large oak desk with his hand extended said, "It's a pleasure to meet you, Mr. Cramer. Thank you for coming. I know it's a long drive from the Gold Coast. Please take a seat, and we'll get down to business."

"Likewise," Luke replied unable to hide his surprise. The man sitting opposite him was at least seventy-five, but his handshake was firm and strong.

"You were expecting someone younger," Webster said, his pierc-ing emerald green eyes gleaming. "I'm used to it. I founded this busi-ness nearly fifty years ago, and they'll carry me out on my last day. This was one of the first warehouses built in Brisbane, and now it's one of the last. People like you have turned them into yuppy apart-ments. Still, you didn't come here to listen to me ramble. Why should I give you credit? You're just a boy. How are old you? Twenty?"

"Mr. Webster, CramerBuild has been in business for more than three years and never failed to meet its debts. A credit check will prove it. Oh, and I'm twenty-six."

"I know you can pay your debts. You'd be surprised how much I know about you and your company, Mr. Cramer. You obviously have something, or Monty Beaurepaire wouldn't be backing you. I want to know about that something."

Luke was annoyed. The old fart was either lonely or a busybody who was just wasting his time. "I don't care to discuss my personal relationships. It should be enough that you know CramerBuild will honor its debts."

Webster clasped his gnarled hands together and smiled. "Be patient, Mr. Cramer. I asked you here to help you. Try to relax. I'm not here to waste your time, and I haven't lost my marbles. Why don't you take a pad and pen from your briefcase? You might want to make some notes."

Luke studied Webster carefully as he reached for his briefcase. The old man's eyes twinkled with vigor not matched by any other part of his body. "You can help me by letting CramerBuild have credit."

"You've been in Queensland for nearly four years. Do you know how organized crime works here?"

What is this old guy smoking? "I was born in Chicago and worked in Las Vegas. I didn't need to come here to find out how organized crime works."

Webster tweaked his mustache and smirked. "I know about Chicago and Vegas. We had you checked out to see whether you were the type of person we wanted to do business with, let alone give credit. What you saw wasn't organized crime. To understand how organized crime operates at its worst, you would need to spend a day watching the Queensland Parliament. It's only a fifteen-minute walk from here."

And the old bugger said he hadn't lost his marbles. Who's he kidding? "I don't think so. I don't have any interest. If they leave me alone, I'll leave them alone."

"Oh, if only it were that easy, young man. They're already looking at you. You can't build a big business in this state without paying."

"You have."

"True, but they're not worried about me. I'm rich, and they know they can't hurt me. If they tried, I'd be in the media shouting about their dirty secrets. Besides, I'll be dead soon enough. Then they'll make whoever buys the business pay."

"'They'? Who are 'they'?" Luke snapped.

"Ah, you think you're listening to the meanderings of a silly, old man. Listen and listen carefully. It might save you money and heart-ache. In the U.S., councils have a lot of power. Here they issue town planning and building permits, collect the rates, pick up the garbage, and repair the roads. That's not to say they don't have any power. Many councilors have become very rich courtesy of property developers, but that's another story. The real power in Queensland lies with the government and the premier. Think of the premier as having far more power than one of your city mayors and the state's governor combined. Make a note of that."

The old man was a compelling raconteur, and Luke found himself involuntarily wanting to hear more. "Go on."

"Every state in Australia has two houses of parliament - a house of the people and a house of review. Every state except one. Queensland did away with its house of review over sixty years ago. Now there's only one house of parliament, and the ruling party can do what it likes. The conservatives, the equivalent of your Republicans, have ruled the roost for the past fifteen years, and the premier and his ministers have become very rich. They're as crooked as a dog's hind leg, and yet they rule the state without any checks or balances."

"What about the police?"

"The premier appointed the chief police commissioner, even had him knighted. Sir Terrence bloody Walsh, a real bastard. You wouldn't find a more bent cop anywhere in the world, and it's spread through the whole force. Every other cop is on the take."

"I still don't understand what it has to do with me."

"Bear with me," the old man said. "You were recently approached by BLMU officials. They wanted you to unionize your sites and fly their flag. You told them to get lost."

"How do you know?"

"When we check someone out, we're very thorough. They haven't been back, but it's only a matter of time. You got lucky when their attention was diverted by the MultiStruct strike, but they'll be back, and the next time they won't be so easily fobbed off."

"Why would they worry about me? I'm small-time. They're more interested in the large employers. MultiStruct and its competitors."

"You wish." Webster chuckled. "You have nearly a hundred employees and subcontractors working on the Opal Shopping Center. You may not know it, but it's probably the largest nonunion site in Queensland. It's a bad example. If you can get away without kowtowing to the union, others will think they can do the same. The BLMU's not going to let that happen."

"None of my sites are ever going to be unionized," Luke said, "but what would change, if they were?"

"Ah, the vital question. The unions see their corruption as a counterbalance to the government's corruption. Once the BLMU flag is flying over your sites, no police force, state or federal, will enter them."

"That's no big d-"

"Let me finish," the old man growled. "Once that happens, your sites will be in the business of selling drugs, security, and protection. They'll become bases for the worst motorbike gang in the country, the Ferals. The union will insist you use insurance companies it nominates, and it will receive huge kickbacks. They'll demand that you pay your employees' pension contributions into a union fund where the directors are former union officials. They'll choose which subcontractors can work on your sites, and they'll be getting a kickback. from them as well. No one will be able to set foot on your sites without a union ticket, and if that isn't enough, they'll insist on appointing your health and safety officers and won't tolerate any interference from you. It's a key requirement."

It was obvious that the old man hated the unions, but Luke didn't know whether he was exaggerating. "Why's the health and safety thing so important?"

"A few years back, the unions were dying. They were all but finished. The federal government had introduced tough laws banning wildcat strikes. Some unions were bankrupted by the size of the fines. Then the government introduced health and safety legislation, and the unions latched on to it like maggots on a carcass. Health and safety officers were provided with enormous powers to the point of being able to shut a site down if they thought it was unsafe. It was manna from heaven for the unions. If they could control the appointment of health and safety officers, they could create havoc. Better still, criticizing health and safety was akin to criticizing childbirth – it couldn't be done. How many times do you see a freeway barricaded for miles, to protect a couple of workers filling fifty yards of potholes with bitumen? Plenty, but is anyone ever critical? No! You can't criticize health and safety, and the unions know it."

"I have health and safety officers on my sites. I know about the legislation. They do a great job, and I support them. We've never had any trouble with the government inspectors."

"Not yet, you haven't. You might find the inspectors become a lot tougher when the union flexes its muscles."

"Hang on, Mr. Webster. The government and the unions are on opposite sides of politics. Why would the government inspectors help the unions?"

Webster smiled and slowly shook his head. "You have so much to learn. They all feed from the same trough. There was a time when the Labor Party controlled the unions. Now it's the other way around – the unions tell the Labor Party what to do. Nearly every Labor politician is a former union official. The government would love to hold a royal commission or inquiry into the unions, but it's too scared to bring one on. If they did, there's a chance that land grants and other favors made by the government to property developers would also be exposed.

"Then there are the donations and the cash bribes paid by those developers to the unions to ensure there's no trouble on their sites. It's rumored that the union boss Col Decker's holiday house in Noosa didn't cost him a cent. It built itself. Those same developers made donations to the conservatives and paid bribes to ministers and other government officials so you can see how messy an inquiry might be. It's better for all concerned if the boat isn't rocked."

"Jesus!"

"The buildings here are the costliest in the world to construct. Where else can a builder's laborer earn more than a recently qualified doctor? You're doing the right thing using subcontractors. The last thing you want to do is employ labor."

"Is the mob involved?"

"You mean like how it is in Chicago and Vegas? No. The union, the government, and the bikers are the mob, except they're much worse. They have nothing to fear from the police. Half the cops in the state are on their payroll."

"You're telling me the union runs the state."

"No, it runs the building industry, but there are three hoodlums it won't cross. Charlie 'Butcher' Gorman, his two partners, and their gang run prostitution, illegal gambling, and soft drugs in Brisbane. They launder cash by building office blocks and parking garages. Gorman's a stone-cold killer who uses bolt cutters to remove his victims' digits when he can't get his own way. His gang's known as the toe cutters. There's never any trouble on their sites."

Webster laughed. "On the plus side, if there is one, Gorman likes to boast that he's never killed an honest man. It's rumored that he subcontracts to the police. A few years back, there was a lunatic, enforcer nicknamed Hire-A-Kill who committed a spate of killings that captured the media's attention. He was bad for the state and bad for business, but the cops couldn't nail him. Rumor has it that Gorman summoned the nutcase to a meeting in a dark alley on the outskirts of Brisbane on the pretext of selling him the latest submachine gun.

"When they found Hire-A-Kill's body, it was shredded beyond recognition. That gun fired a thousand rounds a minute, and Gorman supposedly emptied the magazine. That's a hundred rounds. The cops interrogated a few bums before releasing them. No one was ever charged. Make a note of Charlie Gorman's name and resolve to be very careful when you hear it."

"That's all very interesting," Luke said, "but I still don't see how it concerns me."

"The BLMU's going to come after you hard. The delegate who saw you last time has copped a lot of crap about being unable to sign up a kid. Next time they'll have their enforcers with them, maybe a few of their biker mates. They're going to threaten, bribe, cajole, and coerce, but they're not going to take no for an answer. If the worse comes to the worst, they'll do everything they can to put you out of business."

"Will Gorman work for them?"

"Everyone has a price. I don't know. His specialty is leaning on other crooks. You know, a smarty pulls off a heist or bank job, and Gorman wants a cut. Some tried to tough it out, but it's hard to walk without toes. Beating up or killing law-abiding citizens is bad for business, and Gorman rarely does anything that's bad for business. The union would have to pay him a small fortune, and he still might say no. The good thing is that it probably thinks you're too insignificant, so it won't try to hire Gorman. It has its own thugs and, if they fail, the Ferals biker gang."

"I don't understand why you told me about him then."

Webster laughed. "Forewarned is forearmed. I know you're a tough guy, and you're going to fight the union. Just be extra wary if you find out Gorman's involved."

"I have to get back on site," Luke said, getting to his feet. "I still don't know why you wanted to see me."

"I like to personally assess the people who I do business with and, more importantly, to whom I give credit."

"You're giving CramerBuild credit?"

"That's what I said. Thirty days."

"Thank you," Luke said.

"Feel free to call or come and see me anytime, young man. There's a lot of knowledge in this old head. Good luck. I'll have my fingers crossed for you."

Chapter 12

Early on Monday morning two weeks later, a late-model, black Ford pulled up in front of the Opal Shopping Center site. Four men, including the flabby union delegate whom Luke had told to get lost, sauntered across the site. "Hey," Flabby shouted at Luke, "we want to see you."

Luke looked up from what he was doing and said, "I'm busy. Make an appointment. I'll see whether I can find time for you."

A slim, middle-aged man wearing a white business shirt and black pants strolled over to where Luke was standing and handed an envelope to him and said, "I'm Dennis Bartlett, assistant secretary of the union. That's a notice saying we'll be on site tomorrow at lunchtime to address your men. We don't want to cause you any trouble. If you cooperate, we'll get along just fine."

As Luke was reading the notice, he felt Flabby and the other two men crowding around him. They were heavyset, unsmiling, and dressed in all black. "You're wasting your time. My men are happy and well looked after. They don't want or need a union."

Before they could respond, Luke heard someone behind him and turned to see the towering figure of George Simpson with his hands behind his back. "What Mr. Cramer said is right." George grinned. "I took a vote yesterday. No one wants to join the union."

"As if your vote counts," Bartlett sneered.

"Why wouldn't it?" Luke demanded.

"Look, I'm trying to be reasonable," Bartlett said. "We're not going to interfere with your business. You're too small for us to worry about. However, we do want you to tell your men to join the union, and we want you to deduct the dues from their wages and remit them to us. Also, we want to make it a union site – no ticket, no work, and –"

"You don't need to go on," Luke said. "It's not going to happen

- not ever. I won't discriminate against those who want to join the union, but I won't help you or them either."

"This is a big job for you. Your first shopping center. Twenty-six shops. Nice job. I guess you've locked in a healthy profit. You've poured the slab, and you're making good progress. Imagine where you would've been if you'd poured half the slab and suddenly there were no more concrete trucks."

"Or if one of your workers met with an unexpected accident," one of the thugs butted in.

"Yeah," the other thug said, his face so close to Luke's that he could feel the spittle.

Buoyed by the presence of the thugs, Flabby stepped forward and jabbed his forefinger into Luke's chest. "You can do it the hard way or the easy way, but you are going to do what we want. Get used to it. This is gonna be a BLMU building site!"

Every man on site was now watching, and a vision of Vince Sordi and his lecture about fear flashed before Luke's eyes. Without warning, he grabbed Flabby by his suit lapels and hurled him into one of the thugs, shouting, "Get off my site! Now!"

As the other thug raised his fist, George Simpson brought his hands from behind his back to reveal a four-foot piece of lumber. "I wouldn't if I were you," he said.

"We'll go, but we'll be back tomorrow," Bartlett said. "You're a fool, Cramer. You can't win. We'll close you down. Put you out of business. Send you back to the U.S. with your tail between your legs."

"Move," Luke roared, "or you'll be carried off!"

Flabby looked like he was going to cry, and Bartlett backed rapidly away. The two thugs appeared unmoved, standing with their huge arms across their chests, but their eyes betrayed their apprehension. No one is comfortable around a madman. As they crossed the road to their car, Bartlett turned and shouted, "You've made a big mistake! We'll be back!"

The car pulled away, and George turned to Luke. "Jeez, Luke, I thought you were gonna burst a blood vessel," he said. "Your eyes were rolling, and your face was purple. I'm here to help you, but at one stage, I thought I was going to have to help them. It's not for me to tell you what to do, but your temper's gonna land you in trouble if you can't control it."

I never lost my temper, George. It was an act for them, you, and every other man on site. By the looks on their faces, I must be a good actor, Luke thought. But out loud, he said, "George, if I want your advice, I'll ask for it. Now get back to work."

Simpson scowled and eyeballed Luke for a few seconds before turning to return to where he had been working. When he was about ten yards away, Luke yelled, "Thanks, George, it was mighty comforting knowing you had my back! Thanks a lot!"

The big man spun around, and his face lit up in a huge grin. "I'm happy I could help. Sorry I overstepped the mark."

Fear without losing loyalty. Something not even Sordi achieved, Luke thought, with some pride.

At midday the following day, the union representatives returned in force – Bartlett, Flabby, and six enforcers. Luke knew there was nothing he could do but warned them to be off site before 12:30 when the lunchbreak ended. Flabby shouted into a megaphone ordering all workers to attend a meeting in the open area at the front of the site. Of the hundred-strong workforce, fifteen shuffled forward to hear what the union officials had to say – the fifteen whom George Simpson had agreed to let attend the night before, knowing that none would sign up. The big man leaned up against a wall, surveying the two groups.

Bartlett and his cronies positioned themselves in front of the windows of one of the shops. He was a fiery orator and told the men the only reason they were well paid was because of the union and the sacrifices that had been made by its members over the years. He claimed that it was the unions who had forced the forty-hour week, the thirty-eight-hour week, the thirty-five-hour week, and four weeks' annual leave. Without the union, who would protect them when they were sick or injured? Without the union and the union's pension fund, who would look after them when they retired?

The bosses could not be trusted, and their boss, Luke Cramer, was young, inexperienced, and looking to exploit them by making a fast buck before returning to America. If he were looking after his workers and paying them fairly, he had nothing to fear from the union. The problem was that he appeared to have something to hide, and that was the reason for his temper tantrum yesterday.

Bartlett finished by saying, "I know he's done sweetheart deals with you and is supposedly sharing profits. He's giving you the crumbs off a rich man's table. You shouldn't be grateful; you should be insulted. You've all heard the old saying, 'beware of Yanks bearing gifts,' haven't you? Does anyone have any questions?"

No one raised a hand or said a word.

"Speak up. Tell me if you've been intimidated or threatened. It's against the law, and there are serious penalties for those who breach it!" Bartlett yelled, unable to contain his frustration.

Again, he was greeted with silence.

"Okay, how about a show of hands from those who want to join the union?"

Some of the men looked around, but no one raised a hand. George Simpson grinned while picking his teeth with a tiny toothpick.

"I know you're scared," Bartlett said, stepping forward and pushing a bundle of union literature into the chest of the man nearest to him. "These are application forms and booklets about what the union can do for you. If you call us, rest assured the conversation will be confidential. Don't be afraid; the union can protect you."

It was 12:28 when Luke said, "Mr. Bartlett, you and your henchmen have two minutes to get off my site."

"If-if I find you've threatened any of these men, you'll feel the wrath of the law."

After they left, George Simpson said, "They're coming for you, Luke. The work's too far advanced on this site to hurt you, but they're gonna raise hell on the next big job you win."

"They don't know what hell is, but they'll sure find out if they take me on."

Chapter 13

Four weeks before completing the Opal Shopping Center, CramerBuild won two contracts: the first for a significantly larger factory outlet shopping center in Sunnyside, and the second for a car dealer's showroom and office in Burleigh Heads. Luke had allowed $300,000 for NFR on the Opal quote which turned out to be pure cream because there were no unexpected costs. The client for the Sunnyside Factory Outlet was the Barclay Property Trust, and the anchor tenant was the huge Barclay Clothing & Apparel. It was a major breakthrough because the Trust owned and was building shopping centers all over Australia. The deadline was tight, but Luke knew that, if he delivered a quality product on time, it would lead to further contracts.

He was on the Sunnyside site watching the surveyors peg it out when Dennis Bartlett pulled up in his Ford. For once, he was by himself. He strolled over to Luke, extended his hand, and said, "Look, we got off on the wrong foot. Can we start again? We don't want to hurt your business. Why would we? All that would do is put our members out of work."

Luke ignored the outstretched hand. "Mr. Bartlett, you can't hurt my business, and none of your members work for me."

"Call me Dennis. Can I call you Luke? If you encourage your men to join the BLMU and make your sites closed shops, we won't seek to fly our flag and will guarantee that you won't be subject to any industrial disputes."

"I don't understand. If you're not going to do anything, why would the men want to sign up? Surely, you're not in it just for the dues."

Bartlett shifted uneasily and tugged at his shirtsleeves. "It's a bad look for us. CramerBuild is the only builder between Brisbane and the coast with more than a hundred workers that refuses to make its sites closed shops. The other builders haven't objected to us partici-pating in the appointment of their health and safety officers."

"Participating?" Luke laughed. "You don't participate. You stand over them, and if your nominee – make that stooge – is not appointed, you make trouble for them."

"Hear me out," Bartlett persisted. "The BLMU has a lot of influence with one of the largest insurers in the country. I've been authorized to offer you a position on its board. You'll find the remuneration to your liking."

"Jesus! A bloody bribe. I don't know anything about insurance, hazards, or investments. There's nothing I can bring to the table of an insurance company. Thanks, but no thanks."

Bartlett's face was flushed, but he kept his composure. "Don't let me have your answer now. Think about it. You'll make a lot of contacts. There are some important people on the board, and it's advised by top investment firms. It's a great opportunity."

"I don't need to think about it. The answer's no. I know what you'll do once you're on my sites. I'm sure you're familiar with the old saying, 'give 'em an inch, and they'll take a mile.' Well, you aren't ever going to get that inch, and you can forget about having any say in appointing our health and safety officers."

"You're making a big mistake. We want to work with you, not against you. You don't need to fear us."

"Oh, I don't fear you." Luke smirked. "I just want to control my own destiny, and, in that regard, I don't want to work with you. It's nothing personal. I don't want the bank telling me how to run my business either."

"You don't employ any union members. Despite what you say, you discriminate against them. Worse, you employ that big lout to intimidate them."

"Wrong, wrong, and wrong. I've employed plenty of union members, but after they hear what I have to offer, they can't see the benefit of remaining in the union. George, unlike your thugs, is not a lout and has never threatened anyone. All he does is explain how I reward top-quality, hard work."

"I came here holding an olive branch," Bartlett snarled, "but you have chosen to spit in my face. You said we couldn't hurt you. You'll live to regret that. This is going to end badly for you. Don't come crying to me when CramerBuild is in liquidation, and the bank's calling in its personal guarantees. You think Chicago was tough? You haven't seen anything yet."

"Go back to your bosses and tell them to forget about me. We have one thing in common. We don't care about the law. You take me on, and I won't be running to lawyers. I'll be coming after you personally, so, if it ends badly, it'll be you who'll be doing the regretting."

"Have it your way. You've just declared war on the BLMU – a war you can't win."

The messages the tea leaves were sending were obvious, but Luke didn't read them. With two major projects to undertake, CramerBuild recruited additional labor and subcontractors. Six of the new workers employed on the Sunnyside project were BLMU members, and despite George's persuasive efforts, they wouldn't resign. The union was careful to comply with the law, but its delegates, having given the proper notice, were, much to Luke's chagrin, regularly on site. George Simpson let it be known that the union members would adversely affect the bonuses that CramerBuild paid at the end of each project, and tension permeated the site. Despite this, the union did nothing to jeopardize work on the Sunnyside site until the first of two huge suspended slabs was poured.

The pour was proceeding smoothly when Luke received a panic-stricken call from the Burleigh Heads site informing him of a serious accident. He jumped into the company's SUV and sped to the site. He wasn't worried about leaving Sunnyside because George was far better at supervising concrete pours than he was.

When Luke left, Rapidmix concrete trucks lined the street, and the pour was going as scheduled until the slab was slightly more than half complete. George was pushing the men hard and waiting for the next truck when he looked up, and the street was empty. He had been there when the union organizers had warned Luke, and now they were carrying out their threat. He quickly called the Burleigh Heads site but knew that, whatever Luke did, it would be too late. Then out of anger and frustration, he launched on the union members, subjecting them to a tirade of foul, verbal abuse in a futile attempt to coerce them into fighting him.

Luke called Rapidmix as soon as he heard George's news, but he couldn't get past the receptionist before jumping into the SUV and driving at breakneck speed back to Sunnyside, all the while knowing that he would be too late to do anything. As he drove past other construction sites, he saw Rapidmix trucks discharging their loads. By the time he reached Sunnyside, he knew exactly what had happened. He charged into the site office, grabbed a phone, and called Rapidmix again. This time he was put through to the sales manager. "Sorry, Mr. Cramer," he said, "we had a breakdown at the plant and were unable to supply."

"You're a lying bastard," Luke snarled. "I saw your trucks delivering to other sites when they couldn't deliver to mine. How did the BLMU threaten you?"

"Don't use that tone with me," the executive said. "Those trucks were probably dispatched before the plant breakdown."

"You grub. I'll talk to you any way I like. I have a good mind to drive to your office and beat you to a pulp," Luke shouted, before he heard the clunk of a phone being slammed down.

His next call was to Monty who said, "Luke, it's known as a secondary boycott. Do you know what that is?"

"I don't have time for this. Just tell me."

"As a matter of fact, you now have all the time in the world. The BLMU must have approached the builders that it's done sweetheart deals with and told them that, if they wanted to avoid industrial disputes, they should call Rapidmix and threaten to take their business away if they continued to supply you. The nasty twist with you is that they must have told Rapidmix to make sure they stopped supplying after you'd poured half the slab."

"Bastards! That has to be illegal!"

"It is. The Australian Consumer and Competition Commission (ACCC) will investigate and probably prosecute. Plus, you have grounds for civil actions against the BLMU, Rapidmix, and the builders who put them up to it. The problem is that I think they're all Federal Court actions, and the defendants will seek to drag them out with adjournments. The longer they can keep you in court, the more it's going to cost you. They'll also ask for security for their costs."

"What's that?"

"They'll ask the court to make an order forcing you to lodge an amount with the court sufficient to cover their legal costs and fees, if your actions are unsuccessful. It could be up to half a million."

"I'm screwed."

"No, you're not. You have me. I'm going to call Tim Dixon. He's a Carr & Carr partner and the best industrial-relations lawyer in the state. He's also a close friend of mine. His office will call you within the hour. Hang tough, Luke. I'll make sure he sees you tomorrow."

"Can I see you after I've seen him?"

"Sure. You might have to wait if I'm with someone, but it would be good to catch up."

Luke put the phone down and stared at the muddy floor. No matter what happened with the legal action, there was no way he could meet the Sunnyside Factory Outlet completion deadline. The Barclay Property Trust had taken a risk with him, and he'd let it down. *Maybe I shouldn't have opposed the union. I wonder whether it's too late to undo the damage. God, what am I thinking? If it gets its feet on my throat, I'll be a slave to it. No, I'm going to fight like I've never fought in my life*, he thought.

Thirty minutes later, Tim Dixon's personal assistant called and said that he was in court, but that he could see Luke at midday tomorrow. He felt like he had aged ten years. As he thought about the day's events, he cursed. His desire for retribution had made him overlook the obvious. Anxious to remedy his oversight, he called George Simpson into the site office and told him to hire ten jackhammers and waste containers for delivery first thing in the morning. "George, make sure your men don't waste any time breaking up that slab."

It was 6:30 P.M. when Luke left the site and walked toward his car. He was thirty yards away when he heard an enormous explosion and was thrown to the ground. He felt a surge of heat envelop him, and when he stumbled to his feet, his ears were ringing, his hair and eyebrows were singed, his face was black, and his car was a smoldering mess. Within fifteen minutes, the police arrived on the scene and asked him whether he had any idea who had bombed his car. When he told them of his union problems, the senior detective said,

"Mr. Cramer, that's most unlikely. This is Australia, not America. Our unions aren't run by the Mafia."

What did that old guy Webster say? Every second cop is bent. "You're right," Luke replied. "It was probably some nutcase."

After George Simpson left Sunnyside, he went straight to his local pub, hoping that a few cold beers would ease his disappointment. Fifteen glasses later, he wobbled out onto the sidewalk and started the short walk home. He turned off the main road and was stumbling along his street past a poorly lighted park with a lot of trees, when he felt the agony of someone crashing a steel bar across his knees. As he was going down, he was struck with another heavy blow, this time to the back of his head.

When he regained consciousness, his face was a bloody mess, and the pain in his smashed knees was unbearable. Fortunately, he blacked out again. When he awoke, he was in the Surfers Paradise Community Hospital, his legs encased in plaster.

Chapter 14

When Luke arrived home, Kiara was waiting for him on the front porch. "Thank God you're all right," she said, choking back sobs as she wrapped her arms around him. "You could have been killed. I saw what's left of your car on the news."

"No, I couldn't. They were sending me a warning. They must have been watching the site and detonated the bomb after seeing me leave. They're trying to scare me."

"It's worse than Las Vegas," Kiara sniffled.

"No, it's not even close. I'll have to take your car in the morning. Is that okay with you?"

"Of course. Carlos can miss a day of school. Besides, in all the turmoil, I forgot to tell you that Roxy must have gotten out today. Instead of school, we'll go for a walk and see whether we can find her. Let's go inside. Your dinner's getting cold."

"Sure," Luke said, putting his arm around her. "I hate it when I miss seeing our little man. What time did he go to bed?"

"You only missed him by ten minutes. He was crying for Roxy. He's worried that some bad people stole her." Kiara smiled. "I hope we find her."

"I'll go for a walk after I've eaten. She might be lost," Luke said, fighting the bile building up in his throat. "Can you get me a flashlight and her leash?"

Thirty minutes later, he said, "Don't wait up for me, honey. If I don't find her right away I'll be a couple of hours. I need a long walk to clear my head."

He walked briskly until he was out of sight of the house and then slowed to a casual stroll. He was almost certain he wouldn't be finding Roxy, at least not alive. The urgent call that had taken him away from Sunnyside to Burleigh Heads was about a worker who'd fallen from a ladder and broken his neck. However, when he arrived at Burleigh Heads, the supervisor who made the call said that the man who had been lying prone on the ground had suddenly stood up, said that he wasn't seriously hurt, jumped into his car, and presumably drove home. *It was a setup to get me away from Sunnyside*, Luke thought. *We won't see that guy again.*

Thirty minutes later, he turned and headed back to his house. Other than the light on the porch, it was in total darkness. He crept down the sideway to the backyard and then scanned the lawn from fence to fence in five-yard intervals. When he got to the back fence, he shone the flashlight on a small pile of dead palm fronds. He couldn't see anything, but when he lifted the top two fronds, the innocent little face of Roxy stared back at him. Her throat had been slashed.

Fighting back the urge to vomit, Luke crept into the house and found a towel. He carefully wrapped Roxy's little body in the towel and put it in the trunk of Kiara's car, along with a shovel. He vowed that Kiara and Carlos would never find out what had happened to Roxy. *How dare they threaten my family. Someone is going to pay for this*, he thought, shaking with rage.

It was a few minutes to five when Luke tersely answered the phone. "Luke, Luke, I'm sorry to ring you at this time of the morning," an obviously distraught Maggie Simpson said. "George didn't come home last night. I just had a call from the Gold Coast police. He's in the Surfers Paradise Community Hospital. Some thugs attacked him on the way home. They smashed his kneecaps and fractured his skull. Why would anyone do that? George is a harmless, gentle giant. Does it have something to do with your car getting blown up?"

"That's terrible, Maggie. I don't know. I'll shower and head to the hospital. Keep your chin up. George is a tough cookie."

"My sister has just arrived to babysit the kids," Maggie sniffled. "I'm leaving now. I'll see you there."

It was quiet when Luke arrived at the hospital, and when he entered the foyer, Maggie was deep in discussion with a doctor. As Luke went over to them, the doctor stopped talking and Maggie said, "It's all right, Doctor. This is Luke Cramer, George's boss."

"Well, as I was saying, Mrs. Simpson, he's sustained a massive blow to the back of his head, but fortunately, there's no brain damage and –"

"He's going to be okay then," Luke butted in.

"I didn't say that," the doctor said, miffed at being interrupted. "We've patched his knees as best we can, and there's an orthopedic surgeon on her way from Brisbane. Your husband will have to go back into the OR as soon as she arrives, Mrs. Simpson. It will be a long time before he walks again, and no matter how successful the procedure, he'll never walk the way he did."

"My poor George. Why would anyone want to hurt him?" Maggie asked, staring at Luke.

"The police will be here soon," the doctor said. "They might be able to provide you with some answers."

"What time were they called?"

"When he was admitted, just before 3 A.M."

Luke frowned. "They're still not here. Can we see him?"

"He needs rest. You can see him for a few minutes when he wakes up, Mrs. Simpson. It would be better if you came back tomorrow, Mr. Cramer. We don't want to excite him."

"Fair enough," Luke replied. "Did he say anything about who it was that attacked him?"

"He said that it was dark, and he didn't see anyone. He mumbled through the operation about someone called Maudie, Jordy, Gordy or something. We couldn't make out what he was saying. Do those names ring any bells?"

Luke shook his head and looked at Maggie. "No," she said. "George has a lot of friends at the pub, but I've never heard him mention anyone with names like those."

After the doctor left, Maggie said, "There's no point in you waiting, Luke. I'll call you after I've spoken to George. Do you want me to ask him about Maudie or Fordy or whoever it was?"

"I'll leave it up to you," Luke said, looking at the floor. "I'm not sure how to say this, but be careful about what you tell the police. I don't know whose side they're on."

"You're not telling me anything new. I've lived in Queensland all my life."

"I'm sorry about George, Maggie. I want you to know that CramerBuild will pick up all his medical bills, and he will receive full pay until he returns. If you have any money problems, just call me."

"Thanks. George says you're the best boss he's ever had. Now I know why. Be careful, Luke. You're the one they really want."

"I'll be fine," Luke said, kissing her on the cheek. "I better get going."

As Luke was leaving, a police car pulled up at the front of the hospital. It had been over four hours since they were called.

He drove away from the coast and up into the brilliantly green hinterland. After four miles, he exited the main road onto a gravel track before stopping under a huge Bangalow palm. He climbed out and dug a shallow grave, rewrapping Roxy carefully in the towel before laying her to rest. After he'd filled in the grave, he packed it with gravel and compacted it with the shovel. He didn't want a feral cat or forest animal digging up his son's little pet.

Standing back from the grave, he looked down and said, "Sorry, I couldn't protect you, Roxy. I know it doesn't help, but those who did this to you are going to pay. Oh, how they're going to pay. Rest in peace, little girl."

Chapter 15

When Luke arrived at the Sunnyside site, he was greeted with the sound of jackhammers and sledgehammers, and he gave silent thanks to George. It took two days to remove the slab and steel mesh and another three days to replace the formwork and reinforcing before the slab could be poured. *How am I going to make sure the unions don't use their muscle to stop the concrete trucks midway through the pour?* Luke thought. He looked out the site office window and saw a black Rolls-Royce pull up on the other side of the road, and wondered whether it was the principals of the Barclay Property Trust.

Two huge men climbed out of the car, and he instantly knew they weren't from Barclay. He had seen them – or, more precisely, their types – in Chicago and Las Vegas. It was overcast and humid, but they wore expensive, three-piece suits and dark sunglasses, and the man who got out the passenger's side had a heavy gold chain hanging from his vest. They sauntered across the road, surveying the site before entering the office without knocking.

"Sol Menadue" the man with the gold chain said, extending a meaty hand with fingers adorned in gold rings. "This is my assistant, Toby Wilson."

Wilson nodded and positioned himself against the wall.

"What can I do for you?" Luke asked.

"Ah, Luke, may I call you Luke?" Menadue smiled, revealing an ugly, gold front tooth that contrasted starkly with his oily olive skin. "It's not what you can do for us but what we can do for you."

"I'm listening."

"We're industrial relations consultants," Menadue said, handing Luke an embossed business card – *Sol Menadue, Chief Executive Officer, Menadue & Partners. Industrial-Relations Consultants.* "If you retain us, we can make your union problems disappear."

"You're lawyers?" Luke facetiously asked.

"No, as you well know, we're not. We solve problems without lawyers or courtrooms. We do it expeditiously and guarantee the results. Lawyers can't do that."

"I don't know why the BLMU's even interested in me. I thought I was too small to worry about."

"Don't play dumb. It doesn't work. CramerBuild's no longer a small business, and you're screwing up the whole system. All the other builders on the coast run closed shops and, wherever possible, employ union labor rather than subcontractors. You do it differently, and it's upsetting the equilibrium."

"I use subcontractors because I get more out of them. The only way they make money is by ensuring their costs don't exceed what they quoted. The alternative is to pay some lazy prick $1,500 a week, and then, when I want to fire him, I have to give three warnings before I can show him the door."

"Yeah, yeah, we know all that. In case you missed it, we're experts," Menadue growled. "Now, listen to me. For $75,000, we can guarantee you'll have no further problems with the two projects you're working on. We'll give you an invoice for $50,000 for industrial-relations consulting, and you'll hand the other $25,000 to us in cash. It's less than what your lawyers will charge, and there's no guarantee they'll be successful."

"What happens after the two projects are complete? How far does your guarantee extend?"

"We renegotiate. That's what we do. You have two choices. You deal with us, or you deal with the BLMU. What happened yesterday was just a sample. You don't want to take them on. Make it easy for yourself. We both know you have far more than seventy-five thousand up your sleeve on those two jobs."

Luke looked at his watch. "I'm sorry, gentlemen. I'm running late for an appointment with my lawyers in Brisbane. I'll get back to you."

"I hope it's not about taking the BLMU on in court." Menadue smirked. "They can't help you. We can. Don't leave it too long though. The price is going up by the day. It'll be a hundred thousand by Friday."

Chapter 16

As Luke drove north along the Gold Coast Highway, thoughts of the BLMU and Menadue had him simmering. Despite his efforts to maintain self-control, he found himself gripping the steering wheel of Kiara's Volkswagen Golf and shouting, "Bastards!" They were squeezing him from all sides, and he had to find a way to fight back. He racked his brain until the glimmer of an idea came to him, but it would take money – big money.

Seventy minutes later, he drove into a parking garage on Turbot Street, immediately under the Federal Bank Building, which was home to Brisbane's professional elite. Carr & Carr's offices were on the thirtieth floor, and the elevator doors opened onto a large foyer and reception area with the almost obligatory black leather chairs, coffee tables, and magazine racks filled with newspapers and business literature. Gold-bound legal tomes that looked like they'd never been opened completely covered one wall while portraits of stern-looking judges took most of another.

Luke presented himself at the white marble reception counter where one of the three receptionists said that he was expected and asked him to follow her down a long corridor to Mr. Dixon's office. Large windows overlooked the Brisbane River, a towering cathedral, and a park thick with trees. The man behind the desk cluttered with files stood up, smiled, and extended his hand and said, "Tim Dixon, Luke. I've heard all about you, but by the look on your face, you were expecting someone different."

He was no more than thirty, about five feet three, with a small frame and little meat on his bones. "I thought you'd be older."

"Nice response," Dixon said, running his hand through his unruly, mousy brown hair as his wire-framed spectacles slipped down his nose. "I'm used to it. It's not the size of the dog that counts. It's the size of the fight in the dog. Monty's briefed me so let's get down to business."

"Sure," Luke replied, "but before we do, you should know that I had a visit from two thugs posing as industrial-relations consultants this morning."

"Sol Menadue, no doubt. He's a hoodlum with a rap sheet as long as your arm and a close friend of Col Decker, the union's boss. They supposedly met while doing hard time in Boggo Road Prison. They're a mean pair of bastards. Let me tell you how a Federal Court judge described the BLMU," Dixon said, flicking through some of the documents covering his desk.

"Ah, here we are. Justice Murray Freehill described the union as, and I quote, 'an embarrassment to law-abiding unions. It has repeatedly ignored the law and has shown total contempt for the rights of this court. It is not possible to imagine worse union behavior. The BLMU has been infiltrated by criminals pursuing their own illegal interests rather than the interests of its members. It has engaged in racketeering, coercion, blackmail, and violence and is a blight on society. The federal government should give serious consideration to de-registering this union.'

"They won't because the BLMU is the largest donor to the Labor Party and the Greens. There used to be a time when the government was the dog, and the BLMU was the tail. Sadly, the roles have been reversed, and the Labor Party wouldn't be in power were it not for the BLMU's largesse. The Labor Party's never going to de-register its main source of funds. I'm telling you this because the law means nothing to the BLMU, and if you take them on, they're going to go after you with everything they have. Once I commence legal proceedings, nothing will be off limits, including the health and safety of your family. Do you understand? Are you sure you want to proceed?"

"Are you sure you want to proceed, counselor?" Luke asked, cracking his knuckles. "Won't they go after you too? Won't you be putting your family at risk?"

"They'll threaten, and there'll be intimidating calls in the middle of the night, but so far, they've drawn the line at physically attacking lawyers. I'm not worried."

"Good, because I want you to hit them, Rapidmix, and the builders with everything you have. My biggest fear is that Rapidmix will stop their trucks in the middle of my next pour. What can we do about that?"

"I can get restraining orders from the court, but the BLMU will ignore them, and there's no certainty Rapidmix will comply. They'll make their decision based on what will cost them less – defying the court or defying the union."

"Jesus, maybe I should pay Menadue his seventy-five thousand to make sure I can finish Sunnyside."

"You'll be paying for the rest of your life. Don't do it. Besides, it's illegal, and eventually, there's going to be a day of reckoning. You won't want to be on the wrong side of it."

"It'll be a one-off payment. I have plans to ensure they never stop another pour. I can't afford to let the Barclay Property Trust down again. I promised I could meet their deadline, and now I'm not going to make it."

"Let's go with the court order," Dixon said. "I'll write to Rapidmix threatening them with all hell if they breach it."

"Okay, but if they ignore the order, I'm going to be in all sorts of trouble," Luke said, putting his hands to his forehead and massaging his temples. "Tim, I'll likely never win another job from Barclay. How do I get compensated for that? Who knows how many contracts I might have won?"

"Loss of goodwill is terribly difficult to calculate, and who's to say you won't win work from Barclay in the future?"

"I had a call from one of their managers this morning. They're not happy. He said they'd taken a risk with me, and it had backfired. He said it's not something they'll do again. We can put him in the witness box."

Dixon shook his head and laughed. "Luke, Barclay has thirty, partially completed projects, and you think you're going to get one of their managers to testify on your behalf? It's not going to happen. The BLMU would close Barclay's sites overnight, and they know it. There would be mysterious accidents, health and safety issues, and disputes on their sites. Anyone who helps you will be seen as trying to hurt the union. You're going to have to win by yourself, and before it's over, it's going to get dirty. I'll ask you again. Are you sure you want to proceed?"

"Certain."

"Okay. The actions for damages against Rapidmix and the builders will be heard in Queensland's Supreme Court. The actions against the BLMU will be before the Federal Court. All the judges of the Supreme Court were appointed by conservative state governments, and they'll most likely be sympathetic to your cause. There are eleven federal court judges sitting in Queensland, and nine of them were appointed by the Labor Government. They're former lawyers and barristers who made their names acting for and defending the unions. We want one of the two appointed by the former conservative government."

"Jesus, even the courts are stacked."

"Not stacked, but they do reflect the philosophies and ambitions of the ruling political party of the day, be it left or right. Sorry, I must fly. I'll be in court this afternoon. I'll commence action first thing tomorrow morning."

Chapter 17

Five minutes later, Luke entered the Venetian Tower, took the elevator to the twenty-seventh floor, and alighted in the foyer of Hall Samuel. He had been there many times since first meeting Monty, but as he strode toward the reception counter, he was still taken aback by the quiet, the calm, the deep plush carpet, and the expensive paintings adorning the walls. He could almost smell the money. "Hi, Connie," he said, "I don't have an appointment, but Mr. Beaurepaire said that he'd try to fit me in."

"Oh, Mr. Cramer, I'm sure he'll see you. I'll let him know you're here," the attractive brunette gushed. "He never stops talking about you. Oh, I shouldn't have said that, should I?"

"I won't tell him if you don't." Luke smiled.

"Thanks, Mr. Cramer, I'm sorry."

Montgomery Beaurepaire bounded into the reception foyer, saying, "What are you sorry about, Connie?"

"She saw the pictures of my car on the news last night. It's all right, Connie, cars are easily replaced." Luke winked.

"Quite so. My office is a mess. Please bring salad sandwiches, coffee, and orange juice to the boardroom, Connie. How did you get here, Luke?"

"Kiara's car. I have a rental car getting dropped off at home in the morning."

"Bad business, that. You're going to need to be very careful. Have you thought about a personal security guard?"

"You're kidding. How would that have helped? The guard would've been watching over me while the BLMU planted a bomb in my car. No, that's not the answer."

As they sat down at the top of the seventeen-seat, mahogany board table, Monty asked, "How well do you know those pulling the strings at the union?"

"I don't. I've met Dennis Bartlett, but I don't know anything about him."

"You can't fight your enemies unless you know them," Monty said, resting his chin in his hands. "You need to find out all you can about those making the decisions at the BLMU but don't stop there. Find out about those who are next in line too, and that way you'll be prepared when you have to deal with them."

Monty's right. I should have thought of that. Decker looks like a criminal on television, Luke thought. *He's sure to have skeletons.* "I'll do that."

"How did your meeting with Tim go?"

"All right. The true test will be in the results he achieves."

"You're not impressed. Don't judge him by his size. He's savvy, street smart, and a real fighter. He won't let you down. What is it that you wanted to see me about? How can I help?"

"I'll get straight to the point. How much money are you prepared to lend me? I can put the house and business up as collateral and probably put my hands on half a million."

Monty pressed his thumbs into his braces and pushed himself back into his chair. "Luke, I once told you that there was nothing I wouldn't do for you. If it were not for you, my life would have ceased that dreadful day on the Spit. I still cry when I think of Edward. That aside, you've come a long way and proven yourself to be an astute businessman which makes your question easy to answer. I will loan you as much as you want, but I would like to know what you have planned. I might be able to provide some input."

"I want to buy two businesses, and I need your help with the negotiations and payment. The first is a cast-iron foundry. It needs to be within range of the Gold Coast, preferably in a quiet, industrial area. I'm not looking for modern furnaces but something that vents through a stack – the taller, the better."

"A foundry? What does a foundry have to do with building shopping centers or high-rise buildings? What are you thinking, Luke?"

"I'm looking to diversify. I don't expect to make a fortune - the smaller, the better. See whether you can find something where the proprietor or manager will stay with the business. If it breaks even, that's fine, and if there's a small profit, that's even better."

"I don't get it. You don't have time to oversee another business."

"I know. I'm employing someone to help me. Part of his job description will be to keep his eye on the foundry. He's a friend of mine from Chicago. I'll need your help with a work visa."

"It's a bad business employing or working with friends."

"You think so?" Luke grinned. "Aren't you and I friends, Monty?"

"That's different."

"No, it's not. He's one of the two closest friends I have – you're the other."

"I'm flattered, Luke, but it's not a good idea."

"Maybe not, but you're still going to help me, aren't you?"

"If you insist."

"Good. This is very important. I can't be seen to have any connection with this business - not as the owner, an investor, a director, or a manager. You and my other friend will be the only ones who'll know I'm the owner. Can you hide my involvement?"

"You know I can. Why don't you tell me what you're really up to?" Monty said, getting up from his chair and resting his hand on Luke's shoulder.

Luke was about to answer when there was a knock on the door, and Connie entered with a platter of sandwiches, a jug of orange juice, plates, glasses, and serviettes which she laid out on the table. "Thanks, Connie," Beaurepaire said. "Help yourself, Luke. Now, where were we?"

Luke slowly poured two glasses of orange juice. "I was about to say the less you know, the better. Trust me. It's for your own good."

"But your other friend will know."

"Yes, but that doesn't make you any less trusted or any less of a friend. You could say that he specializes in areas outside normal business parameters." Luke grinned.

"All right. I don't like it, but I'll find you your foundry," Monty said, as he nibbled on a sandwich.

"Good. I'm sure you won't have to guess why I want to buy Farrugia Concrete & Quarries."

"No, that's obvious, but it won't come cheap. I've dealt with Tony Farrugia, and he's built a nice little business. He might be the smallest concrete supplier, but he has at least thirty trucks; plus, he employs subcontractors. He may not want to sell."

"You're right. He may not, but I know how persuasive you can be. Persuade him, Monty. Persuade him."

"I'll do my best not to disappoint you."

"Disappointment is the mating call of losers. Do better than your best. Tony's nearly seventy and can't go on forever. Pull this deal off, and those union thugs will never be able to stop another of my concrete pours. Their industrial-relations mates will never try to blackmail me again."

"I understand, Luke, but Tony might not be a seller at any price. You know how those old Italians are. They love to work. He doesn't need the money. He probably started the business with a hundred bucks and a pick and shovel."

"Yes, you may be right. Here's the deal. We buy Farrugia Concrete & Quarries but keep it secret. Tony stays on as if there's been no change in ownership and manages the business, but now he has a heap of cash for his kids and grandchildren. There will be some builders who'll be reluctant to buy from Farrugia if they find out that I own it. It's a win-win."

Montgomery Beaurepaire's sense of gratitude to the young man sitting opposite him was overwhelming, but there was more than that. Monty respected his business acumen – the rough jewel who had saved his family had turned into a diamond and was just as tough. Monty knew that he wouldn't be able to buy Tony Farrugia's business for less than ten million, and while that wasn't a large sum by Hall Samuel's standards, it was a huge commitment to someone less than thirty who had never worked in a quarry or concrete business.

"You'll need to take out some life insurance, Luke. After we've bought the foundry and Tony's business, you'll be into us for at least twelve million."

"I told you that I can put my hands on half a million."

"Keep it. You'll need it for fees and costs. I wish you'd tell me why you want to buy a foundry."

"I told you. It's better that you don't know."

"I don't like it."

"Yeah, you've made that clear. Monty. There's one other matter I'd like you to handle. We need citizenship."

"That won't be a problem, but why now?"

If I'm going to build a big business in Australia with less than scrupulous methods, I want to remove the possibility of being deported, Luke thought. "I love the place, and there's no time like the present," he said, getting up from his chair. "I have to get back to Sunnyside."

Chapter 18

That night when Luke got home, Kiara looked miserable, and Carlos was crying. "We've walked the streets all day and checked with the neighbors. Someone must have stolen Roxy. I called the police, and they told me they had better things to do with their time than look for dogs. They said to paste posters with a picture of Roxy offering a reward for her return on lampposts and shop windows. I'm going to offer a five-hundred-dollar, no-questions-asked reward."

Kiara told me she was going to look for Roxy, but I didn't anticipate her being this persistent. What am I going to do now? Luke thought. He knelt next to Carlos and cuddled him saying, "Don't worry, buddy. We'll get you another puppy just like Roxy."

"Don't want another puppy," Carlos wailed. "I want Roxy."

"Time for bed, little man," Kiara said. "Give Daddy a big kiss."

When she returned, she said, "Fancy saying that in front of Carlos. How could you be so insensitive? No other dog is going to replace Roxy. I'm going to keep looking for her. If she's been stolen, I'm sure my reward will smoke the thieves out. When they find out they can get an easy $500, they'll return her. You'll see."

Luke felt his gut twisting. "I'm sorry."

"I can always tell when you're hiding something," Kiara said.

"I'm not hiding anything," Luke lied, shifting uncomfortably under Kiara's gaze. He had never lied to her before. "I just feel sorry for Carlos."

"I'll get your dinner."

"I'm not hungry. Don't worry about it. If I get hungry, I'll have a snack before I go to bed."

"You're not hungry? You're always hungry. I've never known you not to eat dinner."

"I have a lot on my mind. George is in the hospital. My car was blown up. I have plans I must go over, and if I can't get that suspended slab poured at Sunnyside, we'll be in real trouble. Sorry, hon, I'm not with it right now."

Kiara held her hands in front of her face as if she were praying and said, "Could the union have taken Roxy?"

Luke cringed and was about to answer when the phone rang, and he dove to answer it. "Luke, it's Maggie Simpson. The surgery was a success, but it will be two months before George can stand and start physiotherapy. He'll limp for the rest of his life, but at least he'll be able to get around. The doctors don't think he'll suffer long-term pain," Maggie sniffled.

"That's good. How was he when you talked to him?"

"You know George. He appeared to be in good spirits, but it was probably an act for the kids and me. I asked him about Gordy or Jordy, or whoever it was he was muttering about under the anesthetic. He had no recollection and doesn't know anyone with a similar name. Sorry."

"That's okay."

"Luke, I haven't made the kids' dinner. I wanted to call and let you know how George was. I have to go."

"Thanks, Maggie, I'll call in to the hospital and see him in the morning. Goodnight."

Kiara was sitting on the sofa listening. "How's George?"

"The operation was a success, but he's facing a long period of rehabilitation. Maggie and the kids are holding up remarkably well."

"At last some good news. Do you remember what I asked you before Maggie called?"

How could I forget? It was all that was on my mind while I was talking to Maggie, Luke thought. "I don't know. It's possible."

"Are you going to look for her tonight?"

"I can't. I told you, I have plans I must go over. If I don't get finished, the sites will come to a standstill."

"If it were Carlos who was lost, would you go looking for him?" Kiara sneered. "Or would you just offer to buy a new son?"

She had never ridiculed him, and they'd hardly exchanged a cross word in nine years. "What's that supposed to mean? If you want me to go out looking, I will."

"Do what you like. I'm going to bed."

Luke went to the study, poured himself a bourbon, sat down on one of the recliners, closed his eyes, and threw his feet up on the desk. He hated lying to Kiara, but it was better than the alternative. He picked up his glass and sipped slowly, enjoying the burning sensation in his chest. If he were going to stay on the Gold Coast, he had to fix the union problem. He had a plan, a good plan, but it largely relied on Ratsy.

It was 11:15 P.M. when he called him, and a bleary voice answered, "If this isn't a matter of life and death, hang up now."

"Ratsy, it's me."

"Jesus, Luke, it's quarter after six. Go to bed and call me when ya wake up."

"I can't. I don't want Kiara to hear me, and it is a matter of life and death."

"Okay, hang on. I need a cigarette, or I'll likely fall back to sleep. I only got home three hours ago."

Luke heard cursing and drawers being opened and closed before Ratsy said, "I'm all ears, Luke."

For the next ten minutes, Luke related everything that had happened with the BLMU and finished by offering Ratsy a job.

"I wanna help ya, but I like Chicago. I don't wanna leave. I'm doin' okay."

"You'll earn far more with me, and the work won't be as dangerous." Luke paused for a few seconds and added, "Well, it probably won't."

"Tell me again what the job involves."

"You'll be overseeing a foundry, handling security, and helping me with union negotiations."

"I've never worked before, let alone in a foundry. The closest I came was walking around that shithole where yar old man works. I know a bit about security, though, and I've had some experience with the unions. What is it that ya really want me to do?"

"It's hard to say over the phone."

"Is it the type of negotiation Vince Sordi had with that druggie all those years ago?"

"Yeah. Do you do that type of work?"

"I do, but it's usually a two-man job."

"I can help you."

"Luke, yar a businessman now. Ya delegate. Ya don't do yarself what ya can pay others to do. Even I know that."

"What do you say?"

"I'll think about it. As I said, I'm doin' okay. I only do the occasional job for which I'm well paid. Besides, I'm as white as a ghost, and I have skin that burns under a streetlight, and ya tell me it's as hot as hell down there."

"You drive a hard bargain. I'll throw in a sombrero and a tube of sunscreen." Luke laughed. "How's that sound?"

"That's funny, Luke, but I'm not sold. Call me in a week, and I'll let ya know. Right now, I'm thinking that I don't want to move."

"Okay, Ratsy," Luke said, hanging up the phone and cursing.

Chapter 19

Kiara hadn't thawed out in the morning, which was unusual. She wasn't one to hold grudges after one of their rare tiffs. When the Avis girl knocked on the front door with the keys to Luke's rental Ford, Kiara was downright rude to her. Carlos was rubbing his eyes when he staggered into the kitchen and asked, "Daddy, did you find Roxy?"

"Sorry, buddy, I–"

Before Luke could finish, Kiara said, "Daddy was too busy to look, little man. We'll go looking again today."

Luke glared at her but bit his tongue. "I'm going now. I'll try to get home early."

There was no response from Kiara. Carlos had his hands in a bowl of cereal saying, "I want the bad people to bring Roxy back, Mommy."

Luke climbed into the rental, looked up at the cloudless blue sky, and heard the newsreader say, "It's going to be another glorious day in paradise. The forecast is for a light northerly wind and a top temperature of eighty degrees. For surfers, there's a good swell at Coolangatta. We are truly blessed."

Yeah, real blessed, Luke thought. Ten minutes later, he entered George Simpson's private room to see him propped up watching the early morning news. "Hello, George, how are you feeling?"

"I've been better," the big man grinned. "The chief surgeon told me I had the toughest skull he's ever seen. He said that anyone else hit as hard as I was would've suffered brain damage. I dunno whether to take that as an insult or a compliment."

"Maggie said they kept smashing your kneecaps after you were unconscious. You're lucky you'll be able to walk again."

"Lucky?"

"Sorry, poor choice of words."

"That's okay, Luke. I know what you meant. I just want to get off the painkillers and get out of here."

"If you're worried about the cost of the hospital, don't."

"Yeah, Maggie told me what you said. There are not many bosses like you. Thanks, but that's not the reason I want to go home. I'm gonna get bored. I know it. There's only so much television a man can watch. There's always someone around at home, and if there's not, I have the dog."

Luke's mind immediately turned to Roxy, and he grimaced as he related what had happened to her. "You need to be careful, George. Maybe you should keep your dog in the house."

George laughed. "Czar's a male German shepherd who tips the scales at just under a hundred pounds. I've trained him since he was a pup. He'll only eat food prepared by Maggie or me. If anyone tries to hurt him, they're going to end up in a horrible mess. These pricks aren't going to try that. They're cowards. They'll smash a man with a chunk of wood or steel pipe from behind and kill a tiny dog. Nah, they're not gonna tackle Czar."

"He sounds like a great dog. Maggie said that the doctors told her you were muttering a name while on the operating table but that you couldn't remember it."

"That's what I told her," George said, shifting ever so slightly and wincing in pain. "I didn't want her to worry. The last thing I heard as I was going down was 'now, Cordy.' Maybe they wanted a clear shot at my kneecaps, but it's obvious that Cordy, whoever he is, was the one who hit me from behind."

"Cordy? It could be a Christian name or a surname, but it's unusual, and he shouldn't be difficult to track down. Did you tell the police?"

"Nah. To be honest, they didn't seem all that interested in what I had to say. They said there'd been a recent spate of muggings in the area, and that I'd been unlucky. They asked me whether I could identify my attackers, and when I said no, they lost interest. When I'm up and about, I'm gonna find Cordy and have a little conversation with him. I don't want the cops linking what's gonna happen to him to me."

"Good thinking, but don't worry about Cordy and his helper. I'm almost certain they're the ones who killed Roxy. I'll take care of them."

"That's not gonna stop me finding them when I can walk. I want to mete out my own punishment."

Luke slowly shook his head, his mouth creased in a grim line. "Sorry, George."

The big man looked confused and took a few moments to grasp the import of Luke's words. "Oh, Jesus!"

"I'm through messing around."

"Jesus, be careful, Luke."

"I will. I must go. I have a shopping center to build. I'll try to get back later in the week."

When Luke arrived at the Sunnyside site, he was greeted by a cacophony of jackhammers. More than half the slab had been smashed, and the men, who never looked up, were working at breakneck speed. They wanted to help him, and they wanted to preserve as much of their bonuses as they could.

Back in the site office, Luke pondered the next pour. If Rapidmix let him down again, he'd be smashing another slab to pieces next week. He briefly thought of ordering from Tony Farrugia, but the job was too big for him at such short notice. No, he was stuck with Rapidmix. Tim Dixon had promised to put the fear of God into them, but what if the BLMU and the other builders were more threatening? He had also promised to get an order from the court restraining the union from coercing the other builders and Rapidmix.

Luke ground his teeth, knowing that the BLMU had a history of ignoring court orders and had gone to too much trouble to walk away now. No, unless he did something, Rapidmix would screw him again. As he pondered his limited options, a vision of Sordi appeared saying *There is no other motivator like fear.*

He pulled out the Yellow Pages, called Rapidmix's head office, and asked to speak to the CEO. His PA said that he was out all day but would be back for a meeting at four o'clock. "What is it you'd like to talk to him about?" she asked. "I may be able to help."

"I'm a customer with a query about a delivery."

"Oh, Mr. O'Dea doesn't handle delivery inquiries, but I can put you through to our sales department. They'll be able to help. Would you like me to transfer you?"

"Thanks, but on reflection, it's not urgent. If I have a problem, I'll call back."

Chapter 20

Luke flicked through the index of his Business Who's Who looking at entries for O'Dea. There were three, and only one was the CEO of Rapidmix – James O'Dea. Luke didn't fancy another fifty-mile drive to Brisbane, but the inconvenience of that task was nothing when compared with the effects of Rapidmix stopping its trucks midway through the replacement pour. At least, he wouldn't have to leave until after three o'clock, and that would give him a chance to get to the car dealer's showroom in Burleigh Heads, a project that he'd neglected since the concrete pour debacle.

It was 4:30 P.M. when he entered Freshwater Place's six-level parking garage on Ann Street while a steady stream of early leavers vacated the garage. An attendant manning a small, glass office lifted the automated gate and told him he'd find plenty of spaces on Levels E and F. Luke knew that Rapidmix occupied the twenty-first and twenty-second levels, but he was more interested in Levels A and B of the parking garage – those levels would be allocated to tenants.

After he parked, he entered an elevator and hit the button marked Parking A and was whooshed up to the top level of the parking garage. There were now two attendants in the glass office at the front, but there appeared to be little in the way of security. He strolled around unchallenged, looking at reserved signs for banks, insurance companies, and other professionals until he found a cluster of signs marked Rapidmix.

A silver BMW 7 Series was parked in a slightly larger space between two concrete pillars, and as Luke walked toward it, he already knew whose it was. The reserved sign read James O'Dea, CEO, Rapidmix. As he reached the rear of the BMW on the passenger's side, he knelt as if to tie his shoe and slowly released the air from the tire. He smiled as he wiped the valve clean with his handkerchief and wondered whether he was watching too many crime movies.

Because of the lateness of the day, there were a dozen empty spaces offering unimpeded vision of O'Dea's car. A few minutes later, Luke was back on Level E and driving up the ramps to a space almost directly opposite the BMW. He slumped down behind the wheel and turned on the radio. A few minutes later, he turned it off. He was on edge, and thoughts of what could go wrong flashed through his mind. *What if O'Dea has someone with him? What if someone sees what's happening and interrupts? What if he calls my bluff? Should I drive out the garage while I still can? God, I hope I don't have to put my hands on him.*

It was just after six o'clock when a tall, slim man in his early forties with wispy, black hair receding at the temples walked briskly toward the BMW. He was dressed in a tailored charcoal gray suit, white shirt, and smart black shoes, and he could well have passed for a lawyer rather than the CEO of a concrete and aggregate business.

Luke watched as O'Dea drove about three yards and then jumped out of the car, smacking the sides of his legs with his hands when he saw the flat tire. Another car couldn't get past and beeped impatiently. O'Dea shook his fist, climbed back into the BMW, and reversed back into his space. By the time Luke had sidled over to him, he was out of the car again. "Got troubles?" Luke asked.

"Yes, I must have a nail in my tire. I'm just going upstairs to call the Auto Club for assistance. I have a function to attend and can't get dirty," O'Dea said. "Hey, I don't suppose you could change it for me? It's worth twenty."

"You didn't get a nail in it," Luke said, closing the distance between them to about a foot. "I let it down. I've been waiting for you."

"What? What are you? I'll call the police. They'll take care of you."

"It's not what I am, Mr. O'Dea. It's who I am. I'm Luke Cramer. Does the name CramerBuild ring any bells?"

"It didn't until this morning. Then we received your writ. We're going to tie you up in the courts for years. The legal fees will break you before we get to a final hearing. I'm sure the court will be pleased to hear about this little stunt. Now get out of my way."

Luke leaned forward until his face was only inches away from O'Dea's. "Let me tell you what you and your friends did besides stopping my pour when it was half complete. You broke the knee-caps of one of my supervisors and knocked him out. He's still in the hospital and will never walk without pain again. You blew my car to smithereens, and then you totally crossed the line when you went after my family. One of your thugs slit the throat of my son's puppy and left it in the backyard so he'd find it. What kind of sick bastard does that?"

"I-I don't-don't know what you're-you're talking about," O'Dea said, wiping flecks of spit from his face as he tried to back away, but there was nowhere to go.

"My family!" Luke shouted, his eyes rolling. "You went after my family. I ought to kill you right now."

"It-it wasn't me. It wasn't."

"No, but it was your company and someone employed by you. Doesn't the buck stop with the CEO?"

A little of O'Dea's early bluster returned. "I'm not going to take this. I'm calling the police. You'll be in a cell within the hour."

"No, I won't. Listen, Mr. O'Dea, and listen carefully. I want a guarantee from you that your trucks will deliver as promised when we re-pour the slab. I want a guarantee that they'll deliver and won't stop mid-pour again. I want a guarantee that you'll settle my claim for damages. If it helps, details of the settlement can be kept confidential. Give me those guarantees, and I promise I won't hurt you or your family. Fail me, and my guarantee to you is that one of your family will die."

"Get out of my way, you cheap hoodlum. You'll get nothing, not a thing. Now move."

"You're not listening," Luke snarled, his face virtually touching O'Dea's. "It was a big mistake going after my family because now the gloves are off. You have two daughters and a son, and I know exactly where you live in Hamilton," Luke lied. "It won't be me who comes for them. It'll be a paid professional."

"I didn't know the BLMU would attack your family, beat up your supervisor, or blow up your car. I'm a businessman."

Fuck. He's not folding. What am I going to do? Luke thought. "Like it or not, you became part of it when you stopped sending your trucks. You and those piss weak builders did the BLMU's bidding. Now you're gonna fix what you did."

"I won't be threatened," O'Dea said, again, attempting to push Luke away.

Luke's left hand moved like lightning. O'Dea gasped, and pain tore through his groin. His legs buckled, and it was only Luke's other hand that kept him upright. "Last chance," Luke whispered menacingly, his eyes rolling insanely, as he squeezed a little more tightly. "Think about your kids. Can you see their smiling faces? How will you feel when they slowly lower the coffin into the damp earth, knowing you killed one of them? It'll rip your guts out, and when your wife finds out you could have stopped it, she'll do more than crush your balls. Are you going to help me?"

"Yes, yes," O'Dea wheezed, sweat breaking out on his forehead and his eyes filling with tears. "Let me go. Please let me go. I'll do anything you want."

Jesus, he's shaking so badly he might have a stroke or heart attack. "All in good time. Do I get my concrete? Do I get my guarantees?"

"Yes. Yes."

"If you fail to honor your guarantees or call the police, one of your children will die. Capiche?"

"Yes. Please, please let me go."

It was true. When you have them by the balls, their hearts and minds will surely follow, Luke thought. "Don't make the mistake of thinking that I'm bluffing," he said, releasing his grip.

"I-I won't," O'Dea sniffled.

Luke turned and walked back to his car. As he drove away, he saw O'Dea grasp the BMW and vomit violently. Luke felt a tinge of sorrow for him. There was no way he would hurt O'Dea's kids, but how could O'Dea know that?

Chapter 21

It was dark when Luke arrived home, and Kiara was sitting on the sofa watching television in the family room. "I thought you said you were going to be early. Carlos was waiting. He tried to stay awake for you. You know it would be better if you didn't say anything. That way, he wouldn't get his hopes up."

Jesus, with so much on, I'd forgotten, but it wouldn't have made any difference if I'd remembered. "Honey, I was called away to Brisbane for a late afternoon meeting. I'm sorry," Luke said, sitting down and putting his arm around her. "Tell me what I can do to make it up to you."

"I'd love it if you went back to being the man I married. You cared about us then, but now all you're worried about is your business. We hardly ever see you."

"I'm doing it for us. Don't you want a better life? Once Sunnyside is completed I'll have more time."

"You know that's not true," Kiara sighed. "You'll just replace it with an even bigger project. I don't want more money. I want a baby sister or brother for Carlos. I'm sorry for giving you the cold shoulder, but I'm tired and have annoying aches in my arms and legs. I think I'm getting old."

"Have you seen a doctor?"

"Of course not, silly. It's the heat and humidity. It's thinking about those union thugs and what they did to George and your car. It's wondering whether you're going to come home in one piece. It's worrying about the police knocking at the door to tell me that you've been hurt or worse. If I can stop worrying and get one good night's sleep, I'll be fine."

"I can look after myself. Please don't worry about me. Why don't you go and have a checkup and get some sleeping pills as well?"

"I'm not putting chemicals in my body. Anyhow, I felt better this morning after having a little nap when Carlos was at school. We pasted reward posters on lampposts and in the shops this afternoon. That's why he fought to stay awake. He told me that Daddy wouldn't let anything happen to Roxy. I think he was expecting you to walk in tonight with her in your arms."

"Poor kid."

"Yes. Oh, and I'm missing my favorite towel. The big black fluffy one. You didn't take it to work, did you?"

Luke felt himself starting to color and dropped his eyes to the floor. "No, I haven't seen it."

"I wonder where I put it," Kiara said. "Luke, why didn't you ask about Roxy when you came home? I told you that we were going to look for her."

He felt her deep brown eyes piercing his soul and shifted uncomfortably. "Lately, all I seem to be doing is saying sorry. I was concerned about you. I was concerned about us. I would've gotten around to asking about Roxy, but I knew that if you'd found her, you would have told me as soon as I walked in the door."

"Gotten around to asking?"

"Jesus, Kiara, cut me some slack. I might not be a wordsmith, but I care. I really care."

Her expression was quizzical and filled with doubt, a look he'd never seen before. "I hope so."

"Honey, as soon as the slab is re-poured, I'm going back to Chicago for a few days. I'd love it if you and Carlos could come with me."

"You're going to try to convince Ratsy to work for you. I heard you talking to him on the phone. I know what he does, and you wonder why I worry."

God, how much did she hear? "With George in the hospital, I need someone I can trust," Luke lied.

"How long will you be gone?"

"Three days?"

"Three days? That's two days travel and one in Chicago. It's hardly worth going."

"I can't be away from the business any longer," Luke said, immediately regretting it. "If you and Carlos come with me, we'll stay for another day. You can see your mom."

"Why would I want to see her? Why? Besides, it's too much travel," Kiara said. "It would exhaust Carlos, and I'm not sure I could cope. You go. We'll try to get some rest while you're gone. I'll get your dinner, and then I'm going to bed."

"I'll leave you Ratsy's number if you need to contact me."

Chapter 22

Two days later, Rapidmix concrete trucks lined the road adjoining the Sunnyside site. Luke pulled on a pair of gumboots and joined the workers, taking George Simpson's place. He wasn't needed but wanted to send a message that nothing was going to stop him.

He seized the gyrating pump hose which fought to break free from his grasp, but it was no match for him. Within a few minutes, sweat was dripping from his chest, and he tore his saturated T-shirt off. His ripped torso and chiseled arms glistened under the hot sun as he sprayed concrete and cajoled and encouraged the laborers around him to work faster. He glanced at the trucks dumping their loads, knowing that there would be no stoppages today. *Sordi had been proven right again. Nothing motivates like fear.*

Near the end of the day, Luke sent one of the men to the pub to fetch six dozen cold cans of XXXX. He had driven them hard, and they had responded out of fear, respect, and a desire to maximize their bonuses. They deserved to be rewarded with a few refreshing cold ales.

As Luke was getting changed in the site office, there was a rap on the door. "Mr. Cramer?" enquired a young man dressed in all black with his shirt embossed Stratton Security and a large pistol hanging from the belt around his waist.

"That's me. Who are you and where are the others?"

"Bob Stratton. As Mr. Beaurepaire requested, five of my men are reconnoitering the site as we speak."

"Reconnoitering?" Luke laughed.

"It means–"

"I know what it means. Why didn't you say 'checking out the site' or 'inspecting it'? Reconnoitering? Christ, you're a security company, not a team of commandos. Oh, and you didn't answer me. Who are you? Where do you fit in?"

"I'm Steve Stratton's son. I handle major corporate clients in southeast Queensland."

"The boss's son. I thought as much." Luke grinned, pulling on a clean T-shirt. "Now listen to me, Bob Stratton, and listen carefully. I know you must give your men breaks. However, your prime responsibility is to protect the site from sabotage until the center's completed so stagger the breaks and make sure there are always four of you on site. Remember, I'm paying you until 6:45 A.M. If I turn up at 6:40, and there aren't six of you here, it'll be you who needs security. Understand?"

"We won't disappoint you, Mr. Cramer."

Luke was about to say that disappointment was the mating call of losers but instead said, "Make sure you don't."

The following morning, he was on site at 6:30 A.M. to see six security guards strategically positioned around the site. Bob Stratton greeted him with a cheery "good morning" and, before Luke could ask, informed him of the weekend schedule. "We'll be here from four o'clock tomorrow afternoon until seven on Monday morning."

"Be alert on Sunday, particularly Sunday night."

"Don't worry, Mr. Cramer, we know what we're doing. Do you have anything planned for the weekend?"

"Nothing," Luke said, as he stepped inside the site office.

By noon, he had booked a business class flight with Tourworld on Qantas to Los Angeles departing at 9:15 that night with a connecting flight on United to Chicago. He booked business class for one reason - the size of the seats. Being able to sleep would save a day and see him back home on Monday night. He would be in the air for forty hours just to spend one day in Chicago. He didn't tell anyone where he was going. Instead, he told his employees that he had to go to Sydney on Monday and might not be on site until late in the day.

As he was leaving the phone rang, and he reluctantly picked it up, saying, "CramerBuild."

"Let me speak to Luke Cramer," a man with a distinctively raspy voice said.

"Speaking."

"Ah, Luke, Detective Bert Trask here. I'm investigating the George

Simpson assault and need to talk to you. I can come to your house tonight, or you could call into the Surfers Paradise precinct on your way home."

"Sorry, I can't tonight. I've made other arrangements."

"All right, what about tomorrow morning?"

"No, that's no good. I won't be here. I'm going away for a few days. The earliest I can see you is Tuesday morning."

"You can't see me for a few minutes tonight?" Trask growled.

"No, I have a flight to catch and want to spend some time with my family before I leave."

There was a long pause. "Where are you going?"

"Detective, I don't see what that has to do with your investigation. I'll see you on Tuesday morning," Luke said and hung up.

Book 3

RATSY

Chapter 23

UA 654 landed at O'Hare just after 5 A.M. on a bitterly cold and windy day. A grim-faced Ratsy was waiting in the terminal. As they shook hands, Ratsy said, "Bad news, Luke. Kiara called. She's a real mess. Someone dumped a dog on your porch with its throat slit. A few hours later, some deadbeat called saying that she was wasting her time with the posters. Carlos's dog had met with the same fate, and you'd found her body in the backyard but hadn't said anything. She called the cops, and they took the dog's body away. They said it was probably kids playing a nasty prank."

"Shit!"

"It gets worse. Come on, my car's in a no-parking area at the front of the terminal. We'll go to my place, and you can call her."

"What do you mean, it gets worse?"

"In the morning, she was awoken by the roar of motorbikes out the front of your house. Then, when she tried to reverse out the driveway, the bikers blocked it. She called the police again, but it took them three hours to respond. Five minutes before they arrived, the bikers disappeared. Kiara could barely speak when she called. They shook her up badly, very badly."

Luke pulled his coat up around his ears as he climbed into Ratsy's late-model Caddy. He normally would have said something, but his mind was in a turmoil. "What time did Kiara call? Did she say anything about Carlos?"

"She called four times. Said she had no one else to talk to. I could barely understand the first call. She was crying, screaming, and ranting, all at the same time. She got it together for the next two calls. I know all about Roxy and what the union is trying to do to you. The last call was about the bikers, and she completely lost it. I tried to calm her, but she was weeping uncontrollably, and I couldn't get through to her."

Luke hung his head while gripping the dashboard. "If I were there, I'd kill the bastards. I never anticipated they'd go this far. Someone's going to pay for this."

"Before you think about retribution, you need to salvage your marriage. The way Kiara was talking, she and the little dude may not be there when you get home. Jeez, Luke, why didn't you tell her about Roxy? You must have known that as soon as she started pasting those posters, the union would figure out what you'd done. It was obvious and so was what they'd do, but killing the second dog to make a point is sick. At least, I now have a better idea of why you want me down there."

Ratsy pulled up at the parking garage of an apartment block in the upmarket River North District and as they got out of the car, said, "Welcome back to Chicago, Luke."

"Yeah," Luke said, kicking the ground. "Bastards!"

Ratsy's two-bedroom apartment was on the twentieth story of the twenty-five-story building, and as they entered, he said, "Kiara said you were to call her the minute you arrived."

"What time is it in Brisbane?"

"About midnight. She said you were to call no matter what time it was. There's a phone in the kitchen, or if you want privacy, there's another in the spare bedroom." Ratsy pointed.

"The kitchen will be fine," Luke said, picking up the phone and dialing. "Hello, honey, it's me."

In response, Kiara shouted, sobbed, and screamed for the next five minutes, accusing him of being a liar and untrustworthy. Then she told him about the dead dog dumped on the porch, the threatening phone calls, the bikers, and the police ignoring her calls.

"I was trying to protect you. Yes, I found Roxy and buried her because I didn't want you to see her. I wrapped her in the towel you've been looking for."

"Did-did she have her throat cut?"

Luke paused for just a second. "Tell me," Kiara demanded.

"Yes."

A fresh burst of sobbing erupted. "Poor little Roxy. She must have been terrified! She was so loving and harmless. How could anyone do that?"

"There are some evil people in this world."

"I don't know whether I want to stay here. I'm scared. The creep with the wheezy voice said that he'd slice Carlos's throat in the same way that he'd sliced that poor dog's throat that they dumped on our porch. Poor Roxy. Poor little Roxy."

"We can move if you want to. We don't have to stay on the Gold Coast. We can always come back here."

"Luke, I don't know whether I want to live with you anymore."

"Don't say that. I can make things right. I'm sorry I never told you about Roxy. I promise I won't ever keep anything from you again."

"It's not the Gold Coast. It's the industry you're in, and building is the only thing you know. The only difference from Chicago, and Las Vegas is the degree of violence. I never knew it, but it's an industry that criminals control, no matter where it's located."

"I wouldn't go that far. It's –"

"You wouldn't go that far?" Kiara screamed. "You aren't here. You didn't see what they did. You weren't here calling the police and not getting a response, because they're paid to look the other way."

Luke held the phone away from his ear, shook his head, and looked at Ratsy. "It'll never happen again."

"That's why you're there seeing Ratsy, isn't it? You're going to offer him a job, aren't you? He knows nothing about building. What's he going to do?"

"He'll oversee security."

"Security?" Kiara laughed derisively. "Don't you mean retribution? Will he bash those in the union like poor George Simpson was bashed?"

He'll do far worse than that, Kiara – far, far worse – but you'll never know, Luke thought. "No, he won't. Promise you won't do anything until I'm back home and we've talked."

"All right, but you should know that, if it weren't for Carlos, I wouldn't be waiting. He loves you, and I don't think I could stand to see him hurt again."

"Thanks, hon. Love you."

"Thank Ratsy for taking my calls, Luke. Bye."

"Rough call?" Ratsy asked.

"Yeah, can I make one more call? Then we'll go out and have some breakfast."

The call was to Steve Stratton. Luke told him to have men discreetly watch his house and to follow Kiara and Carlos if they went out.

"There's a fifties-style hamburger shop on the next block. Will that do?" Ratsy asked.

"Sure, let's go," Luke said, pulling on his overcoat.

After they'd ordered, Ratsy said, "You have some big problems."

"Yeah," Luke said, carefully studying his friend. He'd been skinny but had put on a few pounds, and now he was wiry. There was a hardness about him, and the boyish, cheeky face that Luke remembered had disappeared. His dark eyes mirrored those of the wise guys who worked for Sordi. "That's why I'm here. I want you to work with me, but I have a few questions that I couldn't ask over the phone."

"I know, and I know what they are."

"You're not a made man?"

"Nah, I could have been, but I didn't like the idea of being told to kill someone without having any choice but to do it. I prefer freelancing where I choose to accept or reject a contract."

"So you have kill-"

"Yeah. It's no big deal. I haven't killed anyone who didn't deserve to die. There was a junkie dealer stretching his score with dirty talc and God knows what other shit. Two young girls and their boyfriends shot up. Three of them died. It was on the front page of the newspapers and the lead story on the evening news. It was very bad for business, and I was asked to make the problem go away. I did."

"How many?"

"That's unimportant. Why don't you ask me what I'd do to those who slit the throat of Carlos's puppy?"

A tired-looking waiter served them their meals - bacon and eggs with OJ for Luke, and toast and a triple espresso for Ratsy. "I couldn't drink anything like that," the waiter said, brushing a loose strand of hair from his forehead.

"Am I asking ya to?" Ratsy said, eyeing the man.

It was just five words, and Ratsy had hardly raised his voice, but it was menacing, and the waiter's eyes filled with fear. "I'm sorry, sir," he said and scurried away.

"Where were we? Oh yeah, you were about to ask me a question, and I was about to say, I'd kill the son of a bitch without a second thought. Why? Two reasons. Firstly, I don't like my friends being threatened, and secondly, I get along better with dogs than I do with people."

"I need you, Ratsy. I'm about to make it big. Every builder on the Gold Coast is paying someone off. I'm not. The BLMU members are earning a fortune whether they're productive or not. I use subcontractors who only make money if they're productive. I can cut the other builders' quotes to ribbons and still make a fortune - enough to pay you very well."

"I guess with all the stress you didn't notice my apartment. Everything's marble, gold, and stainless steel – the best materials and the best workmanship money can buy. I own it. There's no mortgage. I change the Caddy over every two years. I own it. I work when I choose to work and have a healthy bank balance. Lastly, I like Chicago. I know every alley in the city. I know the cops. I know the bums. I know the movers and shakers. I've been successful. I don't need money."

"I knew that it was going to be a hard sell, but I hadn't expected such a quick no." Luke frowned. "Is there anything I can offer you that will change your mind?"

Ratsy grinned. "I didn't say no. I was gonna until Kiara called, and then I started to waver. I know what you'll do if I don't accept. You'll find someone else. Someone who you don't know and can't trust. Someone who'll sell you out to the highest bidder. You're my buddy, Luke, and you need me. I just never knew how much until now. I'll come down, but for no longer than a year. I'll need four weeks to tidy up my affairs. Is that okay?

"Fantastic." Luke reached across the table and gripped Ratsy's hands.

"I've never had a reaction like that before."

"Ratsy, do you remember me telling you about the foundry? Well, that's where you'll spend your first week," Luke said and then explained why.

"That's clever, but I think you're overreacting to that DNA shit. Do you really think they're gonna be locking up perps in thirty years' time for crimes they did today?"

"I'm sure they will."

"Okay, if that's what you think. I'm gonna need someone to help me."

"Yeah, I know. We can re-create the old partnership."

"Jesus, for a guy who's a big businessman and who watches a lot of television, yar not very bright. When does the boss, the tycoon, the big wheel ever get his hands dirty? Never! That's what yar hiring me for! Do ya remember Castel Herrera running with the Taipans? He's a few years younger than us."

"Yeah, vaguely."

"After ya disappeared, I started knocking around with Cas. He's a good kid. He spent two years as a sniper in Afghanistan and could kill a sparrow from a thousand yards. I was in terrible trouble one night, and he bailed me out. I'd trust him with my life. I want to bring him with me."

Luke laughed. "You're my head of security. If you need to hire others to help you, you don't need to talk to me. Just do it."

"We won't be able to get our guns through customs. I'll give you a list of what we'll need before you leave, and, Luke, don't get a private detective involved or make any inquiries about Cordy. It'll just lead back to ya. I'll find him, and I won't leave a trace," Ratsy said, smiling grimly.

Luke wiped his plate clean. "Can you drop me off at my father's place? I don't think I'll be long. I'll grab a taxi back to your place when I'm finished, and we can spend the rest of the day catching up."

"The rest of the day? Ya mean until I drop ya back at O'Hare tonight. Surely, ya could have spent more than a day here. On second thoughts, I can understand yar need to get back. That'll change when I get down there. Come on, let's go."

As they walked back to the apartment block, the wind cut through Luke's coat like a knife. "I don't know how you can like weather like this. I haven't experienced a day under sixty-eight degrees in the past seven years."

"You get used to it. You've gotten soft, Luke. Does your dad know you're coming?"

"No, but I doubt he's working Saturdays anymore. Can you wait in front until you see the front door open?"

It was a forty-minute drive to Chatham, or, as Ratsy called it, Shitsville. The houses were old, run-down, and small. As Luke glanced out the window, he thought of the mansion he was living in on the Gold Coast and resolved, no matter where he went, he'd never live in Chatham. The house where he had been raised hadn't changed. Moisture clung to the faded, gray siding, and the grass in the tiny front yard was a foot high. "What a shithole," Luke said. "Do you ever come here anymore?"

"It's better than where I lived, and yes, the club's still around the corner, and that's where I do my business."

"The mob never upgraded?"

"The club's okay. It looks like crap from the outside, but the inside, particularly Vince Sordi's office and the living area, is not much different than my apartment. The bar hasn't changed much since you were there last, but the last thing they want is customers."

"I thought he might have moved. Has he changed?"

"If anything, he's worse. You don't know how lucky you were that day. If he hadn't been able to prove that druggie stashed that envelope with newspaper cutouts, he would have killed you both. Luckily, I don't have much to do with him."

"He taught me an important lesson," Luke said, getting out of the car. "Something I'll never forget."

Chapter 24

A minute or so later, the front door opened, and Luke was shocked to see a bent-over, frail old man. "Dad," he said. "It's me."

"I'm not blind. I kin see you," his father said, glancing around. "You don't have her with you, do you?"

"Kiara's in Australia."

"Good. You better come in out of the cold. Why did you come back? I never thought I'd see you again. Sit down."

It wasn't much warmer inside. The sofa was stained and tattered, and there were dark patches of mold on the walls. The carpet was threadbare. A coffee table was cluttered with what looked like unpaid bills and papers. How can anyone live in this? Luke thought, his conscience pricked. "I had business in Chicago. I'm only here for the day."

"Ah, you're the big businessman now, are you?" his father scoffed.

"I'm doing okay," Luke said, and then told his father about his business. "I have a son. Carlos. He'll be seven on his next birthday."

"Your own little spicracker."

Luke flushed. "Don't call him that! Jesus, why are you such a racist? The area's full of African Americans, and you work with them every day."

"Nothing wrong with African Americans. It's the Hispanics I can't stand. They steal our jobs and live off the welfare our taxes provide, and then you take off with one of them. My son's a bean dipper! Who would've thought?"

"I love Kiara. If you're going to keep talking this way, I may as well go."

"Once she was in the family way, her mom couldn't get rid of her fast enough," the old man chuckled. "Disowned her. She was just waiting for a sucker and along you came."

"You're a nasty old man. I don't know why I came to see you," Luke said, getting to his feet.

"Don't go," the old man said, putting a withered hand on Luke's arm. "Things haven't been easy. I was laid off. Replaced by a bloody robot. The whole place is run by robots. I was lucky. They let me have two days' work a week as a cleaner. You should see all the houses with for sale signs on them."

"What did the union do?"

"What could it do? Management said they'd have to close the business without the robots, but with them, they could salvage a hundred jobs. I was one of the nine hundred they let go."

"You must have received a decent severance package."

"Decent?" his father laughed. "We were screwed. The company's management said that, if we didn't accept their measly offer, they'd file for bankruptcy. The union recommended we accept."

"The union officials were paid off," Luke muttered.

"Don't say that! The union fought tooth and nail for us, but, in the end, it had no choice but to accept. Corporations. I hate them."

Luke was about to unleash but instead bit his tongue. His father loved the union and wouldn't hear a word said against it. *I wonder how many others have been brainwashed like you*, he thought. "Dad, why isn't the heater on? It's freezing."

"It costs money. Sometimes I turn it on at night but prefer to wrap myself up in blankets."

A pang of sorrow coursed through Luke as he looked at what his father had become. He had aged twenty years in just eight. This was the man who had slaved in the steel factory to put food on the table. The man who'd done his best to bring him up. "Dad, let me have your bank details. I'm going to deposit fifty thousand into your account. Keep the heat on. Get the house fixed up. Get rid of the mold. Replace the carpet and buy some new furniture."

"Fifty thousand? You can afford to give me fifty thousand? You really are a successful businessman. I'm sorry I mocked you," his father said, riffling through the papers on the coffee table. "Here, take this. It's one of my bank statements. As you can see, there's nothing in the account."

"Would you like to visit us in Australia?"

"Thanks, but no thanks. I'm never gonna like your wife. She

shoulda been on the pill. Did all right for herself though, didn't she? Picked up a nice meal ticket."

"Dad, enough! Surely, you want to see your grandson?"

"I'll pass on that."

Luke rolled his eyes. "I'll just use your phone. I have to get a taxi to Ratsy's."

The old man turned a shade of red and lowered his eyes. "I'm sorry. I can't afford no phone, son."

"Get one installed with the money I'm depositing. You never know when you might have to make an emergency call," Luke said, getting up and walking to the door. He knew he probably wouldn't see his father again and that he should give him a hug, but he couldn't. *How can I hug a racist who hates my wife and doesn't care whether he ever sees my son?* "I'll hail a taxi."

"Be careful on the streets. You're not dressed for the area, and there are those who'd like that fancy coat you're wearing."

"I know these streets like the back of my hand. If anyone tries to steal my coat, they'll be making a big mistake."

"Thanks for the money, Son."

"That's okay, Dad. Take care."

When Luke returned to Ratsy's, Castel Herrera was there. Luke immediately took a liking to him. About five feet ten and strongly built, he was quiet, but there was an air of confidence about him that belied his age. "Before you ask, Luke," Ratsy said, "the answers are yes and no."

"What?"

"Cas's said yes to coming with me, and no, he's not a virgin when it comes to the business."

"Great. One thing I need to know for the firearm license. Cas, do you have any criminal convictions?"

"I'm like Ratsy. I'm clean. I've never even had a speeding fine."

It was hard to believe that the fresh-faced young man was a killer. No matter, Ratsy had vouched for him, and that was good enough for Luke.

At 10 P.M. UA 542 departed O'Hare for LA. Luke had been in Chicago for just sixteen hours and was well pleased with what he'd achieved. The flight home from Los Angeles gave him time to think. Other than the travel agent and Kiara, no one had known that he would be in Chicago for three days, yet the union had terrorized her, knowing that he wouldn't be there to protect her. He closed his eyes and racked his brain trying to work out how they knew.

After a three-hour nap, he woke up, and the answer was obvious. It had to have been the copper supposedly investigating the assault on George Simpson. Luke cursed himself. He would have to be more careful in the future. There was no point trying to get back to sleep, so he had a snack and read some newspapers.

He was dozing when a flight attendant nudged him and said they were fifteen minutes from landing. As QF 16 started its final approach, the captain announced that they were back in paradise, and that it was a balmy seventy-three degrees in Brisbane. It was nearly midnight when he climbed into a taxi for the hour-long trip home.

Chapter 25

He wasn't surprised to find Kiara on the sofa watching television. She looked tired, her face was drawn, and her normally slim, defined arms were gaunt. "We need to talk," she said. "You can't put us at risk just to further your ambitions. You're twenty-six, Luke, a successful businessman and a millionaire. Most people would be happy with that. You're not."

"Wait, that's not—"

"I thought about why you didn't tell me about Roxy. You knew I'd be scared, and that I might want to leave the Gold Coast and your precious business. You decided it would be safer if I just thought that she had gotten out and ran away. That's right, isn't it?"

"As God is my witness, it never entered my mind. My only motive was to protect you and Carlos. If you want me to, I'll put the business up for sale tomorrow."

Kiara had her hand under her chin and was staring at him. He could tell by the look on her face that she did not believe him. "I wonder what you would do if I called your bluff. Would you stay with us, or would you keep the business?"

"I just told you what I'd do."

"Words are cheap, and even if you are sincere and sold, you'd carry a cross for the rest of your life. I don't want to be on that cross. No, if we're going to make this work, we need a set of rules."

"Rules?"

"Yes, you need to find a way to keep the business and your problems away from our home life. Carlos and I need to feel safe. In return, I won't ask any questions that I think will result in you telling me lies." Kiara yawned, her eyes heavy.

"I'm sorry, I don't understand."

"One of the questions I won't ask is why you're bringing Ratsy to the Gold Coast because I know your answer will be a lie. I'll avoid any questions where I don't think it is possible for you to tell me the truth. Is that clear?"

"Yes."

"If I stray, you can say, 'It would be better if you don't go there,' and I'll drop it. Is that fair?"

"Yes."

"Luke, don't forget the conditions. You are to keep us safe, and I never want to be threatened or under siege by a gang of rogue bikers again."

"We might have to move to another house."

"I can live with that, but what we had has gone. I still love you and always will, but I doubt that I'll ever trust you again. That's why I'm making it easy for you not to tell me lies."

"That's unfair! I—"

"I'm really tired. I had to fight to stay up. I must get to bed. Goodnight, Luke."

"Goodnight, hon," Luke said, kissing her on the forehead. "You've been through a terrible experience, but it'll get better. Don't give up on me. Don't give up on us."

When he got to Sunnyside the following morning, the first call he made was to Steve Stratton to ask him to extend his family's security for another four weeks. Surprisingly, Stratton declined the assignment, saying that he couldn't give a hundred percent guarantee that he could keep Kiara and Carlos safe. Luke put the phone down knowing that someone had gotten to Stratton and that he'd have to arrange fresh security not only for his family but also the two construction sites.

Stratton had said that no one could guarantee his family's security, but Luke knew that wasn't true. There was one man who could make that guarantee. He took the Webster Glass file from his desk drawer and read the notes that he had made in his meeting with old Frank Webster before calling Monty and asking him for Charlie Gorman's phone number.

"Luke, what makes you think I'd have that hoodlum's number, and why do you want it?"

"I didn't expect you to have it, but there's nothing you can't find out. Call me when you have it, and, Monty, I need it pronto."

"You didn't tell me why."

"No, I didn't. It's a private matter. Have you found my foundry yet and have you started negotiating with Tony Farrugia?"

"We're looking at two foundries that might be suitable, and we have an appointment with Tony on Wednesday. We don't want to appear to be overeager."

"Good. I need another favor. I have two new employees from the U.S. starting with me in four weeks. I need you to handle their visas and, while you're at it, to get them licenses to carry firearms. I'll fax you their details later today."

There was a long pause before Beaurepaire said, "I hope you know what you're doing, Luke. I'll be back to you within the hour."

Charlie Gorman was surprisingly articulate and said that he had been waiting for Luke's call, but he was not prepared to discuss business over the phone with someone he had not met. Luke stressed that the matter was urgent, and they agreed to meet in the bar of the Trident Hotel on Roma Street in Brisbane at midday. Three hours later, Luke asked a barman whether Mr. Gorman was in the crowded bar, and he nodded to a small table in the corner of the room.

For the second time that day, Luke was surprised. The middle-aged man wearing suit pants and a white business shirt with the sleeves rolled up was about the same size as Ratsy. Gorman stood up and extended his hand. "Charlie Gorman, young man, but my friends call me Butcher. What are you drinking?"

"It's good to meet you, Mr. Gorman. I'll have a beer, thanks."

Gorman snapped his fingers, and a barman materialized. "Another Jack Daniels for me and a beer for my friend … colleague. Now what's so urgent that had you running around looking for my phone number and rushing up from the Gold Coast?"

On the face of it, there was nothing particularly fearsome about Gorman. He had cropped sandy hair, no scars on his face, no tattoos on his forearms, no sign of his nose having been broken, and he weighed about a hundred and sixty pounds. The one similarity that he had with the wise guys in Chicago and Vegas was his eyes. His smile was all teeth, but his eyes remained hard and cold.

"I need security for my wife and son for four weeks," Luke replied. "I was overseas last weekend, and the BLMU and the Ferals terrorized them. I'm almost certain a detective based in Surfers Paradise tipped them off that I wouldn't be there. I want a guarantee that it won't occur again and that they'll be safe. I've been told that you're the only one who can give me that guarantee."

"I thought as much, and what you were told is right."

"You knew?"

"Do you think I see any mug who calls? You could be a plant. You could be wearing a wire. I had you checked out as soon as I found out that you were looking for me. You were in the same business as I was in Chicago." Gorman grinned.

"You're very thorough."

"That's why I'm still alive and not in prison. Who's the copper, and how do you know he gave the union the nod?"

"Bert Trask. He wants to question me about an assault on one of my men. Thugs hired by the BLMU did it. I told him I'd be away for three days. No one else knew. Do you know him?"

"I know what happened to your man, and I know Tricky Trask. He's been on the take for years, and the union's rewarded him handsomely. He wants to talk to you to find out what you know and what you're going to do. He's a stooge who'll try to intimidate you. Don't tell him anything."

"I won't."

"Good. Now tell me, why only four weeks?"

"I have my own security coming in from Chicago."

Gorman's eyes narrowed. "I hope they don't have any ideas about taking over my territory. You know three Mafioso from Orlando came out here because they saw Brisbane as being easy pickings. Only one returned, and he no longer had a nose. I run Brisbane, and nothing happens without me knowing about it."

"My source told me what happened to the guys from Orlando. I have no interest in your business, Mr. Gorman. The men who are coming from Chicago are friends, and their only responsibility will be to provide security for my family and my business. If they ever set foot in Brisbane, it will be fleeting."

Gorman looked over the rim of his glass as he slowly sipped his whiskey. "Fleeting? That's fine. If they need hardware, I'm your man. Serial numbers removed and untraceable. Let me know what they need. There's nothing I can't supply."

"I have to get them firearm licenses before I worry about hardware."

"Licenses? Are you mad? You'll just draw attention to them and yourself. It's less expensive and far more sensible to pay their fines. Forget about licenses."

Luke put his hand under his jaw and pondered what Gorman had said. "I don't want to run the risk that they might get deported."

"Have it your way. Will you use your friends to retaliate against the BLMU and the Ferals?"

"Yes, if I have to. Is that a problem?"

"No. I might even let you quote on our next project. Can you handle a large amount of cash?"

"My quote would be far less than my competitors, but my financiers wouldn't go for it. I have to do everything by the book. I digress. Can you – will you – look after my family's security for the next four weeks?"

"A pity about the cash. Yes, looking after your family won't be a problem. It'll cost you thirty thousand."

"That's acceptable. How many men will be involved? I'd like them to be discreet. My wife thinks she's living in a fishbowl, and seeing strange guys hanging around will just make it worse."

"That's funny." Gorman laughed, as he got to his feet and shouted, "Freddy, bring me a phone, another Jack Daniels, and a beer for my colleague!"

As the barman crawled under the table to plug the phone into the conveniently located phone plug, Gorman said, "I have to call my office."

Luke was perplexed but merely nodded as Gorman dialed.

"Brent, it's me," Gorman said, "we have a new client. Luke Cramer. We're providing security for his family. Call Col Decker at the BLMU and let him know. After you've done that, call that red-headed meathead who leads the Ferals and tell him. Then call Tricky and let him know that we don't want him harassing Mr. Cramer or his family. Okay?"

There was a pause, and Gorman said, "I'm just finishing up. I'll be back within the hour."

"You didn't answer me when I asked you how many men you would be assigning to my family's security."

Again, Gorman burst out laughing. "The man I spoke to, Brent Stoker, is one of my partners. He's completing the assignment as we speak. You're not going to have to worry about discretion because there won't be anyone hanging around your house or family."

"I don't understand."

"Once word is out that we're looking after your family, you'll have nothing to worry about. No one is going to terrorize them or make their life hell. You know why? Because they know that, if they do, they'll most likely be found in a dark alley with a bullet in the back of their head."

"You're charging me thirty grand for three phone calls," Luke said, open-mouthed.

Gorman's demeanor visibly changed, and his lips almost disappeared as he hissed, "No, I'm charging thirty grand to guarantee your family's safety. I can only give that guarantee because of my reputation and past deeds. If you don't like it, find someone else."

"I'm sorry," Luke quickly said. "I'm not looking to find anyone else. The way you operate ... it just surprised me."

"You shouldn't look for anyone else. Your family's safer than the crown jewels, and not even your friends from Chicago will be able to give the guarantee I have."

Not initially, Luke thought, *but in time they will.* "What will you do if the union offers you more to walk away from our deal, and in four weeks' time, asks you to work for it, will you?"

"You know, kid, in the first few minutes after you sat down, I thought, 'Jeez, this is a smart young fella.' I was wrong." Gorman scowled. "My reputation is everything. How many customers do you think I'd have if I double-crossed them? The union could offer me a hundred thousand, and I'd still stick by our deal. I don't know how you Yanks work, but here a man's word is his bond.

"Now I don't know what you were told, but I'm not a hitman. If someone were to harass your family, I'd kill him, but that's different. It would be reactive. You do know the difference between proactive and reactive, don't you?"

"Yes," Luke said, turning red.

"Pleased to hear it. In answer to your second question, yes. I'm running a business, and if the union wants to use my services, I'm happy to provide them. However, do you think the union bosses are ever going to knock on my door and ask for protection? It's never going to happen. Do you have any more questions?"

Gorman's sure to be able to find Cordy, and unlike a private detective, no one will ever be able to trace it back to him, Luke thought. "If I give you a name – I don't know whether it's a first name or a surname – of someone who does work for the union, could you trace him?"

"Yeah. What's this guy done?"

"He's the one who put my man in hospital. The poor bugger will never do heavy work or walk properly again. The same bastard slit the throat of my son's puppy and left it in our backyard for him to find."

"That's easy. I could tell you with one call, but I know you're not sure whether you want to go ahead. When you make up your mind, my fee is five thousand. Think about it."

"Talking about money, how do I pay you?"

"One of my companies will send you an invoice. It'll all be on the up and up."

"Thanks, Mr. Gorman," Luke said, getting up, and holding out his hand.

The little man's grip had been insipid when they had first met, but this time, Luke momentarily flinched when his hand was squeezed with unexpected force. "I'll be waiting to hear from you." Gorman grinned.

Chapter 26

Hebron Castings, the foundry and metal shop that Monty's people had located, was on a small street in Southport. According to Monty, the equipment was old but well maintained. The business had run a double-shift operation for years but had fallen on hard times. However, it was still making enough to pay the owner a generous salary and leave a little left over.

Luke was pleased to hear that it took three days to fire up the furnace, and that the only time it was shut down was at Christmas for maintenance. It sounded perfect, but to be sure, he needed to see it.

When he called, Monty said, "I thought you said you didn't want anyone to know of your involvement."

"I don't, and they won't," Luke replied. "Tell the owner you need to make another inspection before you submit an offer. I'll throw on a suit and tag along as one of your consultants. I only need to see one small area of the factory."

"It's all small. If it's what you want, I think seven hundred thousand will buy it."

"Get your people to set up another inspection, preferably in the evening. You don't need to be there."

"Yes, I do. It's my money."

"No, it's not, it's the bank's." Luke laughed.

"You're being pedantic. It's my ass on the line if things go wrong."

"And to think, Monty, I wouldn't have known what pedantic meant, had I not met you. How are the negotiations with Tony Farrugia going?"

"He'll sell. He likes the idea of continuing to manage the business and keeping the sale confidential. It's a good business, better than I anticipated. He wants twelve million. We're at ten and not budging. We'll get it for ten and a half."

"Tell your people not to lose it for half a mil."

"My people." Monty laughed. "I don't let my people negotiate ten-million-dollar acquisitions. I had dinner at Tony's a few nights back, and ended up drunk on his homemade grappa. Nearly blew my head off the following day. The things I do for you."

"Thanks. I appreciate it."

"Talking about things I do for you. Did you meet with Charlie Gorman?"

"Yes."

"And?"

"He's providing my family with security. He also recommended another security company to look after my construction sites. He said they can't be coerced or bought. I don't think he's as bad as his reputation portrays."

"He earned that reputation. You won't be wrong if you think of him as being as bad or worse than any of your Chicago mob friends. I hope you know what you're doing, having him look after your family."

"I do. Oh, I nearly forgot. Don't worry about the firearm licenses. They're not needed."

"Sure, Luke," Monty sighed.

A few minutes later, a gushing Tim Dixon called. "Luke, Monty told me the slab was poured without any hassles. I told you Rapidmix would cave when we dragged them into the Supreme Court."

"Yeah, they must have." Luke grinned. "Well done."

"I have the BLMU in the Federal Court tomorrow."

"That's the court stacked with left-wing judges, isn't it?"

"Some might say that. I wouldn't. Do you know the exact amount of your additional costs yet?"

"I thought we were suing for three hundred thousand."

"That's an ambit claim, or what's better known as a bullshit claim. The court's not going to award us a number we've pulled out of thin air. Can you fax me your calculations this afternoon? The union's lawyers are sure to seek an adjournment. I don't want to give them any wriggle room."

"How much do I put in for loss of future contracts?"

"Leave that to me," Dixon said. "They haven't made an offer, but I have a feeling that Rapidmix wants to settle. They asked me what the rock-bottom figure we would accept was."

"I hope you said three hundred thousand."

"I said I'd seek instructions from my client and get back to them. Even I know you didn't lose three hundred thousand."

"Tim, if Rapidmix settles, what happens to our actions against the union and the builders?"

"You can only get paid once. If Rapidmix settles, you haven't sustained a loss, and therefore the actions against the other parties are at an end."

"Damn! I didn't think of that."

"Why does that upset you?"

"I thought you said that the evidence raised in our case might lead to the Australian Consumer and Competition Commission launching an investigation into the collusion that took place among Rapidmix, the BLMU, and the big builders. You told me what they did was illegal. What did you call it?"

"A secondary boycott, and yes, it is illegal. Look, the ACCC doesn't need us to take legal action before commencing an investigation or laying charges."

"No, but the media coverage of our action will intensify the pressure on them."

"The ACCC doesn't respond to external pressure."

"Bullshit! The unions, including the BLMU, are huge donors to the Labor Party. In other words, they funded the election of the federal government. Do you think the Labor Party members want their mates in the BLMU investigated? I'm betting they're exerting plenty of pressure on the ACCC not to investigate."

"The ACCC is an independent statutory body. I told you that it doesn't respond to pressure."

"Did they teach you that at law school, counselor?" Luke laughed. "I want you to screw Rapidmix. I'll be pleased if it fights. Make it as tough for them to settle as you can."

"You'd rather take the union and builders on in court than settle with Rapidmix?"

"Now you're talking. Call me after the hearing tomorrow," Luke said, before hanging up. *Tim thinks the legal action against Rapidmix resulted in the company supplying concrete to me, and that his threats are why it's looking to settle.* If only he knew, Luke thought. As he pondered this, a little light bulb went off in his head. *It's the BLMU putting pressure on Rapidmix to settle. The union knows that, if settlement is reached, I won't have an action against it. Yes, that's it. Bastards! I don't think I'll be using lawyers again. Once Ratsy and Cas are here, I'll have my own way of resolving the union problem.*

Chapter 27

Life at home improved a little after Luke bought a female Shiba Inu puppy who Carlos named Gumby after the cartoon character. Luke would have preferred a German shepherd, but the Shiba, while only slightly larger than a fox terrier, was known to be fiercely protective.

Kiara was still strangely lethargic, had lost more weight, and said that she felt sore in her limbs. When Luke again suggested that she see a doctor, she wouldn't hear of it, saying that she was too busy with Carlos and that it was just the sticky weather. She perked up when Luke told her that he had found a house in the gated community of Sanctuary Cove thirty minutes north of Surfers Paradise.

Fully secured by a gatehouse at the only entrance and by the ocean on the other side, it had its own shopping center, a small brewery, a magnificent golf course, an upmarket recreation club, a marina, and a hotel. The house – rather, the mansion – on Marine Parade had its own pool and was fronted by a river that led to the sea. It also came with a mooring, and the real estate agent said that, for another two hundred thousand, the owner would throw in his cabin cruiser. The price of eight hundred thousand was more than Luke wanted to spend, but if Kiara liked it and it brought harmony back into their lives, it would be a small price to pay.

They stopped at the gatehouse before driving onto a brick driveway lined by magnificent, mature palms and surrounded by acres of freshly manicured lawns. Kiara said, "I like the estate. I feel safe here."

"Wait until you see the house."

Strangely, she did not embrace the house in the way that Luke had hoped she would. While agreeing that it was magnificent, she thought that it was too large for the three of them. "It might be too large now, but we're going to be adding to our family soon, aren't we? Don't worry about how big it is. We'll get a cleaner."

"I'd love more kids," Kiara said with a wan smile. "I'd be happy with a small house on this estate, but I can tell you love it."

Luke laughed. "Did you see any small houses on the way in? I know you haven't seen all the properties, but this house is at the smaller end of what's available. The agent told me that they flew Frank Sinatra and Whitney Houston out on the night they opened the estate. They were paid a million dollars each to belt out a few songs. There's nothing else like it."

"You're selling to yourself, Luke. Why don't you make an offer?"

Before the inspection was completed, the Cramers were out nine hundred and fifty thousand but were the proud owners of a Sanctuary Cove mansion, a mooring, and a cabin cruiser.

Late the following day, Luke received another call from Tim Dixon. This time the young lawyer wasn't so self-assured. "The BLMU's a very bad union, Luke. The hearing was adjourned, and as I was walking down the steps, one of its thugs said that it would be good for my health if I dropped the action. When I didn't cower, another one showed me two photos. They were of my daughters. Then he told me what school they attended and the bus they catch to get there."

"Did he threaten you?"

"No, he just smiled. They know they don't have to threaten. I called the police as soon as I was back in my office. They said they were surprised I was reporting it because no offense was committed that called for their action. When I asked them whether they could patrol my house for the next few nights, they said they didn't have the resources. My wife is paranoid. We're staying in a hotel tonight."

Maybe I should tell him about Charlie Gorman, Luke thought. "I'm sorry to hear that. You told me you weren't worried about them. I take it that's no longer the case?"

"I'm not worried about myself. It's my family. I'm going to settle with Rapidmix which effectively finishes the actions against the BLMU and the builders. I know that's not what you want. If you want to use the services of another firm, I'll understand."

"Go ahead and settle, Tim. Your family comes first. It's been a learning experience for me. I've learned that the law is a blunt tool when it comes to the BLMU. I'll have to find some other tools."

"I underestimated the lengths they would go to. Don't make the same mistake, Luke."

"I won't."

Chapter 28

When Luke got home that night, there was a check from the insurance company waiting for him. He'd been so busy that he'd almost forgotten that he was driving a rental. But the gleaming, silver Sports Quattro in the showroom window of the local Audi dealer that he passed every day, jolted his memory. He would have to double the insurer's check, but it was worth it. The Audi was a big step up from the Ford in class and power but unlikely to cause worker envy like a BMW or Mercedes. He would visit the dealer on his way to Sunnyside in the morning.

The smell of the interior and the power under his foot lifted his spirits, and when he arrived at the site, rather than park on the street, he parked right next to the site office. When he'd been on other sites, he'd seen workers resent their bosses' luxury cars and was pleased that he had chosen the Audi. There was no rancor, and most of the workers seemed pleased; a few of the older hands even offered their congratulations.

Since meeting with Charlie Gorman, he had not heard from the union or Detective Trask and work on the two sites was progressing on track. After getting Rapidmix's check for damages, CramerBuild would clear more than $1 million on Sunnyside, but the work was starting to take its toll. The only time he got to prepare quotes was late at night, and he knew that he was losing business because he couldn't meet submission deadlines.

If CramerBuild were to grow, it needed to employ a project manager who could alleviate his workload. Luke's mind immediately turned to Max Tilson, his night-school buddy. He was perfect – loyal, bright, hardworking but lacking the balls to do his own thing. Yes, Tilson would always be an employee, but Luke would never have to worry about him stealing a gang or a project. He made a note to call him when he got home.

When Monty's PA called to ask whether three o'clock tomorrow afternoon would be okay to inspect Hebron Castings, Luke wondered whether the day could get any better.

The following day, Luke left the Burleigh Heads site just after midday to go home, where he showered, put on a clean, white business shirt, his only suit, and a tie. Carlos was at school, and Kiara was sitting at the kitchen table, head in her hands, reading the local newspaper.

"You don't look well, hon. How much do you weigh?" he asked.

"I'm fine. I'm just a little tired. I've spent ages packing, and there's still so much more to do."

"I thought we agreed that the carriers would do all the packing and unpacking."

"I feel bad getting others to do what I can do, and the thirty-day settlement doesn't leave us much time."

Luke crunched his lips together and rolled his eyes. "How much do you weigh?"

"If you must know, ninety-six pounds."

"God, you were one hundred and ten when we arrived on the coast. You've lost fourteen pounds, and you had nothing to lose. You should have seen a doctor."

"I've been too busy with Carlos, and lately we've had all that drama. I haven't had time."

"You're going to see a doctor, and I'm going with you. Make an appointment."

"I'm not going to argue with you, but I know there's nothing wrong with me. Now why don't you go to your meeting? You should wear a suit more often. You look very smart, but I don't like all that oil in your hair. It's as if you're trying to disguise yourself," Kiara said, smiling weakly.

"Hon, I love you," Luke said, kissing her, "and I worry about you. If anything were to happen to you, I don't know how I'd go on."

"I love you, Luke Cramer, and nothing's going to happen to me."

Monty and one of his assistants were waiting at the front of Hebron Castings when Luke pulled up. "Great-looking car, nice suit, pity about the hairstyle," Monty said.

"It's—"

"I know what it is, Luke. It's a crummy disguise. I don't think you're going to have to worry. Old Mr. Hebron was worried about the number of inspections so there's no one working. If we do the deal, he has a holiday house in Port Douglas, more than a thousand miles north, where he's going to retire. No one's going to know of your involvement."

"Good, let's not keep him waiting."

The factory wasn't that old, but the equipment was, and the smell of molten metal hung in the air. Hunched over and totally bald, Mr. Hebron was only sixty-two but looked much older. *Just like my dad*, Luke thought, *the result of a lifetime spent in a metals factory.*

They started their inspection in the machine and tool shop at one end of the factory. It was equipped with lathes, drills, and shapers and held little interest for Luke. As they walked toward the furnace and castings area, it became progressively dirtier. "Did you buy the equipment secondhand?" Luke asked.

"Some of it. My grandfather started the business in Brisbane, and my father continued it. About ten years ago, we realized we could no longer afford the rent so we shifted the business and equipment down here."

"How old is the furnace?"

"I don't know. My father purchased it secondhand. As I told Mr. Beaurepaire, we've only recently had it relined. It might be old, but it's still efficient."

No, it's not, Luke thought, *but it's perfect for my needs.* "What's its maximum temperature?"

"I don't know, but we melt scrap iron, and its melting temperature is a thousand degrees Celsius."

"Eighteen hundred degrees Fahrenheit," Luke said. "Do you leave it on twenty-four-seven?"

"It's not the type of equipment you can turn off at night and restart in the morning," Hebron said disdainfully.

"How do you feed it?" Luke asked, ignoring the sleight.

"See the bucket attached to the overhead crane? We fill it and then maneuver it above the furnace. It has a door in the bottom that we can automatically release. It's a simple operation."

"You could throw scrap metal into it."

"You could, but it would be dangerous and inefficient."

"I was making an observation, not a suggestion," Luke said. "Do you pour directly from the cupola?"

"Yes, it's tilted. Are you the buyer?" Hebron slyly asked.

"No. I have a manufacturing background. Our client specifically requested that I ask you those questions."

Monty was quick to take his cue. "Mr. Hebron, I think that answers all our queries. Can we have a few minutes?"

"I'll be in my office," Hebron replied.

After he had left, Luke said, "It's perfect. My only concern is his retirement. Will we still have the people to operate it? Is there someone we can make CEO or general manager? This is strictly an investment for me. I can't – and don't want to – get involved in the day-to-day operations."

"I thought you had someone lined up."

"I do, but he won't be hands on. He'll have an overseeing role."

"I wish you'd come clean. It's a lousy investment," Monty said, "but you're not worried because you're buying it for another reason. The plant manager has been with the business for years, and the sales guys know how to win orders. Hebron doesn't do much, other than sit in his office and drag out a hundred and fifty thousand a year. You could give the two main men fifty grand and have a hundred left over for interest and loan repayments. If I'm lucky, my loan might be repaid in eight years."

"Ah, Monty, don't be a pessimist. According to you, Farrugia Concrete & Quarries makes more than enough to repay both loans, and if it doesn't, the high-rises I build will. I must get going. Try offering Hebron six hundred thousand, but if you must, go to seven-fifty. I want this business. Oh, and let him know we'd like him to stay on for thirty days after settlement."

Chapter 29

That night, Luke called Max Tilson, and they agreed to meet for a drink in the birdwatcher's bar the following evening. Then he spread the plans out for a five-story office block in Coolangatta and started working on the quote. He was tired, but there were only two days left to submit it, and he knew that his quote would be the lowest. He reasoned that, after he'd won and completed the office block, he'd be another step closer to building high-rises. After all, if he proved that he could successfully build a five-story building, there was no reason why he couldn't build a thirty-story high-rise. It was midnight when he turned the study light off and went to bed. The moonlight was coming through the bedroom window, and Kiara was sleeping fitfully. He didn't have a religious bone in his body, but, as he stared at her drawn face, he said a silent prayer.

Monty called the following morning to say that Hebron had accepted six hundred and seventy-five thousand for a speedy settlement. Luke was elated. All the pieces were coming together. "Have you closed with Tony Farrugia yet?"

"We're getting closer. He's on the hook. Be patient."

"I was thinking last night. Tony's not getting any younger. Do we have a backup if something happens to him?"

"Need you ask? It's my money. Do you think I'd fund a deal like this on the security of a seventy-year-old's health? Domenic, his nephew, has been with him for fifteen years. He's part of the package, but don't worry. There are plenty of good managers who can run the business. Good managers have no difficulty running good businesses, but bad businesses are something else. Even Jack Welch couldn't make a decent profit out of Hebron Castings. When are you going to tell me the real reason you bought it?"

"I want to diversify."

"Bullshit!"

Anytime Monty swore it made Luke smile. His refined, English voice destroyed the impact of his cussing. "Let me know the minute you close with Tony," Luke said, immediately biting his tongue.

"I would if you had a cellphone. Have you thought about what I said?"

"Sure, I looked at a Mitsubishi. It weighed twenty pounds and would barely fit in my briefcase. You know what they're calling them? Bricks. Bricks! You're the only person I know who has one. They want five thousand for the Mitsubishi."

"Everyone will have them in the future."

"I agree, but right now, hardly anyone has one. They're an extravagance."

"Luke, before the month is out, you'll owe me twelve million. By comparison, five thousand is chickenshit. I need to be able to contact you 24/7. I want you to go back to the dealer and buy the Mitsubishi."

"I'll think about it," Luke said. He had no intention of lugging a brick around. "Is there anything else I need to know?"

"Have you been following the Surf Coast's elections?"

"I didn't know there were elections. Anyway, I'm not interested in politics."

"You should be. There's a young guy about five years older than you who is running for council. He's very smart, a conservative, and the council's just a stepping stone to either the state or federal parliament. He could end up premier or even prime minister. If you get to know him while he's on the bottom rung, you can climb all the way to the top with him."

"Who is this genius?"

"Russell Hannan. I've told him that you're good for twenty thousand toward his election campaign."

"You told him what?"

"Trust me. It'll be the best money you'll ever spend."

"What do I get out of it? Is he going to pull strings when I'm having trouble with building and planning permits?"

"It's subtler than that. He'll help you when he can, and he'll never block you, but there'll be times when he'll have to sit on his hands. He won't ask you for anything directly, nor will you ask him for anything, but there'll be an understanding."

There was a long pause before Monty followed up with, "When have I ever led you astray, Luke?"

"Yeah, okay. Do I send him a brown paper bag?"

"Definitely not. Everything must be aboveboard and declared. There might be some flak in the media about a builder and property developer cozying up to a politician, but it won't last long. Can I tell him that your check's in the mail?"

"Yeah," Luke reluctantly said. "I have to go, Monty. I have another appointment."

Max Tilson was propped up at the one-way glass window in the bird-watcher's bar nursing a beer, and there was another on the table next to him. Famous with the locals, the bar overlooked the main drag where an abundance of beautiful and scantily clad women did their shopping or just paraded themselves. They shook hands, and Tilson passed Luke a glass of beer, saying, "I take it you're still on XXXX? Where else can you get a floor show without a cover charge?"

"Thanks. You look well, Max. Yeah, the girls sure look good," Luke said, glancing out the window and hoping that he wasn't aging as badly. Tilson's thick black hair had receded, he had a distinct paunch, and worry lines were etched into his forehead. "How's work?"

"Hectic. We have two towers, a shopping center, and a twenty-story office block on the go. I barely have time to scratch myself."

"It's better than the alternative. How are Lizzie and the kids?"

"You know what it's like. I work too many hours. I don't get paid enough. I don't spend enough time with the kids. I don't spend enough time with her. I can't afford and can't get time off to take a holiday. We haven't been on one for years. Besides that, great. What about you and Kiara?"

"We're good. We're moving to Sanctuary Cove in two weeks. Things got a little rough with the union, and I don't want to have to worry about Kiara and Carlos."

"I heard about the concrete pour debacle."

You should have, Luke thought, *your employer, Suncrest*

Developments, was one of the companies that threatened to blackball Rapidmix if they supplied CramerBuild. "It was a hiccup that we've managed to resolve. It won't happen again."

"I hope you're right, but that's not what I'm hearing. You pissed the union off big time by opting not to join the club. They're not going to put up with a maverick, Luke. The other builders won't let them."

Luke laughed. "Doesn't it strike you as strange that the union and the builders are in bed together?"

"Not really. That's how things have happened here ever since I've been involved. There have been a few holdouts like you, but they've either been brought to heel or have gone broke."

"Neither's going to happen to me. We're well financed and have plenty of quotes in the pipeline. Surely, you don't support the current fix up?"

"No, but it's way above my pay grade. You're taking on some very powerful people."

"Perhaps. Did you ever think of going out by yourself, Max?"

"Are you kidding? I have a wife, three kids, and a dirty great mortgage. No way. Luke, things are a bit tense with Lizzie right now, and I don't want to get home too late and be accused of having a good time at the pub while she's cooking and minding the kids. What is it that you wanted to see me about?"

"I'd like you to work for me. I can offer you a very attractive package."

"If you'd made your offer before I got married and had kids, I would've said yes. I can't run the risk no matter what you offer me. I need security, and that's something you can't offer. I heard one of my bosses say that CramerBuild won't exist by Christmas. I can't run the risk."

"Look, Max, I know what you're earning, and I'm prepared to offer you another thirty percent. As far as security goes, I'll provide you with a bank guarantee for two years' salary. Can we talk turkey?"

"I'd be secured for two years? I don't know. I have a long-term career path with Suncrest. Who knows what's going to happen to CramerBuild?"

"I do! CramerBuild will be the biggest builder on the coast within ten years. You reject my offer, and you'll live to regret it."

"I don't know."

I never realized you were so weak. Maybe I can use it to my advantage, Luke thought. "You said you haven't had a holiday for years, and Port Douglas is very nice this time of year. Join CramerBuild, and I'll pay for you and your family to have a two-week, all-expenses-paid holiday before you start." Luke paused and smiled – Tilson's eyes said, *I finally have some good news to tell my wife.* "Don't give me your answer now. Think about it tonight. Talk to Lizzie and get back to me tomorrow."

As he climbed into the Audi, he knew that Tilson would accept. His wife would see to that. He mused that good men were hard to find and felt a sharp conscience pang when he thought of George Simpson. He made a mental note to visit him at his home tomorrow.

Thinking of George immediately regurgitated the name of his attacker, Cordy. He had promised Ratsy that he wouldn't seek him, but that was before he knew Charlie Gorman. Besides, Ratsy and Cas would be here in a week, and he wanted to put them to work immediately.

Chapter 30

The first thing Gorman asked when Luke called was whether he had experienced any trouble. "None, Mr. Gorman," Luke replied, "but you already knew that."

"Yeah, I did," Gorman laughed. "but it's always nice to hear it from the mouth of a satisfied client."

"Yeah, yeah. When can I see you?"

"What's it about?"

"Several matters I'd rather not discuss over the phone. We talked about them the last time we met."

"You're a fast learner, Luke. Maybe I'll reassess you and put you back in the smart category. Where are you?"

"Southport."

"If it's urgent, I can fit you in, if you leave now. If not, I have most of Friday free."

"I'm on my way. Same place as last time?"

"Nah. Now that I know you, you can come to my office. Kittens on the corner of Ernest and Bond streets. You can't miss it. You'll be able to park at the front."

An hour later, Luke pulled up at the front of a converted old double-story bank building, with a garish green neon vertical sign that screamed Kittens. A billboard next to it featured five young girls wearing G-strings, negligees, and high heels. He entered the double doors and sank into a gaudy, multicolored carpet.

To the right, leaning over a small red pool table, was a long-legged brunette, while the guy she was playing stood behind ogling her. To the left, three pole dancers ground out their stuff before a few bored patrons. A blonde wearing a red negligee and little else got up from her chair at the horseshoe bar, told him her name was Linda, and asked whether he'd like to buy her a drink.

"Another time. Could you please let Mr. Gorman know that Luke Cramer is here?"

"I'll do that, love," she said, strutting over to the bar and picking up a phone.

"Thanks."

"Maybe when you're finished with Mr. Gorman, you can buy me that drink, or perhaps you'd like a little more. I do a terrific lap dance," she said, nodding toward the dimly lit cubicles on the other side of the bar. "You won't be disappointed."

"I'm sure I wouldn't be, but I'm married."

"You're kidding! Ninety-nine percent of the guys who come in here are married, not that they admit it, and they're all hoping they'll get lucky."

"I must be in the other one percent." He grinned, as Gorman shouted from the top of the stairs, "Up here, Luke."

Gorman's office was large and luxuriously fitted out with a wall constructed of floor-to-ceiling one-way glass that provided him with an unimpeded view of the bar and the activities below him. "Pull up a recliner," he said, as he sat down at a coffee table adjacent to his desk. "Would you like something to drink?"

"Thanks. I'll pass. We have a lot to discuss, Mr. Gorman, and you don't have much time. Last time we met you said you knew the name of the man who assaulted my worker?"

"Ace Cordy. He's a bum. Set himself up as a tough guy for hire. Big, ugly bastard with a mohawk and decorated in tattoos. Here's a bonus for you. He never works alone. - too gutless. His partner's name is Ryan Quade. You can't miss him. A few years back he picked on this little guy - big mistake. The little fella was a real goer and bit one of Quade's ears off - perfect job. He might just as well have used a scalpel." Gorman laughed.

"Where do they live?"

"What is this? You might as well pay me to do whatever you have planned. I said I'd give you one name for five gorillas, and I've given you two. They live in Fortitude Valley, but I don't have their address. It's Brisbane's tough-guy area where the locals don't go out at night. Cordy and Quade are losers. They've beaten up a few drinkers in my territory, but luckily for them, they weren't patronizing my bars. They're bad for business."

"Thanks. It sounds like I might be doing you a favor."

"Kid, don't get ahead of yourself. I need you doing me favors like I need another asshole."

Luke felt himself turning red. It was the second time Gorman had put him in his place. *I'll have to be more careful. He might be more personable than Sordi, but he's just as dangerous.* "Sorry. No offense meant."

"Apology accepted." Gorman smiled. "How else can I help you?"

Jesus, this guy changes like the weather. "I'd like to know the name of the red-headed guy who leads the Ferals."

"Why?"

"He terrorized my wife. I'm not going to let him get away with it. Do you know him?"

"Of course. He was only doing what he was paid to do. It was just business."

"You could say the same about Cordy and Quade."

"You have a point," Gorman said, cracking his knuckles. "Do you really want to make enemies of the Ferals? They can cause you a lot of trouble."

"They already have. Look, if you don't want to tell me, that's fine. I'll find out using my own resources."

"Let me think about it. Is there anything else?"

Luke had done nothing about digging up dirt on his enemies, but Monty's comments were locked in his psyche. "I need the name of a good private detective on the Gold Coast, and before you ask, I'll only be using him to do background checks on some of the union bosses. You know - family, residential addresses, and criminal convictions - basic stuff."

Gorman flicked through his business cards before handing one to Luke. "Tom Coughlan. He's careful about who he works for. I'll call him and tell him you're kosher. Are you all done now?"

"No. I need two pistols - a Smith & Wesson .38 Special, and a Beretta Cheetah, and silencers."

"Ah, that's more like it," Gorman said, his face lighting up. "Ankle guns, aye? I have the Smith & Wesson in stock, but I'm not sure about the Beretta. Follow me."

Gorman took the stairs to the basement two at a time and, after striding down a passageway, stopped in front of a vault. He punched in a combination, spun a wheel, and swung the door open. "When we bought the place," he said, "the door weighed twenty tons, and it took two of us to open it. We replaced it with titanium, scrapped the dial, and made it electronic. It cost a fortune, but now it's far more secure than it was when the bank owned it. Come inside."

Luke had never seen so many guns, not even in Chicago. Glass cases surrounded three walls of the vault, not unlike a jewelry store, but diamonds and gold were replaced with firearms. A large pair of bolt cutters was propped up against the wall adjacent to the door. "Jesus!" he exclaimed, picking up a gun from an open-topped box.

"They're Glocks. They just arrived. They need work before they'll be available for sale."

"Removal of the serial numbers and identifying marks?"

"Yeah. This is what you're looking for," Gorman said, taking a Smith & Wesson from a glass case.

"What about the Beretta?"

"I'll get one in the next shipment. It'll be another six weeks though."

"Shit, how do you get them past customs?"

"Silly question, as if I'm going to tell you. I can let you have another Smith & Wesson if it helps."

"Silencers?"

"Of course."

Ratsy had ordered the Smith & Wesson, and Cas had asked for the Beretta. *It's more important to keep Ratsy happy than Cas,* Luke thought. "Yeah, I'll take them. How much?"

"For you, ten thousand."

"What about shoulder holsters and ankle holsters?"

"I'll throw them in."

"And five body bags?"

"Shit! You're serious. I thought you wanted the guns to scare them. You don't. You're going to kill them, aren't you?"

Luke compressed his lips and didn't respond.

"Why don't you get the bags yourself? You can get 'em from a funeral parlor or one of the medical equipment suppliers."

"I don't want them traced back to me."

"And I use them every day, so no one will query me," Gorman sarcastically replied. "Why five?"

"I may not use any of them. I just want to have them if I need to."

"Bullshit! I know you're going to use two. That little, silent act of yours was a dead giveaway. They'll cost me a hundred and fifty, but I'm going to charge you two grand."

"That's fine."

"Is that it, or do you have another surprise for me?"

"What's the biker's name?"

"Nice try, kid. You're more dangerous than I gave you credit for. The Ferals frequent my clubs. They're big spenders, so what you want me to do is bad for business, and I never do anything that's bad for business. Let's go upstairs, and you can put the guns and ammo in your briefcase. Are you all right with an invoice for seventeen grand for personal security?"

"Sure. You said 'clubs.' How many do you own?"

"There's not a girlie bar in Brisbane that we don't own, and there's no one likely to compete." Gorman smirked.

"I wouldn't like to be paying your weekly wages."

"You mean the girls? They don't work for me. I provide them with a place to work and security. They pay me half their tips – the money the patrons shove down their G-strings for lap dances and flirting. In an average week, a girl will get three grand in tips. There's no explicit sex on the premises, and the girls are warned about fraternizing after hours. That's where my chain of brothels comes in."

"Unbelievable."

"Yeah, it's good. Luke, I would have liked to have had lunch, but I have another meeting - next time."

"Yeah, next time," Luke replied, shaking Gorman's hand. The club was filling with the lunchtime crowd, and he smiled when he saw the blonde leading a happy patron to one of the private cubicles.

The last thing Luke wanted was to be pulled over by a motorbike cop on the way back to the Gold Coast, so he drove slowly. As he trundled along the highway, his mind turned to Gorman. He didn't doubt that the Brisbane crime boss had earned his reputation with the bolt cutters but knew he wouldn't last ten minutes on the streets of Chicago. Conversely, Sordi and his baseball bat wouldn't survive in Brisbane.

They both ruled because they had infrastructures comprising cops, politicians, judges, and snitches on their payroll, and nothing happened in their territory without their knowledge. Sordi had more depth because of his Mafia connections, but their power came about because they each dominated the territory in which they had chosen to operate. *Perhaps, I should do the same and confine myself to the Gold Coast*, Luke thought.

Chapter 31

By the time Ratsy and Cas landed at Coolangatta Airport, Luke owned Farrugia Concrete & Quarries, had shifted into his new home in Sanctuary Cove, and had sent Max Tilson on a holiday before his start with CramerBuild. However, his security contract with Charlie Gorman had expired, and the union and bent cop Bert "Tricky" Trask were again chasing him.

As they drove away from the terminal, the sun beat down on the Audi. It was a typical Queensland day: a cloudless blue sky and a balmy eighty degrees. "Welcome to paradise, fellers," Luke said.

"It was freezing when we took off from O'Hare," Cas said.

"I like it better than this," Ratsy said, squinting. "I'm not a sun lover."

"You'll get used to it, and you'll grow to love it. It's impossible not to. It's God's country."

"Yeah, maybe. Do you have a plan for us?"

"Of course, but I want you to spend a few days familiarizing your-selves with the coast between here and Southport. Also, take a drive up to Brisbane and have a look around. I've rented a house for you in Surfers Paradise. The fridge is full, the cupboards are stocked, there's $1,000 in Aussie money on the kitchen bench, and there's a minivan with the keys in the ignition in the garage. You'll find the house very comfortable, but more importantly, it's secured by a six-foot-high wall and even taller bougainvilleas."

"You seem to have thought of everything, Luke. What are bougain-villeas, and more importantly, what do they have to do with security?" Cas asked.

"Beautiful tropical plants with glorious purple flowers. They're covered in semi-poisonous spikes, and there's no way anyone can climb through or over them. If they try, you'll most likely find them unable to move and impaled by spikes."

"Did you get the guns?"

"I got yours, Ratsy. Sorry, Cas, what you wanted was unavailable. I got you a Smith & Wesson too."

"When do we start work?" Ratsy asked.

"Not until you've completed your seven-day, foundry apprenticeship." Luke laughed. "I'm going to have you introduced as the owner, Ratsy. You'll be his assistant, Cas. You need to learn how the furnace works, get a set of keys to the foundry, find out how the security system works, get yourself an office, and put two clothes lockers in it. You'll only ever keep changes of clothes in them, but I don't want anyone nosing around. Let the managers know that you might visit after hours to inspect the premises. Get a combination lock put on the door and make sure it's tamperproof. Don't skimp, get the best."

"I might have to delegate the work to my assistant." Ratsy smirked. "I've never had a real job. This will be a first."

"Wear suits, and I'll give you clipboards and legal pads. All you need to do is observe, look intelligent, make notes, and ask questions when appropriate. From what I saw, the furnace operation is simple."

"Don't worry, Luke, me and my assistant will work it out. When do we start the real job?"

"The following week - I found out their names: Ace Cordy and Ryan Quade."

"Jesus, you didn't go to a private dick, did you?"

"Give me some credit, Ratsy. My source is untraceable. There's nothing to worry about. I'm going to use a private detective for a related matter though."

"Where do they live?"

"I don't have their address, but they live together in a suburb bordering Brisbane, Fortitude Valley. It's a rough area. Think of it as Brisbane's Englewood. You should check it out when you're up there. I'm going to drop you off now. Get a few hours' sleep. I'll pick you up for dinner at seven."

Private detective Tom Coughlan answered his phone on the second ring. "I've been expecting your call, Luke. I hope Charlie told you that I skirt the law, but never break it."

"Tom, what I want is on the up and up. Nothing illegal."

"That's what I like to hear. Shoot."

"I want separate dossiers on BLMU officials Col Decker and Dennis Bartlett. Residential addresses, interests, clubs, wives' names, children, their ages, where they go to school, and, on a separate page, criminal convictions."

"Just the type of assignment I like. I'll come back to you within forty-eight hours. Is two thousand okay with you?"

"Not a problem."

As Luke put the phone down, there was a sharp rap on the site office door, and he looked up to see Dennis Bartlett and two of his thugs. "Congratulations, Luke," Bartlett said, "you're coming up in the world."

"What?"

"Don't play dumb with me. We know you won the Coolangatta office block contract."

That's great news, but no one's told me. How do these pricks know? "Oh, that," Luke said nonchalantly.

"Yeah, that, smartass. Here's what we want. No union ticket, no start. The same with your subcontractors. We want to know who they are, and if we don't approve, they won't be setting foot on site. Don't worry. We have plenty of subbies who we can recommend."

"If my men want to join the union, they can. I won't hold it against them. However, I'm not forcing them to join, and Coolangatta, like the rest of my sites, won't be a closed shop. As far as subcontractors go, I know you have mates who give you and the union an under-the-table payoff. It's not happening with me. They're free to quote, like everyone else, and if their quotes are the lowest, and I think they're competent to perform the work, I'll willingly use them. Oh, and you're never going to have any say in choosing my subcontractors."

"You're not hearing me, Luke," Bartlett said, stepping into the office. "We let–"

"Hey," Luke interrupted, "close the door and tell your gorillas to wait outside."

The two thugs stared daggers at Luke before Bartlett told them to get out. As he started to sit down, he said, "As I was saying, we–"

Again, Luke interrupted. "Don't sit down. You won't be here long enough."

Bartlett's face flushed with anger. "You think you're so smart. You have no idea what we can do to you. We can do worse than stopping a concrete pour. We've let you go on the smaller projects. Coolangatta is too big. You're going to toe the line, like the rest of the builders on the coast, or you're going to wish you'd never been born."

"Are the other builders getting jumpy?" Luke laughed. "Are they going to dump the sweetheart deals they've done with you? Have they realized that there's no way they can compete with me as long as they're paying you off? CramerBuild will be the biggest builder on the coast within ten years."

"You'll do what we want, or you won't be here within a year – forget ten years," Bartlett said, turning to leave. "We'll be back at lunchtime tomorrow to talk to your men. We think that we're going to get plenty of signups, without that intimidating thug of yours scaring them."

Luke thumped the desk with his fist. "You prick! Why don't you tell me how you arranged George's beating?"

"I don't know anything. You just want to make sure the same thing doesn't happen to you."

As Luke got to his feet, Bartlett opened the door and stepped out into the bright sun and the safety of his men.

Later that morning, Detective Bert Trask called to say that he was on his way to the Sunnyside site. Luke watched as a burly, overweight man wearing a gray fedora and a matching suit wriggled his way out of the front seat of an unmarked navy-blue Ford. He waddled across the street like he had all the time in the world and extended his damp, flabby hand. Luke reluctantly took it. "I'm glad we've finally met. I have a few questions to ask you about George Simpson."

"Good. Have you found the thugs who beat him up?"

"I'll ask the questions," Trask said, wiping the perspiration from his jowls. "When Mr. Simpson was admitted to the hospital, he was rambling. The doctors said it sounded like a name, but they couldn't make it out. Did he say anything to you?"

"Not a word. He did say he'd been drinking. Perhaps it was the beer talking."

"Yeah," Trask replied, looking pleased. "Does he have any enemies that you know of?"

"Everyone likes George. He's a big gentle giant."

"Then he doesn't have any enemies?"

"I didn't say that. Shortly before he was assaulted, he convinced his fellow workers not to join the BLMU. Obviously, it upset some union officials."

"You're not suggesting that the union had him beaten up, are you?" Trask smirked.

"Suggesting? No. I'm telling."

"That's a serious allegation you've just made. I hope you can back it up."

Luke laughed. "I've given you a lead. It's your job to follow it up. Are you going to?"

"Don't tell me what my job is," Trask blustered. "I don't answer to the likes of you, and no, I'm not going to follow up on your imaginary lead. as if the union would resort to assault. Tell me why you went to Chicago."

"Only my wife and travel agent knew I was going to Chicago. How did you find out? More importantly, who did you tell?"

"We have our ways, and what do you mean - who did I tell?"

"My wife was terrorized while I was gone, but you already know that, don't you? The mongrels knew that I wasn't home, and when she called you for help, it took three hours before anyone showed up."

"I don't know what you're talking about." Trask smirked. "Did Mr. Simpson have any real enemies that you know of? Not imaginary ones. Any people who actually threatened him in your presence?"

"I told you what happened and who did it, but you're not interested. That doesn't surprise me. If you're quite finished, I have a business to run."

"You have a smart mouth for someone so young. You'd be wise to show some respect. You might have been a tough guy in Chicago. Here you're nothing but another damn Yank. Put a foot out of place, and I'll have you behind bars before you can spit," Trask said, shoving the door open.

Chapter 32

It took Ratsy and Cas less than a day to cover the twenty-five miles of coast between Coolangatta and Southport after stopping at Currumbin, Burleigh Heads, and Broadbeach. As they drove along the Gold Coast Highway, Cas said, "I know why Luke bought us a minivan, but why dark blue?"

"It's obvious, Cas. He doesn't want us seen at night."

"Of course."

"There's not much to see, is there?" Ratsy said. "Sand, waves, and high-rises."

"You have no appreciation of beauty," Cas replied. "We better get you some sunscreen in Southport. You're as white as a ghost. If you're not careful, this sun will fry you."

"Says he with the olive skin. Whatta we gonna do now?"

"Let's head up into the hinterland and find somewhere we can get a cold beer."

"Hold that thought, Cas. We'll have a look at the hills, but let's go to Brisbane for that beer. The faster we get that out of the way, the faster we get on with what we're here to do, and the faster I get home."

"What are you talking about? You promised Luke you'd stay for a year."

"Yeah, I know, but he's not gonna need us for that long. After we've finished, no one's gonna give him any trouble. Follow the sign that says 'Mount Tamborine, Brisbane.'"

Two hours later, Ratsy said, "There's hardly anyone on the streets. It's a dead city. If it weren't for the girlie bars and pubs, no one would be here."

"Do you want to go for a walk? Have that beer?"

"Nah, keep driving, Cas. It's only a mile or so to Fortitude Valley. We'll have a drink there."

"You're the boss."

"Hey, that place will do." Ratsy pointed at an old, three-story hotel. "Shit! Who calls a pub The Elephant?"

There were a handful of drinkers in the bar, and Cas ordered two beers.

"What will it be, mate? Middies, schooners, pots, or pints?" the barman asked.

"Whatever's the biggest," Ratsy snapped.

"That's pints," the barman said, filling two large glasses. "What part of America are you from?"

"Illinois," Cas said.

"I don't think I know it."

"What about Chicago?"

"Of course. If you had said Illinois was part of Chicago, I would have known where you were talking about."

"Of course, you would've." Ratsy grinned, knocking the froth off his beer. "I needed that."

"You prick," Cas said.

"Just having some fun with the natives," Ratsy replied. "This is not a bad drop."

"Yeah." Cas yawned. "Are you ready to head back?"

"Let's have another beer. Hey, barman, another two pints."

As the barman poured their beers, Ratsy said, "Is it always this quiet? It's like a morgue."

"Like a morgue, aye?" the barman replied. "It's Tuesday night. What do you expect? Why don't you come back on Friday or Saturday night? You won't be able to move."

"We might just do that," Ratsy said.

As they climbed back into the minivan, Cas said, "Where now?"

"Let's check out the other pubs. One with a large adjoining parking garage or an alley nearby would be ideal."

"Okay. What's the plan tomorrow?"

"We'll tell Luke we're a week ahead of schedule and want to start at the foundry on Thursday. Is that okay with you?"

"Yeah. I'm tired. Jet lag, I guess. Let's look at these pubs and get out of here. I've had enough driving for one day. I'm gonna sleep late tomorrow."

Old Mr. Hebron told the two Americans that they'd need overalls or dust coats, depending on what they were going to do, before entering the foundry. Then he fobbed them off on the plant manager and went back to planning his retirement in Port Douglas. There was a small office at the end of the corridor where Ratsy and Cas hung up their suit coats and changed into the gray dust coats provided. The men in the foundry looked at their new clipboard-bearing owners and put their heads down, apprehensive and anxious not to draw attention to themselves. *If only they knew,* Ratsy thought.

Two hours later, he was confident that he understood how raw materials were fed into the furnace via the overhead crane, but he also knew that the same result could be achieved manually. Bored, he left Cas in the foundry and told the plant manager to get him a set of keys and show him how to operate the security system. He then instructed him to buy two lockers and also install a new heavy-duty door to the spare office with tamperproof hinges and a combination lock.

At lunchtime, he walked around the yard with Cas, and they familiarized themselves with the external lighting and security gates. "Are you coming back on the foundry floor this afternoon?" Cas asked.

"It's pretty straightforward. Is there anything you've picked up on that you think I need to know?"

"Did you see how they opened the bucket to dump the scrap in the furnace?"

"Yeah, but I'm not sure what buttons to press. I know how to do it manually though. As long as the furnace isn't turned off, it looks easy. We'll come back tomorrow for half a day. Next week we'll drop off a change of clothes and check out the new door and combination lock. If they're okay, we'll be set to go. I just need to clear it with Luke."

"When are we seeing him?"

"Tomorrow night for dinner."

Luke looked out the window of the Sunnyside site office as Dennis Bartlett delivered a sermon to the workers about the benefits of joining the BLMU. Standing behind him were three enforcers with application forms in their hands.

"Unless we appoint the health and safety officer, you can't be sure that you'll be going home to your loved ones tonight," Bartlett was saying. "CramerBuild is no different than the others. It'll sacrifice safety in pursuit of the almighty dollar. You can't trust the bosses. Now is your chance to send a message to CramerBuild by joining the union. Let me have a unanimous show of hands."

Bartlett was a convincing salesman, and without the imposing figure of George Simpson to maintain order, half a dozen hands were raised. "Come on," Bartlett shouted, "you're going to take the pay rises and benefits we negotiate. It's only right that you join."

A few more hands were raised, and when Bartlett stepped into the site office ten minutes later, he said, "There are now eleven of our members on site. Should you attempt to victimize them, we'll close you down. Our members are not happy with your health and safety officer. They want us to appoint a replacement."

"You appoint, and I pay. Is that how it works?"

"Yes. That's how it works with the other builders on the coast. Why should you be any different?"

"We're covering old ground," Luke said. "The overwhelming majority of my employees are happy with CramerBuild's health and safety policies. If they weren't, they would've joined the union."

"They will," Bartlett said. "Today's just the start. When we visit next week, we'll get another twenty. In a few more weeks, we'll have a majority, and in six months, your sites will be closed shops. Get used to it."

Luke knew that what Bartlett was saying was true and suspected that some of his newer employees were union plants. In hindsight, it was obvious that getting rid of George Simpson had been a critical part of the BLMU's strategy.

Chapter 33

According to Luke, Harry's Woodfired Grill on Orchid Avenue served the best steaks in the world. It was an old-style eatery, nothing flashy, with cubicles along three walls surrounding another twenty tables. The only courses on the menu were meat – porterhouse, T-bone, eye fillet, Scotch fillet, and German and Italian sausage pieces for an entrée. A silver-haired man greeted Luke warmly and led him through the packed restaurant to a small private dining room at the rear. "I'll send someone to take your orders. What are you drinking?"

"Thanks, Harry. Beers all around," Luke said, glancing at Ratsy and Cas.

Ratsy nodded, and Harry turned, saying, "Won't be long."

"I thought you'd be another week," Luke said. "Are you sure you know how to feed the furnace?"

"Easy," Ratsy said.

"We'll be fine, Luke," Cas agreed, then related in precise detail how the overhead crane and bucket functioned.

He's thorough, Luke thought. *He makes a good foil for Ratsy. I'm glad he's here.* "Have you thought about how you're going to find them?"

"They're not in the White Pages. I checked." Ratsy grinned. "We'll need another thousand in cash, and we won't worry about finding them. They'll find us."

"How?"

"The less you know, the better. We'll also need some duct tape and a dozen rolls of bulky foam - about twelve feet in width, light, and easy to move," Ratsy added. "Is there something like a Home Depot where I can pick them up?"

A waitress brought their beers and a large tray of assorted sausage meat before taking their orders. After she had gone, Luke said, "Yeah, Bunnings in Southport. When are you going to do it?

"We're going to set it up tomorrow night," Ratsy replied. "We'll get it done early next week. You're not getting cold feet, are you?"

"No. I'm not going to be stood over. They're going to pay for what they did to George and Roxy. More importantly, I want to send a message to the BLMU."

"Are you sure you only want one photo?"

"Yeah. Buy a Polaroid at one of the local pharmacies."

"Okay. What about the biker leader? Do you want us to track him down? It'd be easy."

"Not yet. I'd like to pay him back for terrorizing Kiara, but let's put him on hold. I'd prefer not to upset Charlie Gorman. If what you do has the impact, I expect we might be able to pass on him. Anything else?"

"Nah, that's it," Ratsy said. "Leave the rest to us."

"Good," Luke said, looking up as the waitress brought their steaks. "Let's enjoy our meal, and then you can bring me up to speed with what's been happening in Chicago."

The Criterion Hotel on the outskirts of Fortitude Valley was conveniently located next to a poorly lighted, dead-end alley. "I'll be as quick as I can," Ratsy said, pulling his shirt out from his pants and messing up his hair. "How do I look?"

"Maybe loosen a few buttons on your shirt."

"Yeah. Good idea."

Cas took a long drag on his cigarette as he watched his friend stagger down the alley. The barman at The Elephant had been right – Brisbane came alive on Saturday nights. Ratsy stumbled and pushed his way through the crowd, drawing many curses and snide remarks until he was at the bar. He smacked it with an open hand and demanded service. "Keep that up, mate," a barman said, "and you'll be out on your ass. Whaddya want?"

"Gis a pot," Ratsy slurred, reaching into his pocket and pulling out a huge roll of notes.

Some of the drinkers waiting to be served surveyed the roll with greedy eyes. "Put it away," the barman said. "There are those in here who'd kill for that."

Ratsy peeled off a twenty and shoved it at the barman. "I have plenty and even more owin' to me. Keep the change."

The barman picked up the twenty and hissed, "You've had too much to drink already. Put the roll back in your pocket. I'm trying to help you, you bloody fool."

Ratsy downed his beer in one gulp and thumped the empty glass down on the bar. "Fill it up," he demanded, again pulling the roll of notes out and again peeling off twenty for the barman.

"You'll be lucky if you get out of here with that."

"Don't worry. I have powerful frens who'll look afta me."

"Like who?" the barman sneered.

"Do ya know Ace Cordy? He works for me, at least he's gonna work for me. I heard he was gonna be here. I need some debts collected, and they tell me he's a debt collecta who gets results. That's why I have the cash. To pay im."

Ratsy downed his second beer and appeared to stumble, grasping at the bar for support. "I think you've had enough," the barman said.

"If ya don't want me business, I'll go to The Elephant. I gotta say I like this little bar, but I don't like the crowd. Wass it like on Tuesday night?"

"You'll have the bar to yourself."

"Good. Thiss is for yar trouble," Ratsy said, peeling off another twenty, as he teetered out of the bar. A dozen sets of eyes focused on his back, and twenty seconds later, two sleazy-looking characters followed him out the door. As Ratsy reached the alley, he broke into a light run before climbing into the minivan and ducking down. "The hook's baited. Let's go, Cas."

They had traveled about twenty miles along the highway on the way back to the coast when Cas slowed for roadworks. "Pull over next to that sign," Ratsy shouted, jumping out as soon as the van stopped. He slid the door open and threw the yellow sign and its two plastic supports in the back. "Let's go."

"What the –"

"I'll tell you when we get back." Ratsy grinned and then closed his eyes. "I'm going to have a snooze."

Chapter 34

Kiara felt safe in the gated Sanctuary Cove but didn't enjoy it. She didn't tell Luke that she didn't like living in a cocoon for fear of appearing ungrateful. She told herself that she should love the luxurious house in which she was living, but she didn't. The house, pool, and cabin cruiser meant little to her.

In her eyes, Luke's success had been tarnished by being in an industry only one step removed from organized crime. She didn't know why her husband had recruited Ratsy, but she knew that it couldn't be good. He was small, and she liked him, but she had never met anyone more intimidating. If God granted her only one wish, it would be to have the man that she married back again. She still loved Luke and always would, but he had changed. He was harder, more material, and less attentive.

Carlos was growing up quickly, and Kiara wanted a brother or sister for him, but she had been unable to get pregnant. Worse, her lethargy hadn't improved, and the soreness in her lower arms had intensified. When the pain moved to her shins, and she had twinges when she walked, she turned to painkillers. She still wasn't overly concerned, putting it down to stress and the humid weather.

Luke had insisted on her seeing a doctor, but with everything else on his plate, he had forgotten, and she hadn't seen a need to make an appointment. When the pain in her shins became more acute, she finally called the clinic, confident that she would be prescribed painkillers and be back to normal in no time.

Ratsy and Cas loaded the minivan on Tuesday, then lazed around the house for the rest of the day. They knew exactly what they were going to do and exhibited little in the way of nerves. During the afternoon, the coast was hit by a savage hailstorm, and they watched in awe as hailstones as large as golf balls bounced off the house's triple-glazed windows.

"This is something we didn't plan on!" Ratsy shouted. "It'll be impossible to drive through this. What if it doesn't stop? Beautiful one day, perfect the next. Bullshit!"

"Luke told me if it's not a cyclone, hailstorms only last fifteen minutes." Cas laughed. "And there's no wind, so I guess it's not a cyclone."

"Haven't you heard about the calm before the storm?" Ratsy growled, as the intensity of the hail started to dissipate. Five minutes later, the sun was out, the hailstones had melted, and a haze of steam hung over the road. "Jesus, give me Chicago any day."

It was six-thirty when Cas drove out of the garage, and the sun was just dipping below the horizon. There wasn't a drop of water to be seen. "Crazy climate," Ratsy said. "I'm gonna snooze. Wake me when we get near Brisbane. Oh, and don't forget to give the keys to me."

Seventy-five minutes later, Cas stopped at the top of the dark alley near The Criterion and stacked the yellow sign and two supports against a brick wall where they couldn't be seen from the street. He then reversed to the end of the alley and switched the lights off. Ratsy, dressed in black designer jeans and a matching long-sleeved shirt, climbed out and strode toward the hotel. The barman had said there'd be no one there, yet there were five groups of men drinking. *I wonder whether they're waiting for me.* He smiled, quickly glancing around the bar. No one matched the descriptions of Cordy and Quade. The same barman was there, and Ratsy said, "I'm sorry about Saturday night. I was a little under the weather."

"You were half pissed and making a racket. I was worried about you flashing that roll of notes. Did you get home okay?"

"Yeah, I got home fine. I'll have a pot, thanks," Ratsy said, pulling out his wallet, which had $80 in it.

"You don't have the roll with you tonight?"

"Nah, that was stupid. Thanks for trying to help me."

"That's okay. Ace was in last night, and I mentioned that you were looking for him. He might be in later," the barman said, as he filled another drinker's glass. "Enjoy your beer."

"Thanks," Ratsy said, sitting on a stool and spinning himself around to face the door.

There was a phone at the end of the bar, and while he didn't look at the barman, he felt him walk away and pick it up. I won't have long to wait now.

The bar door opened with a crash, and Ratsy turned to see a big blond guy with a mohawk, ink-covered arms, and a tight, white T-shirt that screamed *look at me, I work out*. His partner was missing an ear. "I hear you're looking for me," the blond guy's voice boomed.

"If you're Ace Cordy, I am."

"That's me. Who are you, and whaddya want?"

"Jim Brennan. I'm a money lender on the Gold Coast. I have some bad loans that I need collected."

"Why don't you go to a lawyer?"

"They're not that kind of loans."

"You're a loan shark." Cordy sneered. "What's a Yank doing on the coast making loans to druggies and deadbeats? Why haven't I heard of you? I know all the crooked moneylenders."

"I'm new, and I've been keeping my head down."

"You're gonna be in a lotta trouble when the others find out. They don't like competition. Anyhow, why do you want my help, and who told you about me?"

"I initially approached Charlie Gorman, but he said it was too small for him and suggested I contact you."

"Charlie Gorman recommended me!" Cordy yelled, letting the whole bar know.

"Barman," Ratsy said, "another pot, and my friends are having –"

"A couple of schooners," Cordy said. "How much are you owed?"

"Twenty thousand. Two loans of ten thousand. Charlie told me that your fee would be five thousand. If you're agreeable, I'll give you two and a half up front, and you can take the balance from what you collect."

Cordy took a long pull on his schooner. "Do you have the cash?"

"I had it on Saturday night, but the barman thought I was stupid carrying so much. No, I only have beer money."

"We don't work for beer money," Cordy's partner snarled.

"And you are?"

"Ryan Quade. Rhino to you."

"Well, Rhino, just because I'm not carrying the money doesn't mean I don't have it."

"What? What are you talking about?" Cordy demanded.

"I thought I'd play it safe," Ratsy said. "I left it in my van along with the names and addresses of the pricks who owe me."

"Oh, you stupid fucking Yank." Cordy roared with laughter. "This is Fortitude Valley. You'll be lucky to have a van when you get back, let alone the cash. Where did you park?"

"Down the alley off Ruthven Street."

"Jesus, you couldn't have picked a worse place. Come on, let's go. If we hurry, we might be able to salvage something," Cordy said, emptying his glass and heading for the door.

"Is it really that bad?" Ratsy asked, as they strode down the street.

"Stupid," Cordy muttered, turning into the alley. "Stupid. I can't see any van. Where are you parked?"

"Right at the end of the alley."

As the minivan came into sight, Ratsy dropped his keys. He slowly bent down to pick them up, and with his other hand withdrew the Smith & Wesson that he'd modified to cope with the length of the suppressor from the ankle holster.

The two thugs were standing a few yards away, and Cordy snapped, "For Chrissakes, hurry up."

Ratsy stood up, took two paces forward and shot Cordy right between the eyes. For a split second, Quade froze, mouth agape. In one smooth movement, Ratsy turned the gun on him and pumped two bullets into his head. Cas jumped out of the van and sprinted to the end of the alley where he placed the yellow NO ENTRY ROADWORK sign between the two orange, supporting bollards.

By the time he got back to the van, the two bodies were lying face up next to each other, and Ratsy was looking at the photo he'd taken. "Get the foam out, and lay the body bags on the ground," he ordered, as he started wrapping Cordy's head in duct tape. "Then you can wrap the other mutt's head." Two minutes later, they dumped the bodies in the back of the van and covered them with the rolls of foam. "Let's go."

When they reached the end of the alley, Cas got out to shift the sign. "Do you want to throw this stuff in the back, Ratsy?"

"Is it clean?"

"I'm wearing gloves," Cas replied, holding up his hands.

"Leave it there. Remember, take it easy. The last thing we want to do is attract a nosy traffic cop."

"You have blood splattered all down the front of you."

"Don't worry. We're not gonna get pulled over, and even if we do, no one's gonna see it against the black. I wish they were all that easy. I killed some bum for Sordi back home. Put three bullets in him, and he kept on coming at me. I like them when they're clean and easy."

Chapter 35

It was nearly midnight when they pulled up at the front of the foundry. Cas deactivated the alarms, opened the front gates and a roller door to the foundry, and drove the van inside. "I hope Luke's right," Ratsy said. "He owns a boat, you know. It would've been faster to weigh 'em down and dump 'em out at sea."

"He knows what he's doing," Cas said, picking up the controls to the overhead crane and the bucket which he lowered right next to the van.

"We don't need the bucket. We can throw them in."

"No, we can't. They're too heavy. The heat's too much. We won't be able to get close enough to the furnace. Come on. Help me lift them into the bucket."

"They're gonna stink," Ratsy said, as Cas maneuvered the bucket above the furnace before releasing the two bodies.

"Okay, that's done," Cas said. "Let's get rid of our clothes."

As they stripped down to their underpants, and put their clothes and the Polaroid in a pile next to the furnace, Ratsy said, "Luke's paranoid about this DNA shit. I'm sure he's watching too much television. How are you gonna get caught in thirty years for something you do today? It's bullshit!"

Cas picked up the pile of clothes and threw them into the furnace. "Better safe than sorry," he said. "Come on, let's get changed. I can't smell much, but we better check outside. Luke said there'd be nothing left after three hours."

"We'll wait until there's nothing. I'd hate someone to turn the furnace off while they're only half cooked. I like my meat well done."

"You're a sicko, Ratsy."

When they reported to Luke the following day, he was dispassionate. "Did you get the photo?" he asked.

"Yeah, of course," Ratsy replied. "Do you want it?"

"No, hang on to it. The union will be at Sunnyside at midday on Friday. Bring it with you. Oh, and wear a suit."

"What about me?" Cas asked.

"Rent a car. I want you at Sanctuary Cove with my family. It might be a gated community with its own security, but that's not going to stop the bikers. You will though."

"Take the van," Ratsy said. "That way you can leave now. I'll get a rental."

"Yeah, good idea," Luke said.

After Cas left, Ratsy said, "That's the first time you've ever killed someone, Luke. How do you feel? Any regrets?"

"None! They were vermin. Were there any problems at the foundry?"

"There was a little bit of a stink, but by the time we finished, the air was clean, and the mongrels were cinders."

"Good job, Ratsy. Let me brief you about Friday. Then you can go home and get some sleep."

"Home?" Ratsy laughed. "I wish."

On Friday morning, Luke called Dennis Bartlett, and invited him to visit Sunnyside thirty minutes earlier than planned. Sensing that Luke was about to weaken, he eagerly accepted. When Bartlett knocked on the site office door, Luke was careful not to fully open it, saying, "Tell your two gorillas to grab a coffee across the street."

"Sure," Bartlett said, before entering the office only to see Ratsy sitting on a stool. "Who's this?"

"Mr. Joe Ratsch, my new industrial-relations and security manager. I thought he should sit in because he'll be involved in future negotiations."

"Fine. Good to meet you." Bartlett smiled, extending his hand.

Ratsy compressed his lips and didn't move or utter a word. Luke, looking on, felt a chill run down his spine. No one projected menace like Ratsy, and Bartlett looked nervously around the office. "Sit down," Luke said, pulling out two chairs, taking one for himself. "I want to talk about your thugs beating up my supervisor and slashing my dog's throat."

"I told you, I don't know anything about that."

"I found out their names. Ace Cordy and Ryan Quade," Luke said, as he watched Bartlett try to conceal his surprise. "I thought you should be the first to know that their services are no longer available to the union."

"What are you talking about?" Bartlett scowled.

"I asked my industrial relations and security manager to point out the error of their ways to them. Can you let me have your report, Mr. Ratsch?"

Ratsy passed Luke the photo, and he held it up in front of Bartlett's face. "Recognize them now?" Luke asked.

Bartlett's face turned stark white. "You-you kill-killed them!"

Ratsy unbuttoned his suit coat, took out a cigarette lighter and lit the photo, his shoulder holster and gun clearly visible.

"There was only the one photo. I hope you committed it to memory," Luke said, handing a dossier to Bartlett. "Read this."

The private detective had been meticulous, and the dossier on Col Decker showed the dates, times, and places that his wife traveled to on a regular basis. She attended book club at the Gold Coast Library every Tuesday morning and played bridge on Thursday afternoons. Decker had two adult children, and there were details about where they lived, where they worked, what recreational activities they enjoyed, the names of their wives and their children, and where the kids went to school. The criminal offenses page revealed that Decker had been convicted more than twenty times on charges of assault, extortion, brawling, offensive behavior, drunk and disorderly conduct, and being a public nuisance, and he had done two stretches of hard time in Boggo Road Prison.

"What-what is this? Are you trying to intimidate Col? It won't work."

Luke was impassive as he passed Bartlett the second dossier and watched as his face collapsed. The details about Bartlett's private life were comprehensive, right down to the times and buses that his children caught to school.

"If you look at the fourth page, you'll see a summary of the affair that you had two years ago with Brenda Gibbons in accounts. Did you ever tell your wife about it? Did Col Decker know? Is that why you fired her?"

Ratsy hadn't said a word, but his presence was ominous, and tension filled the small office. The air conditioner was on full blast, but beads of sweat covered Bartlett's forehead. Luke momentarily felt sorry for him before a vision of Sordi flashed through his mind.

"Wha-what do you want?" Bartlett asked, ignoring Luke's questions. "What are you going to do?"

Luke pulled his chair closer to Bartlett's until he was in his face. Ratsy fidgeted on his stool, his suit coat again unbuttoned and the holster visible. "First, you're not talking to my men today. Second, you're going to tell Col Decker what happened to Cordy and Quade. Third, you're going to tell him about the dossiers and let him know that, if I must, I'll kill someone near and dear to him. Fourth, if you ever set foot on one of my sites again, you'll end up in a photo like the bums who beat up George Simpson and killed my dog. Fifth, if you're stupid enough to sic the Ferals on my family and me, you'll experience pain like you've never felt. Sixth, you'll tell that crooked copper on your payroll to stay away from me, and let him know I have a dossier on him. Seventh, I'm firing all the men who joined the union last week, and you're not going to do anything about it. Eighth, after you've spoken to Decker this afternoon, you will call me and confirm our new arrangements. Should you fail to call, I'll assume there has been a misunderstanding and act appropriately. For you, it will be inappropriate. Have I missed anything, Mr. Ratsch?"

Ratsy shook his head and stared deep into Bartlett's eyes before the union man hung his head.

There was a knock on the door. One of the thugs stuck his head in and said, "It's twelve o'clock, boss."

"Can-can I-I go?" Bartlett stuttered.

"We're not stopping you," Luke said. "Don't forget. Call me."

Bartlett's legs nearly went from under him as he got to his feet and stumbled out the door.

"I think he got the message." Ratsy smirked. "Jesus, I thought I was back in Chicago watching Sordi, Luke. You've come a long way."

He might be wary of me, but he was petrified of you, Luke thought. "We'll know soon enough."

Later that afternoon Luke answered the phone to a deep, throaty voice. "It's Col Decker, Luke."

"I was expecting to hear from Dennis."

"I had to send him home. You terrified him. He could hardly talk. You didn't need to kill those two guys. We could've come to an arrangement."

"I don't know what you're talking about."

"You're a smarty, Luke. You think I'm taping you. I'm not."

"You called me. What is it that you want to say?"

"We'll leave you alone. You're too small to worry about - insignificant, but I'm gonna remember what you did. You're not the only one who can play dirty pool. Now listen–"

"I've heard enough. Let your wife know that my industrial relations and security manager would like to join her bridge club. Can I tell him that she's willing to nominate him?"

"You stay away from my wife, you smart bast–"

"Goodbye, Col. I hope I never see you. If I do, you'll regret it. Oh, and if you have any stupid thoughts, I can fit a lot of bikers into one photo," Luke said, hanging up before throwing his legs up on the desk.

There wasn't another builder on the coast who could compete with him now. Once he proved he could build high-rises, he'd be able to cherry-pick the market. *Life is good*, he thought, but then his mind turned to Kiara. They hadn't made love in months but were still having sex in the middle of the night. She would roll over and spoon him, and feeling her hot body, he would react.

He knew what she was doing. Her desire for another child had become obsessive, but she was so thin that he knew that even, if she got pregnant, she wouldn't be able to carry to full term. She had been skinny, but now she was bony, and because he'd gotten caught up in the fight against the union, he'd forgotten to follow up on the doctor's appointment.

He silently cursed himself. He had neglected her and Carlos, but now that his business problems were behind him, he was determined to make amends. *I hope she's been to see a doctor, and everything's all right*, he thought.

Book 4

KIARA

Chapter 36

When Luke arrived home, he told Cas that the immediate danger had passed and sent him back to Surfers Paradise. Carlos was outside playing with Gumby when he asked Kiara to sit with him on the sofa. Her cotton dress hung on her like a shroud. "Honey, have you been to see a doctor?"

"I made an appointment. I'm going tomorrow morning."

Luke reached over and gently took her hand. "Don't stress. I'm going with you. You'll soon be your old self."

"You don't have to go. I know how busy you are."

"I'm taking a few days off. I want to be with you."

The clinic was bustling, and Luke made a mental note to find a private doctor. When the doctor finally saw them, she looked harried, and a strand of her long dark hair fell across her face. She apologized for being late and turned her attention to Kiara. She asked questions about her diet, her lifestyle, her eating habits, and medications, then gave her a brief physical examination.

Kiara told the doctor that she had increased her dosage of pain-killers, but the relief wasn't what it had been. Luke felt a sinking sensation in his stomach. It was compounded when Kiara said that the pain in her shins had intensified. The doctor was thorough but told them she couldn't make a proper diagnosis without blood tests, and that Kiara was to fast from midnight until the tests were completed.

The following morning, Kiara told Luke that there was no need for him to go to the pathology center, but he wouldn't hear of it. There had been something in the doctor's demeanor that had worried him, and he was again praying as hard as he could.

"Why is the lady pricking Mommy's arm?" Carlos asked.

"She's just taking a small sample of blood. It's nothing," Luke said, hoping he was right.

"Am I going to school?"

"Of course. You'll be there by morning playtime."

"I want to stay with you and Mommy."

"Sorry, buddy, not today."

Two days later, Kiara received an early morning call from the doctor asking her to come into the clinic. When she asked whether it was serious, the doctor said she couldn't discuss it over the phone, but that Luke should also attend. When they arrived at the clinic, they were immediately shown into the doctor's consulting room. "Mrs. Cramer," she said, "I'm sorry, there's no easy way to say this. You have bone cancer."

"What?" Luke said. "How?"

Kiara hadn't known she had cancer, but in the past two weeks, had suspected something bad. She had been plagued with fatigue for months, but recently, her shins, forearms, and shoulders had become more painful. "How-how bad is it?"

"I don't know. I've made an appointment for you to see a Brisbane specialist in the morning. He'll be able to tell you more."

"But how?" Luke repeated. "She's so young."

"I don't know how, Mr. Cramer. No one does. Unfortunately, being young does not protect against cancer."

"Jesus, it's so bloody unfair. So unfair," Luke said, knotting his hands together, before taking one of Kiara's. "We're going to beat this, hon."

"In a worst-case scenario, how long do I have?"

"Don't even think that way," Luke said. "We're going to beat it."

"I don't know, Mrs. Cramer. The specialist will be better able to answer your questions. I'm sorry," the doctor said.

Luke held Kiara tightly as they walked to the car. His head was spinning, and he was scared, but there was no way he was going to show fear. "Everything's going to be all right. We'll get the best doctors in the world to treat you."

The following day, the specialist was no more enlightening than the GP, sending Kiara off for imaging tests and scans. Two days later the specialist called and told Kiara that he would need to perform a needle biopsy before he could give her an accurate diagnosis. The waiting, stress, and uncertainty was getting to Luke, but somehow, he managed to keep his composure.

When the news came, it was brutal and earth-shattering. The specialist told them that Kiara had stage IV bone cancer which was the most advanced form of the disease. It had spread beyond the bones to other areas of her body.

"How do you cure it?" Luke demanded.

"As I said, it's at an advanced stage. We can try chemo and radio-therapy, but you might like to consider the quality of your life, Mrs. Cramer."

"How long do I have?"

"What? What are you talking about?" Luke said. "We're going to beat it."

Kiara was surprisingly calm. "How long, Doctor?"

"I'm sorry, I can't be definitive. Perhaps six months."

"No! No!" Luke shouted.

"And the worst case?" Kiara stoically asked.

"I can't say."

"Could it be less than a month?"

"Yes."

"Why can't you operate? Cut it out?" Luke demanded.

"It's gone too far."

"But you said it could be treated with chemo and radiotherapy," Luke said.

"It might add another three to six months, but it's not a cure, and the chemo might make Kiara very sick. I know it's a terrible shock. Why don't you go home and discuss the options? Don't rush. You're going to have many more questions. Please don't hesitate to call me."

As they waited for the elevator, Luke said, "We'll go back home and see the best specialists in America. We're going to beat this. I promise."

"Honey, we are home, and it's not like Australia is a third-world country."

As they drove back to Sanctuary Cove, Luke had never felt so helpless. The car was deadly quiet as each of them wrestled with their inner thoughts. He had wanted to ask the specialist what would have happened had Kiara seen him six months earlier.

His heart was bleeding, and he could hardly focus, but there was an underlying feeling of resentment. *Why had she waited so long? Why hadn't she seen a doctor when the symptoms first appeared? Why hadn't I insisted?* He thought. *What will I do without her? Poor Carlos. No, no, she's going to beat it. She might not want to go back to Chicago, but I can still get a second opinion. Yes, that's what I'll do.*

By the end of the day, Kiara was exhausted. She tried to remain stolid, but the terrible news had taken its toll, and she was in bed by eight o'clock. Luke wondered what was going through her mind. She was just twenty-six. Life was so unfair. He picked up a bottle of bourbon and stumbled down the hallway to his study. As he filled his glass, tears streamed down his cheeks, and he cursed the unfairness of life. By the time he'd finished his second shot, he'd regained some of his composure.

Monty picked up the phone on the second ring, and Luke poured his heart out between sobs and gasps. "Monty," Luke said, "do you know a cancer specialist in London? An oncologist or surgeon?"

"No, but don't worry. I can use my contacts to access the best in Harley Street. It'll take just a few calls. Get copies of the blood tests, the X-rays, and the imaging. Fax them to me. How's Kiara holding up?"

"It's hard to say. She didn't say anything after seeing the specialist. She's stoic but must be going through hell. I wish I could do something. Anything."

"You can. Don't leave her side. She needs you. We'll keep our fingers crossed that we get a favorable second opinion, but you have to support her."

"What about the business?" Luke asked, immediately regretting asking.

"I'll look after the business. It's lucky that you employed Max Tilson. We have someone to manage your projects."

"He's not an entrepreneur."

"He doesn't need to be. I am. Forget about the business."

"Thanks, Monty," Luke said, refilling his glass. He rarely drank heavily, but the warmth in his chest was helping.

Chapter 37

On the face of it, the following morning was no different from any other. Kiara was up early helping Carlos get ready for school. "We'll take my car today," Luke said.

"Aren't you going to work?"

"Honey, I'm not going back to work until you're better."

"Are you sick, Mommy?" Carlos asked, dropping his spoon into his bowl of fruit loops.

"No, I'm just tired," Kiara said, picking out the spoon from the bowl and wiping his mouth. "I'll make sandwiches for your lunch."

"Can I have jam?" Carlos squealed.

"No, salad." Kiara smiled, but I'll put a chocolate bar in as well if you promise to clean your teeth after you've eaten it."

"I will. I will."

Luke watched and fought off the dreadful choking sensation in his throat. *She can't die. She can't. How will I live without her? How will Carlos live without her?* he thought. When they returned home after dropping Carlos off at school, Kiara said, "We have to talk. What are you going to do after I'm gone?"

"What are you talking about? You're going to beat it. You're not going anywhere."

"Luke, I know you. You'll want to give up the business and go back to Chicago. Don't. Carlos loves it here, and you've been such a success. This is your home now."

"Please don't talk that way," Luke begged. "Do you want to have a holiday and go back home to see your mom?"

"A holiday?" Kiara smiled. "You can't do this, hon. You can't bury your head in the ground. We must plan, and no, this is my home. Why would I want to see the woman who disowned me? The only thing I ask is that you don't let them put me in the hospital. I want to die here in my own bed."

"No!" Luke sobbed. "No!"

"Poor Luke," Kiara said, reaching out and taking his hand. "You gave me a wonderful life and a wonderful son. After I'm gone, I want you to find someone else. You're young, and I don't want you to carry a cross for me. Sorry, I'm feeling a little tired. I'm going to lie down."

Five minutes later, Luke crept into the bedroom. Kiara was asleep and looked at peace with the world. Luke wept uncontrollably, putting his hand over his mouth to stifle the choking. The specialist said that he had been expecting Luke's call, and that he would arrange to have all the test results faxed to Monty. "Please fax them to me too," Luke said.

The specialist sighed. "Mr. Cramer, any oncologist, surgeon, or specialist who looks at those results is going to confirm my opinion. There's no point in sending them all over the world hoping that you'll get a different opinion. You'll eventually work your way down to the quacks and soothsayers. They'll take your money and tell you what you want to hear, but it won't change the outcome."

"You're saying there's no hope."

"That's what I said yesterday. In the absence of a miracle, your wife will pass within six months. I'm sorry."

Luke gripped the phone with all his strength, burning to ask what the prognosis would have been had Kiara seen him six months ago. He didn't, feeling that the question would be a betrayal. Besides, knowing the answer would serve no purpose.

"It's a miracle I ever met her, Doc. It's a miracle she ever married me, so you'll understand when I say that I believe in miracles."

"I'll say a prayer for her."

"Do that, Doc."

Monty used all his contacts to access the most highly regarded surgical oncologist on Harley Street. Initially, the surgeon was reluctant to provide any opinion to a third party about a patient that he had never seen. It was only after he received a call from Britain's minister for health that he became compliant and agreed to help.

Late that afternoon, Monty's receptionist, head down and shoulders drooping, dropped a fax on his desk without waiting for a response. She liked Luke, and it was obvious that she had read it. It was only two pages, and by the time he'd finished the first page, Monty's eyes were watering. There was nothing that could be done for Kiara, and he now had the thankless task of relaying the Harley Street specialist's opinion to his friend.

"Thanks for nothing, Monty," Luke snarled. "Who is this guy? What's he ever done? What would he know? England doesn't have the surgeons that we have in the U.S. I'm getting another opinion."

"Luke, when there was a cancer scare with one of the young princes, the royal family consulted with this surgeon. He's presented at Harvard on many occasions. He is elite. I'm sorry, you must face reality and do what's best for Kiara. Have you thought about palliative care?"

"I told you what I'm doing. I'm going to find the finest cancer surgeon in New York and get another opinion."

Monty sighed. "Do you want me to help?"

No, but how am I going to find the best specialists, let alone get them to talk to me? Luke thought. "Yes, but find someone better than that English bum."

"I'll do my best, Luke," Monty said, knowing that trying to reason with him was pointless.

Luke was paranoid about leaving Kiara alone when he took Carlos to school and picked him up in the afternoons, so he employed a full-time in-house nurse. Despite this, she continued to deteriorate rapidly over the next month, even though she had short periods where she seemed to improve. It was those times that Luke focused on – the times that gave him false hope.

The surgeon in New York confirmed the opinion of his peers in London and Brisbane and, like them, had the status of useless bum conferred on him. Convinced that orthodox medicine didn't know what it was doing, Luke moved on to faith healers. His hopes soared when he met a woman in Coolangatta who convinced him that Kiara could be cured with pumpkin seeds.

She was the first of many. Another told him that Kiara could be saved if she drank her own urine, but that it had to be modified with rare herbs and spices that only the miracle worker could provide. Luke spent thousands and thousands of dollars in the vain pursuit of a remedy and, unlike everyone else, never gave up hope.

Kiara weighed less than seventy pounds but was still lucid in her waking moments, and the morphine drip alleviated the pain. It was another glorious Gold Coast day, and the sun was streaming through the shutters when Luke rolled over and felt her cold body. His piercing scream ratcheted through the house, and a few seconds later, Carlos was at the door closely followed by the nurse. Luke leaped out of bed, picked him up in one arm, and carried him out to the kitchen. "Why are you crying, Daddy? What's wrong?"

Luke's mind was in turmoil. He hugged Carlos and told him that Mommy was still sleeping. When the grim-faced nurse came out, she said, "I'm so sorry, Mr. Cramer. I know it's difficult, but I think you should try to keep the day as normal as possible for the little one."

"I didn't say good morning to Mommy," Carlos said.

"Mommy's tired, buddy," Luke said, fighting to regain a semblance of control. "Go get dressed. I'll take you to school. You can buy lunch today."

"I'll make the arrangements," the nurse said. "Are there any special arrangements or funeral parlors that you prefer?"

"A Catholic burial," Luke muttered, "and I don't know any funeral parlors. You handle it."

That night he replayed the events that had led to Kiara's death, and the tinge of resentment he'd felt toward her disappeared. True, she hadn't gone to the doctor earlier, but he hadn't pushed her because of the trouble that the union had caused.

He punched the pillow and ground his teeth. Ratsy shouldn't have just killed the thugs; he should have killed Decker and Bartlett too. As the seemingly endless night rolled on, his grief was exacerbated by his hatred of the union.

Chapter 38

On the day of the funeral, the weight of losing his mother still hadn't hit Carlos. When he woke up, he said, "Daddy, when is Mommy coming back from the angels?"

Luke choked up and had been unable to answer. Now, as they sat in the front row of the cathedral listening to Monty's heartfelt eulogy, all he wanted was for the day to be over. Veronica Beaurepaire had said that she would look after Carlos rather than have him see his mother's burial.

It took Luke all of his strength to get into the hearse. The cortege slowly wended its way along the roads to the Surf Coast Cemetery where the priest mercifully spoke only a few words before the casket was lowered into the ground. Its gold handles glinted in the bright sun while Luke hung his head and wiped the tears from his eyes.

He didn't look up as the mourners filed silently past the grave, dropping roses on top of the casket. He wanted to be alone when he said his last farewell to Kiara. Finally, after thirty minutes, he raised his head and slowly turned around. There were still two mourners standing under a jacaranda tree about thirty yards behind him. They were his two closest friends, and yet he'd had no idea that they even knew each other.

"I know there isn't a wake," Monty said, "but would you like to go somewhere where we can have a quiet drink and say goodbye to a woman who we all loved before you pick up Carlos?"

"Good idea," Ratsy said. "It'll do you good, Luke."

I just want to be with Carlos, but I know they're trying to help, Luke thought. "Okay. One round at Harry's. Can you use that fancy, cellphone to call him and book the private room, Monty? I don't want to be near anyone.'

Luke was still wallowing in self-pity but was relieved that the shaking of mourners' hands and listening to their condolences was over. The beer was cold and frothy, and as he took a mouthful, Ratsy said, "I propose a toast to Kiara, one of the finest ladies I ever met."

"I'll second that," Monty said, "I'll never forget the day I met her at the hospital. She was–"

"I know you guys mean well," Luke interrupted, "but I prefer to grieve alone. If that sounds bad, I'm sorry."

Monty and Ratsy exchanged a quick glance before Monty said, "We understand. That's fine."

Luke was in a world of pain and not really listening, but he still managed to pick up bits and pieces of the conversation. When Monty had become heavily involved in the business, Ratsy, understandably, had demanded to know who he was. When he found out that Monty was Luke's closest, Australian friend, he had adopted him. For Monty's part, he knew that Luke had grown up with Ratsy, and the fewer questions he asked, the better. George Simpson had returned to work with a walking stick as a purchasing officer but hated the paperwork. Within days, he was back in his role as a supervisor, and while his legs no longer functioned like they once had, his booming voice could be heard all over the site. Luke wasn't focusing, but it sounded like the business was doing just fine without him.

"You should take a month off," Monty said. "Maybe take Carlos back to Chicago and visit your father."

"I'm not going to Chicago. I need to sell the house. I can't stand the thought of being in it without Kiara. There are too many memories, not all good. If only I'd been there to look after her. I'm not going to make the same mistake with Carlos. I won't leave you in the lurch, Monty, but I'm thinking about selling the businesses. I don't care if I don't get anything out of them, just as long as your loans are paid off. I've lost the enthusiasm for business and building."

"Luke, you might not think this now, but time cures everything. It might be years, but by then, you're going to have a different mindset to what you have now. The businesses could be your legacy to Carlos. You've worked too hard to throw it all away, and don't forget all the people who upended their lives to help you.

"Max Tilson left a secure job to join you. Ratsy and Cas dropped everything to come and help you. George Simpson lost the use of his legs because of his loyalty to you. Tony Farrugia sold his business to you because of the undertakings you gave to him. Then there are your workers and subcontractors who stuck with you when you took on the union.

"Business isn't just about dollars and cents. I know you'd never let me down, but there's more to think of than just me."

Luke nodded and took a long drink.

Monty continued. "Oh, Veronica and I are going back to Brisbane tonight so why don't you stay in the penthouse until you find a new place? I can understand you not wanting to go back to Sanctuary Cove."

"Don't worry about Cas and me," Ratsy said, draining his beer. "We can always pick up where we left off in Chicago."

"Thanks, Ratsy. Thanks, Monty, I'll take you up on your offer," Luke said, "but I'll have to grab some clothes and pick up Gumby first. You're right. I'm being selfish. I'll take some time off, spend it with Carlos, find a new house in Surfers Paradise, and think about what I'm going to do. I'm sorry if I appear ungrateful. I'm lucky to have two friends like you."

Each morning for the next two weeks, Carlos asked the same questions, always starting with, "Where's Mommy?"

"She's with the angels."

"When are the angels going to let her come home?"

This was the question that Luke had no idea how to answer, and the innocence of Carlos's expression tore at his heartstrings. "She's helping the angels look after the poor people," he said. "It's very important."

"But when the poor people are all better, Mommy will come home, won't she?"

"There are lots of poor people, little man."

"But I miss her," Carlos said, and the tears flowed.

Luke gritted his teeth, swallowed hard, and somehow managed to hold back his own tears.

Book 5

LUKE 1991

Chapter 39

The house I bought had only three bedrooms, and even though it had an in-ground, salt-chlorinated pool, it was nowhere near as grand as Sanctuary Cove. I enrolled Carlos in Surfers Paradise Primary School which was only a five-minute walk from our new house. The school offered before and after-hours childcare, but I resolved to take Carlos in the mornings and pick him up in the afternoons. I had expected objections and tears from him about having to leave his old school and friends, but there were none.

I thought about the commitments that so many good folks had made to help me build the business, as Monty had reminded me, and I knew I couldn't let them down. However, without Kiara by my side, I lacked motivation and kept pushing my return date back. I was drinking half a bottle of bourbon every night in the vain hope that it would make the pain go away.

I still blamed the union for her death and would lie in bed at night, fighting to get to sleep, tormented, only dropping off when I visualized the bodies of Decker and Bartlett riddled with bullets or pierced with multiple stab wounds.

Ten weeks had elapsed since Kiara's passing, and I still hadn't returned to work. Monty and Ratsy called regularly and kept me informed about the business, but I struggled to show any interest. I had not visited any of CramerBuild's three sites, not even Coolangatta where the five-story office block was nearing completion.

One night I was grilling fish for dinner, and Carlos was in the backyard playing with Gumby when there was a knock at the front door. "Hello, Luke, we must talk," Monty said.

"Not until we've eaten," I replied. "Should I throw a barramundi on the grill for you?"

"Sure. Do you have a nice white chilling?"

"I don't know. Check the fridge. I know I have plenty of bourbon."

Monty poked around in the fridge before saying, "You've surpassed yourself. There's a Margaret River Chardonnay hidden amongst the soft drinks and milk. I didn't expect to see a full fridge."

"Carlos is a growing boy."

"How's he holding up?"

"Better. He's stopped asking questions, but some mornings his pillow is soaked, and it's not perspiration. They were extremely close. I guess that happens if you're unlucky enough to have an absentee father."

"You have to stop that. It serves no purpose and sure doesn't help. Felicity could say the same about me."

"Maybe you should change," I said, as Carlos and Gumby came running into the house.

"Hello, Mr. Beaurepaire."

"Good to see you, Carlos. I love your dog."

Before Carlos could respond, I asked him to set the table.

After Carlos was in bed, we sat on the veranda while sipping our whiskeys. "Get it off your chest," I said.

"The business needs you. I know you're suffering, but life must go on. Becoming a recluse is not going to help you ... or Carlos."

"I thought you said everything was fine."

"It is with the existing contracts, but there's no new work, no quoting, no hustling. When Coolangatta's finished so is the business, and Luke, while CramerBuild is still profitable, it's not as profitable as it would be with you at the helm. It needs your drive, your inspiration, your leadership – after all, it's your baby."

"What about Max Tilson? I had him preparing quotes."

"Yes, he did the grunt work, but you determined the final quote. He's meticulous, his work is faultless, but he's more of an accountant than an entrepreneur. Max quotes because it's part of the job. You quote because you're desperate to win the business. There's a big difference. It's the same on site. He knows exactly what to do, but the men don't jump the same way they do when you're around."

"I don't know. I like taking Carlos to school, picking him up, going fishing, and playing rugby. The stuff I should have been doing when

Kiara was alive but was too busy," I said, shaking my head. "I just don't know."

"You can keep doing all of that. Work from nine to three, and then, after Carlos goes to bed, do another hour or so."

"You make it sound so easy, Monty."

"It is. You've built a great team. They just need a little leadership. If you let them go, it'll take years to build another team like them."

"I'll think about it."

"I was hoping for more than that. At least, visit Coolangatta. It's your first multi-story building, and the guys have done a great job. Even Ratsy said he was surprised you hadn't been down to look at it."

"You and Ratsy." I grimaced. "Talk about the odd couple."

"I like him. You can't buy loyalty like he has for you. I know he's a tough guy, so I don't ask him any questions that might compromise him. He fired the security contractors and replaced them with guys who he personally interviewed. I'd say you have the best security team in Queensland now. I'm sure he's told them that, if there's a security breach, they'll answer to him, and none of them want to face that prospect."

"Who'd believe that? Another drink?"

"No thanks, with the wine I must be close to the limit," Monty said, getting up. "I can't imagine what you're going through, but you're going to have to make a decision soon. If your answer's no, I'll have to get going on the sale of Farrugia Concrete. Oh, did I tell you they're going to tear down Coral Towers on Northcliffe Terrace and replace it with the twenty-five story Ocean View Pinnacle? It's bespoke residential accommodation."

"Coral Towers must be only about ten years old."

"It is, but the property is prime, and it's only eight levels. It never should've been built. How many other beachside allotments that size are available? None!"

"Who's the lucky builder?"

"The plans will be finalized this week, and then it'll go out for bids. It's being funded by a consortium of international investors. Want to guess who the lead manager and investor is?"

I slammed my glass down on the table. "Why didn't you tell me that when you arrived? I'd do anything to win that contract."

"A good hold-'em player keeps his hole cards close to his chest." He grinned. "I had to know you were interested before supporting you."

"You bastard."

"I take it you've made your decision," Monty said, extending his hand. "Welcome back, Luke."

Chapter 40

With all the stress I was under, I paid no attention to the council election results, and were it not for the thank you card I received from Councilor Russell Hannan, I would not have known that he had won. When I returned to work, I was pleasantly surprised to find that Max Tilson and George Simpson were on top of the three projects which left me free to devote all my time to the Ocean Pinnacle bid. The only problem was finding somewhere to work, and when Hannan called, I was at home with the plans taking every inch of the living room floor. "I hope you're feeling better, Luke," he said, "and I'm glad you're back on deck."

"Thank you, Councilor."

"Call me Russell. Let me again express my gratitude for your campaign contribution. It was a tight race, and your check may have made the difference. Thank you."

"My pleasure."

"I want you to know that, if I can repay the favor or do something for you, I will. I'm in your debt."

What is he offering? This isn't how Monty said it worked, I thought. "I'll keep that in mind."

"Good. When can we catch up for dinner?"

I paused. "I'm not sure how to put this. I don't do dinners anymore. I have an eight-year-old son who needs all my attention. I'm happy to do lunch."

"That's commendable, Luke, and yes, lunch is fine. I don't have my diary with me. If it's all right with you, I'll get my PA to call your PA tomorrow."

I laughed. "I don't have a PA. Ask her to call me."

"I'm surprised. You run a large business. I felt sure there'd be someone in your office who …" Hannan trailed off.

"That's okay, Russell. I'm looking forward to lunch. Goodbye."

I sat at my desk and pondered the call. CramerBuild's accounts and payroll were handled by a firm of public accountants. Purchasing was undertaken from cramped and noisy site offices. Changes to drawings and bills of materials were made in engineers' offices, and I was quoting a multimillion-dollar building off my living room floor. *If I'm going to become the biggest builder on the coast, I need my own offices, and I know just the site.*

The block of land on the corner of Ferry and Langton roads, Southport, was prime, but the mortgagees had been trying to sell it – a former service station site – for years without success. The problems were the costs associated with getting rid of the contaminated soil and getting planning and building approvals from the left wing aligned Surf Coast Council.

I knew the mortgagee was desperate to sell. I also felt that I could resolve the problems, and CramerBuild made a lowball offer for the property that the mortgagee couldn't accept fast enough. I immediately submitted plans to the council that included excavating to a depth of fifty feet, and transporting the contaminated soil to a hazardous, materials dump twenty miles south of Brisbane.

But the objections came in thick and fast. The soil would, by necessity, be disturbed by the excavation, and the toxins would become airborne. The workers would be exposed, along with the thousands of drivers using Ferry Road every day. The hazardous materials dump was forty miles north and, despite the trucks using tarps, the Greens claimed poison would be spread all along the freeway. While not close to the water table, other opponents claimed that it would put the Gold Coast's pristine water at risk. Then there were the parents of students at the primary school two miles away who were worried that their kids would be inhaling death and destruction.

I had known that there would be problems, but the ferocity and intensity of the Greens' attack took me aback. Russell Hannan called to say that, while he supported the project, he didn't have the numbers on council to push it through. More than a year had elapsed when Hannan called one night and told me to switch my television to Channel 16.

Councilor John Wiese was speaking. Balding, fortyish, and with horn-rimmed spectacles covering his beady eyes, he was a zealot but an eloquent speaker, and he proposed leaving the land dormant for at least fifty years. His eyes glazed over when he spoke of the dangers of trucks carrying contaminated soil and speeding along the streets of Southport.

When the interviewer suggested to Wiese that his stance was stopping the removal of an eyesore and putting hundreds of jobs in jeopardy, he was contemptuous. "How many of those workers will still be alive when Mr. Cramer's building is completed? That is the question you should be asking," he said. "No one can be certain that the seepage won't continue."

The interviewer laughed and said, "Councilor, if we are to believe you, buildings all across Australia would never have been erected on former service station sites."

Rather than backing down, Wiese condemned the councils and other authorities before saying, "The Surf Coast Council will not make the same mistake."

I scratched my head and wondered whether the property I'd bought so cheap was such a bargain. The environmental dangers expressed either didn't exist or were grossly exaggerated, but Councilor Wiese was taking no notice of the professionals. I didn't know whether Wiese's concerns were genuine or made up, but I did know that if I were going to get anywhere, I had to persuade the councilor to change his mind, so I called Russell Hannan and asked him to arrange a lunch with Wiese.

Surprisingly, Wiese accepted immediately, and along with Hannan, joined me in the private dining room at Harry's. Russell Hannan was a convincing salesman and sold the project hard, but Wiese, while professing to have an open mind, was intransigent. I laid out reports from environmental engineers and consultants, but he paid no attention to them.

There was something about him that I didn't like, and it wasn't just his wispy hair, pallid skin, and inability to hold eye contact. When our meals were served, the room fell into uncomfortable lapses of silence. Wiese picked at his steak nervously and broke out into a heavy sweat, even though the thermostat on the air conditioning was set to sixty-five.

"Councilor," I said, "I'll adopt any additional controls that you believe will make the project safe."

"That's just it," Wiese said. "There are no additional measures that will make it safe. Once the soil's disrupted, you'll be opening Pandora's box. You shouldn't have bought the property without the council's clearance."

"Pandora's box! You know that's not true. Read these," I said, again pushing the experts' reports across the table.

"I don't understand you, John. I thought you'd want to get rid of that eyesore," Hannan said, getting to his feet. "Excuse me, I have to go to the bathroom."

As the door closed after Hannan, Wiese said, "You've done well for yourself since arriving on the coast. You're not even thirty, came here with nothing, and now they say you're a multi-millionaire. I've lived here all my life, I'm fifteen years older than you, and I still have a mortgage around my neck."

"I've worked hard and taken risks, Councilor. What does my success have to do with the planning and building permits for CramerBuild's offices?"

Wiese put his knife and fork down and, for the first time, held my gaze. "You're a taker, Mr. Cramer. I don't like takers. You give nothing back to the community. It's all take, take, take."

"That's not true, but I'm not going to argue with you. It's certainly not grounds to block my office development."

"Do you know how many votes short you are? One. One vote. Mine." Wiese smirked.

"Well, it's obvious that I can't get you to change your mind. Perhaps, I should try to persuade one of the other councilors."

"You're not listening. The lefties vote as a bloc. There's no way you'll turn one of them. I'm your only chance."

I slowly sipped my beer and stared at Wiese over the rim. "But, you've already said no."

"Russell will be back soon," Wiese said, glancing at the door. "Here's what will get you your permits. Two hundred thousand into an overseas bank account that I'll nominate, a fifty-thousand-dollar donation to the Little Nippers Kindergarten that you will give me credit for, and a fifty-thousand-dollar campaign contribution when I run for state parliament later this year. I know you stole that property from the mortgagee. Another three hundred thousand is nothing for you."

I wasn't surprised. Something had smelled about Wiese the minute I laid eyes on him. This hypocrite was just another of the many on the take. "Councilor, I can put the money up for the kindergarten, and I'll support your election campaign. The two hundred will see us both in prison. I can't and won't do it."

"You know that's bullshit, Cramer. There's no way you'll get caught. I'm betting Beaurepaire has set you up with international bank accounts to avoid paying taxes. He and his high-priced accountants are specialists in that area, but you already know that. There's no way anyone could trace a transfer from one of your international accounts. Think about it. You're never going to get the permits unless you come to the party."

"If I make the transfer, what excuse are you going to use to justify your change of mind?"

Wiese laughed and brushed the reports on the table with the back of his hand. "The expert advice is overwhelming. After reading the reports and doing a great deal of soul searching, I decided to support your project. It's easy and proves to the public that I'm open-minded and flexible."

"If only that were true," Russell said, as he rejoined the table.

"Don't be skeptical, Russell. We might have made a little progress in your absence. Isn't that right, Luke?"

I'd like to beat your brains out, I thought. *I've wasted eighteen months and tens of thousands of dollars to solve a problem that never existed.* "Perhaps. Thank you for taking the time to listen to me, Councilor," I said, smiling through gritted teeth.

"Fill me in," Hannan said.

"All in good time," Wiese replied.

It was midafternoon when I brought the lunch to an end, saying that I had to pick up Carlos from school. As we stood in front of Harry's, I shook Russell Hannan's hand warmly and then embraced John Wiese before handing him the file of consultants' reports. "Read these, John. They might change your mind."

Chapter 41

When I got home, I called Ratsy, and Cas answered. "He's not home, Luke. He's out shopping with his girlfriend. He said he'd be back by seven."

"Girlfriend?"

"Yeah, a little ginger-haired firecracker who goes by the same name. He met her when she was serving at one of the local restaurants. I think she's the only living soul who's ever intimidated Ratsy," Cas laughed.

"I can't recall him ever having a girlfriend. Hard to imagine Ginger keeping him on his toes. Ask him to come and see me tonight when he gets back."

When Ratsy knocked on my door, I greeted him with a grin. "I hear your social life's looking up."

"Yeah, she's a great kid - only nineteen so she's a bit young. We're only hanging out together. She's a real live wire and great fun."

"Good for you, Ratsy. Is the Gold Coast starting to grow on you?"

"Perhaps. Why do you want to see me, Luke?"

"Sit down. I'll get you a beer. Then I'll tell you about the lunch I had with councilors Hannan and Wiese today."

Ten days later, the main story on Gold Coast television channels was the mysterious disappearance of Councilor John Wiese. His wife claimed that he had left for work early the prior morning and that he'd called her that evening before attending a meeting of the Surf Coast Council. When he hadn't arrived home by midnight, she called him on his cellphone, but the call went straight to voicemail.

After two more attempts, she called the police and told them that her husband was missing. She would later say the police hadn't taken her seriously, and they had suggested that her husband might be sleeping off a bender. Then there were those who speculated that he'd been caught in an affair with his PA, and that he was lying low.

When I was questioned by the police, I said the last time I had seen Wiese was over an enjoyable lunch, and I had given the councilor some consultants' reports in the hope that he might drop his objections to CramerBuild's proposed office building. There was nothing untoward or acrimonious, and it was an amicable lunch which Councilor Russell Hannan confirmed.

At the next council meeting, CramerBuild's proposed four-story office building was back on the agenda. When the vote was locked at six all, the mayor, a conservative and friend of Russell Hannan, exercised his casting vote in favor of the proposal. Two months later, in the by-election for John Wiese's seat, the conservative candidate won by a handful of votes and put the right wing back in control of the council. I had contributed $50,000 to her campaign, and that had been the difference. Monty had proved himself right again – having politicians onside could be very beneficial.

The dispute with the council was time consuming, but I had never taken my eye off the Ocean View Pinnacle. No high-rise building on the coast had ever gone up so fast, and CramerBuild was going to reap an enormous profit. There had been no serious accidents, the workers were happy, and the BLMU had not attempted to enter the site or stir up trouble.

I continued to take Carlos to and pick him up from school, and I could feel the bond between us growing stronger. We spent every Saturday visiting construction sites, and he showed a keen interest in building. CramerBuild was now the preferred builder for many of the large investment companies and enjoyed an abundance of projects on the coast.

On the personal front, Monty and Veronica arranged several dinners with unaccompanied, single, young women. I enjoyed the company of women, but the attempted matchmaking stilted any opportunity of anything meaningful arising. Then George Simpson got in on the act, telling me that Maggie's younger sister was a real looker, and she had just broken up with her boyfriend. Even Russell Hannan mentioned that the councilor whom I had backed had recently divorced and was very attractive. The pain of losing Kiara had diminished, but her memory had not, and I asked my well-meaning friends to desist from further matchmaking. Besides, with the business and Carlos, I had no time for dating.

Parent-teacher nights at Surfers Paradise Primary School were held in the early evening, and while I waited for Miss Dorsey to finish her earlier meeting, I smiled. She was the first teacher whom Carlos had fallen in love with, and I was intrigued to see what the attraction was. I had my head in a book when she walked over, held her hand out, and said, "Hi, Mr. Cramer, I'm Sally Dorsey. Let's go into my little cubicle."

Blonde, cuddly, and lightly tanned, she had freckles below her eyes which were even bluer than mine. There was a little buzz, and I held her hand for a fraction longer than I should have. "It's a pleasure to meet you, Miss Dorsey."

"Miss Dorsey is how the kids address me, Mr. Cramer. Please call me Sally."

"Only if you call me Luke."

"It's a deal." She laughed, the dimples in her cheeks dancing.

For the next twenty minutes, we talked about Carlos and how he was progressing in grade six. "He's a lovely boy," she said, "and so bright. Do you know he still tells me stories about his mom and how she's in heaven helping the angels? Oh, I'm sorry. I shouldn't have said anything."

"Don't be." I said, "It has been more than three years. I'm glad he's talking to you about her."

"He's a sweet, sweet boy."

"Now it's my turn to be sorry," I said, glancing at my watch. "I've overstayed my welcome."

"You're the last," she said, "and I'm in no rush."

"Is it against the rules for you to have coffee with a parent?"

A bemused look came over her face. "I don't think so. I'll meet you at Vito's on the main drag in five. Do you know it?"

"I'll see you there."

Chapter 42

Two years later I married Sally in a small ceremony on the banks of the Brisbane River. Only family and close friends were invited. I had fervently believed that I would never fall in love again. I was elated to be proven wrong.

She was eleven years younger, and whereas Kiara had been model-slim, Sally was all curves. We couldn't keep our hands off each other, and I would later joke that every time I looked at her, she got pregnant. By the end of the first year's marriage, Sally was carrying Lloyd. Eighteen months later she gave birth to Trent, and three years later the girl she had always wanted was born - Madison.

As my fortieth birthday approached, the media started to speculate that my personal worth might exceed one hundred million. CramerBuild was the largest and most influential builder on the coast. I had realized my dream of building a skyscraper the year before when CramerBuild had completed The Zenith, a fifty-story, luxury apartment complex on Main Beach.

Yet, I was still restless and looking to expand my horizons. As always, the danger lay with the BLMU. It had largely left me alone on the Gold Coast, but would it do the same if I expanded into Brisbane, Sydney, and Melbourne? The risks in the two big cities were probably too great, but Brisbane was only fifty miles to the north.

It didn't take long for word to get out that CramerBuild had won its first bid for a high-rise office building in Brisbane – the Queensland Bank Tower. I had never met Col Decker and hadn't spoken to him in more than ten years, but I wasn't surprised when the union man called to set up a meeting.

CramerBuild's head office was an unpretentious, four-story, prefabricated concrete building. I was a believer in the adage that you should never have better offices than your customers. After we moved in, I indulged myself, took Russell Hannan's advice, and hired a PA. Jill Adams had been with me for years, and I didn't know how I'd managed without her.

My medium-sized office on the top floor was spartan and all male. My desk, coffee table, and bookshelves were carved from twenty-five-centuries-old Huon pine found only in southwest Tasmania. When the craftsmen had wanted to stain it, I wouldn't hear of it, knowing it would darken in time, and I'd been right. It was a darker, richer, and more overpowering color than walnut.

Behind my desk was a huge painting of a gazelle with a trace of blood on its neck, surrounded by a pack of hyenas. The sky was black, there was a flash of lightning, the hyenas looked ravenous, and the gazelle's eyes seemed to be fixed on one tiny opening. Protruding from the walls were the heads of a deer, a water buffalo, and a fox – all feral animals. I had never killed a kangaroo or emu, even though there had been numerous culls. For me, there was something sacrilegious about killing the animals on your country's coat of arms.

All my kills had been with a high-powered, single-shot Ruger, and I lived by the code "If I miss, the animal wins" – but I never missed. I wasn't a great shot, but my ability to hold my nerve when facing a charging boar and to pull the trigger at the last moment compensated for my lack of marksmanship.

I sat in a black leather, high-back recliner, and my visitors' chairs were smaller matching versions. There was only one window in the office, and it overlooked the parking lot at the front of the building. I scowled as I saw the blue Ford pull up, and four men get out. "They've come in force, Ratsy."

"They'll leave with their tails between their legs," Ratsy replied. Eating Ginger's cooking had expanded his waistline and looking after two sons whom he adored had mellowed him, but, when need be – like now – he could still exude menace.

"You better get two more chairs. It's going to be cramped. Tell Jill to make sure they're shown to my office as soon as they arrive. I don't want the goons frightening off our clients in reception. Oh, and watch what you say. I wouldn't put it past Decker to be wearing a wire."

A few minutes later, the receptionist knocked and said, "Mr. Decker and his colleagues are here for their midday appointment."

Decker was big, overweight, and in his mid-sixties with unruly gray hair, meaty forearms, and calloused hands. He looked at the picture on the wall and said, "Is that how you see yourself, Luke? The leader of a pack of hyenas, and I'm the gazelle?"

"You have it all wrong, Col. That picture is to remind me how alert I need to be when dealing with you. Look at the picture more closely. There's only one small opening where the gazelle can make its escape, but, if it hesitates, it's lost. That's how I see myself when I'm dealing with you."

"You see us as hyenas?"

"I never pass judgment on others. Is that what you think?"

Decker ignored my question. "My assistant Bill Kronk and another organizer will be here soon. We're not going to have enough room."

"Do they have to be at the meeting?" I nodded at the three thugs.

"Does he have to be at the meeting?" Decker replied, pointing at Ratsy.

"Yes. Joe is a director of the company, in charge of industrial relations and security."

"My men are union organizers. They're as important to me as he is to you."

"Take them down to the boardroom, Joe," I said, appearing to surrender. "I just have to find a file. I'll be there in a minute."

A few minutes later, Jill took Bill Kronk and an enforcer dressed in a BLMU black T-shirt down to my office. Heavyset, in his late fifties, and wearing a navy-blue suit, Kronk was even bigger than Decker. When we entered the boardroom, Decker was sitting in my chair at the top of the seventeen-seat board table. If he thought that he was annoying me by taking my position, he was wrong.

The head of a sixteen-foot crocodile that I had killed was mounted at one end of the boardroom, and the head of a wild boar looked down on us from the other end. As I took a chair next to Ratsy, Decker looked at him and said, "Your boss is quite the killer, isn't he? Look at the tusks on that boar."

For years, Ratsy had adopted a persona where he intimidated by silence, but this was an opportunity he couldn't resist. "No, I'm the killer. I've killed far more pigs than Luke," he said, slowly turning his head to eye off Decker, Kronk, and the four thugs. None of them could hold his gaze.

"Gentlemen," I said, "you've had a long drive. How can I help you?"

"We heard that you're expanding into Brisbane and that you've won the Queensland Bank bid. Are you going to use union labor?" Decker asked.

"CramerBuild will advertise and certainly won't discriminate," I replied, "but, if you're asking whether the site will be a closed shop, the answer's no."

"We've heard that song. Yes, you employ unionists, and then they either resign from the union, leave the company, or are fired. How many of our members do you employ on the Gold Coast?"

"It's a big business these days. I wouldn't know."

"I can tell you. Zippo, none, zilch. Why do you think that is?"

"Lousy employers create trade unions. I guess my men think I'm a fair employer. There are unions that have their members' interests at heart, and then there are lousy unions. I'm not against unions. I never have been."

"You think we're a lousy union?" Decker said.

I compressed my lips and stared at the union men.

"We've let you have free rein on the Gold Coast," Decker said, "but Brisbane's a union city. We're not going to turn the other cheek this time."

"Let?" Ratsy smirked, undoing his suit coat to reveal a glimpse of his shoulder holster. "Where do you guys get off?"

"What if we join your men up in Brisbane for nothing? They won't have to pay union dues. The only condition is that we appoint the health and safety officer. In the absence of safety issues and accidents, we'll undertake not to set foot on site. The other builders all run closed shops in Brisbane. A non-unionized site will look bad for us."

"You want to buy your way in?" I said. "It's not going to happen, and you're never going to appoint my health and safety officers."

"If you think we're going to let you dismantle a hundred years of sacrifices, you have another think coming. You have no idea of the trouble we can cause, and it won't just be in Brisbane," Kronk said, thumping the table with his fist.

"How long have you been with the BLMU?" I asked.

"What does that have to do with anything?" he replied. "Four years, but I was with the Wharf Workers Union before that. I know my way around a building site."

"It's been a long time since anyone from the union threatened me. Why don't you tell Bill what occurred then, Col? Haven't you told him why you haven't set foot on my Gold Coast sites?"

Decker shifted uncomfortably. "That was a long time ago. I thought we might move forward in the spirit of cooperation."

Ratsy's lips were a thin line, and he tapped his fingers on the table while staring at Kronk who looked down and then nervously glanced around the room. When he looked up, Ratsy's unblinking eyes were still locked on him.

"CramerBuild won't discriminate. It never has. It's the best I can do," I said.

"We turned the other cheek twelve years ago, but we can play your game too," Decker said, nodding toward the four, black T-shirts. "We're not going to let you run a nonunion site in Brisbane."

"Let?" Ratsy said again. "Are you guys hard of hearing?"

"It won't be as easy now, Luke. Twelve years ago you were a Chicago hoodlum. These days you're a supposed pillar of society. You have friends and contacts in high places. Killing your enemies is no longer an option," Decker said.

I scowled. "I don't know what you're talking about."

"I'll see you on site," Decker replied, getting up from his chair. "Make that sites. The days of victimizing our members are over."

"Sit down," I said, raising my voice ever so slightly. "Joe, would you give us a few minutes? Take Col's associates down to the kitchen. Don't let them clutter up reception. Col and I need to have a word in private."

Decker smiled and nodded to his men. "I'm glad you've finally seen the light," he said.

I took the chair immediately to his right and made a show of dropping the file on the table.

"What's this?"

"Do you remember the dossier I had on you?"

"I won't be intimidated," Decker said, again, starting to get up.

"There's nothing intimidating," I replied, "and, if you'd prefer, I'd be more than happy to hand the folder to the media."

"What? What are you talking about?"

"You paid your wife a hundred thousand for secretarial duties last year, but, as far as I know, she did nothing. That is, unless you paid her for driving around in that union-provided BMW."

"That's none of your business," Decker blustered.

"You had four overseas trips with her last year, all on union business. I just wonder what was discussed on the cruise from Civitavecchia to Monte Carlo. Then there was the diamond necklace you bought for her birthday. You celebrated at your holiday house in Noosa. I had it valued - two million and unencumbered. How does a good union man afford a place like that?"

"How-how do you-you know?"

"You can find out anything if you have the money, but, if you had kept your nose out of the trough, there wouldn't have been anything to find."

"What are you going to do?"

"Nothing! It has no effect on me. I feel sorry for your members, but that's their problem, not mine. You stay away from my sites, and your dirty little secrets will never surface. Oh, and the BLMU is a lousy union. Real lousy."

"You're a smart bastard," Decker said, pushing back his chair.

I stood up and opened the door. "You can leave now. Remember, if the police get ahold of that dossier, you'll lose everything and find yourself doing ten years in Boggo Road. Don't cause me any trouble, and you'll have nothing to worry about."

"First it was murder, now it's blackmail. I hope I'm there when you get yours."

Chapter 43

Much to the chagrin of Brisbane's other builders, the Queensland Bank Tower went up in record time without any interference from the BLMU. As it had with the Gold Coast, CramerBuild quickly became Brisbane's preferred builder for investors, banks, and insurance companies.

Tony Farrugia had retired, but Farrugia Concrete & Quarries had trebled in size and value. Hebron Castings had repaid its loans and was making a small profit, and Ratsy and Cas hadn't had to make a nighttime visit to the foundry for years. Ratsy was the consummate family man, while Cas, with his flashy Latino looks and newly acquired penthouse, was a confirmed bachelor.

I outlaid more than six million to acquire a seven-bedroom mansion on exclusive Cronin Island. It backed up to the Nerang River with a rooftop deck and had uninterrupted, Surfers Paradise, skyline views. Included in the acquisition were a cabin cruiser that some described as a ship, jet skis, an infinity pool, a tennis court, and a temperature-controlled, two thousand bottle wine cellar. When I complained about CramerBuild's twenty-million-dollar tax bill, Monty suggested leasing a corporate jet.

"Is that why you bought the Lear?" I asked.

"No. It's because I travel interstate frequently, and it saves waiting time at terminals. I still fly commercially when traveling overseas. If we're going to reduce your tax bill, you need a more expensive jet - a Gulfstream or a 737."

"What good will that do? I'm not building overseas. I won't get a tax deduction."

"Luke, everything is tax deductible for the super-rich. You have international suppliers, and who's to say you won't have international consultants and engineers? You might even offer CramerBuild's services and expertise to the international community. Oh, and think of the political advantages. There's nothing politicians like more than taking their partners and wives away on a private jet. You'd have them in the palm of your hand. Leave worrying about the tax deduction to me."

"If it's a choice between giving it to the government or getting a luxuriously, fully-equipped jet, I'll go with the latter," I said. "See what you can find, Monty."

I was watching television when the program was interrupted by a grim-faced reporter announcing that BLMU chief Col Decker had died in his office of a suspected stroke. He was close to seventy, obese, and a heavy drinker and smoker. If he had been smart, he would have retired years ago, but I guess his lifestyle had been funded by the union.

I felt no sorrow, and my mind immediately turned to his replacement, Bill Kronk. They were like peas in a pod. Kronk was in his early sixties but had the usual qualifications of those who made it to the top of the BLMU: convictions for assault, offensive behavior, and two years' hard time in Boggo Road for extortion and threatening to kill. Like Decker, he had been ripping off the union and living the high life at the expense of BLMU members.

I wasn't worried about him but made a note to call Tom Coughlan in the morning and get Kronk's dossier updated. He had been threatening to come after me for years, and I suspected that Decker had never told him why the union had left CramerBuild alone. I smiled. Now he was going to find out. He was also going to discover that I had the goods on him.

The newly-elected, conservative, federal government finally decided that it could no longer tolerate corruption in Queensland and established a royal commission to investigate the trade unions and the state's socialist government. Monty told me that there was an adage that you should never convene a royal commission unless you knew what its findings would be. Clearly, the conservatives had no idea what the outcome would be because it, embarrassingly, backfired on them.

Headed by a former high court judge, Selwyn Fitzjohn, the royal commission not only delved into the affairs of the current socialist state government but of the prior conservative state government too. It would be two years before the Fitzjohn Royal Commission made its two hundred recommendations, but when it did, they were devastating.

Four former, conservative ministers would be imprisoned for up to ten years, the premier would be tried for perjury, and the chief commissioner of police would lose his knighthood, be fired, and be sentenced to five years in Boggo Road. More than ten police officers would commit suicide during the commission, and my old friends Tricky Trask and Sol Menadue would both get to do hard time. The CEOs of three of CramerBuild's major competitors would also receive heavy fines and be jailed for bribery. Some BLMU officials were prosecuted for dealing drugs and running protection rackets with the commissioner describing the union as an evil, lawless body, and a front for organized crime. Despite this, it was not the result the conservatives wanted, and they might just as well have picked up a shotgun and blown off their own feet.

The BLMU's response to the commissioner was to threaten to shut down Brisbane and the commission if he continued to make what it described as inflammatory comments. He had certainly been right about *lawless*. During the commission, bribery, corruption, and crime all but dried up because those who paid bribes and those who had been on the take shut up shop for fear of being subpoenaed.

It made no difference to me because I had always run CramerBuild on the up and up. My only concern was that Ratsy's and Cas's names might surface, but they didn't. Monty had been right all those years ago. Had I paid Menadue to get the union off my back, I would have found myself in prison. As it was, I wasn't even called to testify before the commission. The old ways of doing business in Queensland were over – at least, until the heat died down.

I still occasionally took advice from the industrial relations lawyer Tim Dixon but hadn't spoken to him for months. I had just finished dinner and was watching a sitcom with the kids when he called. "The ABC's televising a meeting of the BLMU at the Trades Hall Building on Channel 12. I think you should watch it."

I wasn't into party politics and couldn't stand the left-wing propaganda that the ABC espoused. As such, I rarely watched Channel 12 or listened to their radio stations. "Why?"

"I've had a tipoff that Bill Kronk is going to declare war on CramerBuild."

"Okay." I said and trudged down the hallway to my study. I knew that Kronk would publicly attack me but would do nothing to interfere with my sites. I had far too much on him.

Chapter 44

I flicked on the television in my study, poured myself a bourbon, sat down, and threw my legs up on my desk. The hall was packed with chanting BLMU members. Standing on stage were half a dozen heavily muscled henchmen. In the middle of them, was the young, Armani-attired, assistant secretary Winston Broderick. He looked totally out of place among the thugs, and I could tell from their body language that they had no respect for him. He wasn't cut from their cloth and didn't fit in. I had asked Tom Coughlan to dig up the dirt on him, but he'd come up smelling of roses.

He had graduated with a business degree from Queensland University shortly after his twentieth birthday. Academically brilliant, he commenced a traineeship with BHP Billiton, the world's largest mining company. Two years later BHP used its influence to get him admitted to the Harvard MBA program. He was one of the youngest, if not the youngest, ever accepted.

He returned to Australia and worked for BHP for another eighteen months before applying for a position as a research assistant with the BLMU. His salary had to be far less than he had earned with BHP, and, in comparison, his prospects couldn't have been anywhere near as good. Coughlan said that his few friends thought that he was crazy, but he had told them they couldn't see the big picture. What was he talking about?

The music to Rocky boomed through the speakers, and Kronk strode onto the stage wearing a black T-shirt with the white letters BLMU across the front of it. A crescendo of, "United, united, we'll never be defeated. United, united, we'll never be defeated. United, united, we'll never be defeated," echoed around the hall.

Kronk raised his gnarled, heavily tattooed arms and said, "Bruvvers, you know why you're here. CramerBuild refuses to let us appoint health and safety officers on its construction sites, placing its workers at risk. Other builders are starting to try to do the same. Well, your union is not gonna sit on its hands while you run the risk of injury or death. We're gonna bring Luke Cramer to heel."

Shouts of "Yeah, yeah," drowned Kronk out, and then the chant started all over again.

"Comrades, comrades," Kronk shouted. "Some good news. We have negotiated a two-hour, fully paid sobering up and drug recovery allowance with the industry. It means that when one of your mates has had a few too many beers or is suffering the after-effects of a few joints from the night before, he'll be recovering in company provided facilities rather than working and putting you at risk."

"Fully paid?" someone shouted.

"That's right," Kronk said, "you are the highest paid construction workers in the world, and you deserve to be."

More cheers and shouting drowned him out.

One of his henchmen took the microphone and yelled, "A bit of quiet, fellas ... and girls. Bill has some important announcements to make, and if you don't shut up, we'll be here all day. I dunno about you, but I want to get to the pub before closing time."

Good-natured laughing gave way to silence, and Kronk said, "It's not all good news. There's one holdout who refuses to sign, and I think you know who that is. Yeah, it's CramerBuild, and when we put it to Cramer, he said, if any of you turned up pissed or suffering from drugs on his sites, you'd be fired, and he'd personally throw you out on the street. He's a danger to all of you, and that's why we're deter-mined to get union-backed health and safety officers on his sites."

Hisses, boos and yells of "bastard" permeated the room before a stooge in the back row raised his hand, and said, "Can I speak?"

Kronk, knowing that the man was going to throw more fuel on the fire, said, "Go ahead, comrade."

"I was a laborer working on CramerBuild's Roma Street site. About a year ago, I injured my neck. I was on workers' compensation for five weeks, but when I tried to return to work, I was fired. It's not only me. They've done it to others too. Now I have recurring neck problems, and they don't want to know me."

More hisses and boos echoed around the room.

I had a good memory for faces, but I couldn't recall seeing the stooge. I knew that he was lying because CramerBuild never treated its employees in such a disrespectful and disdainful manner. Perhaps Kronk was going to make a serious run at me. If he did, he'd end up in prison.

"I'm sorry to hear that, comrade, but your experience is the norm. The only way we can ensure that your rights and safety are protected is if we appoint the health and safety officers."

"Yeah," shouted another huge man standing on Kronk's left. "We have to show Cramer who's boss."

Clapping and cheering erupted, and the stooge was back on his feet. "CramerBuild's done me over, and it's not just me. The only way we can bring Cramer to heel is by shutting down his sites."

"Strike, strike, strike," reverberated around the hall.

Brendon Murphy, a thick-necked Britisher with a crew cut and the union's number one thug, grabbed the microphone and shouted, "Shoosh up. We want to hear what Bill's saying."

Ratsy had wanted to make Murphy foundry fuel years ago, but I had resisted. He wasn't important enough to worry about. Winston Broderick, however, was something else. He wasn't the typical union leader. He was young, highly qualified, and had no criminal convictions. I had a bad feeling about him.

"Remember, shutting CramerBuild's sites down won't be easy because they don't employ our members. You're going to have to stop their scab workforce from gaining entry to its sites!" Kronk screamed, not trying to conceal his anger.

More cheering and yelling followed.

"Don't ever forget that, without the union, you'd be earning peanuts and being trampled into the ground."

"Yeah, yeah," the lemmings yelled.

Kronk stomped around the stage, microphone in hand, thrusting his fist into the air, shouting, "You'll only be safe when the union flag is hoisted above every construction and mining site in the country."

He was a poor speaker, but the cheering and yahooing reached a new crescendo. I wasn't worried about him. Winston Broderick was an altogether different proposition.

Book 6

WINSTON BRODERICK

Chapter 45

Why would you want to name your kid Winston? I know thousands had. Why my parents did was beyond me. Did they think that their son was going to grow up to rule the British Empire?

If so, their logic escaped my schoolmates who called me Winnie and, even worse, Winnie the Pooh. The only plus was that, just like Johnny Cash's *A Boy Named Sue*, I had no choice but to learn how to fight. I didn't look like I could. As I grew up, this proved to be a great advantage, as the many who underestimated me could testify.

I also resolved very early in life that I would never be poor again. My parents were as poor as church mice, and as a boy, I got around with my butt hanging out of my pants. Underclothing was a luxury we couldn't afford.

While I was earning my MBA, my mainly American classmates talked about running huge corporations like Boeing and GE. Others talked about becoming principals at Goldman's or JP Morgan. I didn't talk much, but my goals were simpler, less competitive, and far more lucrative. I wanted to own my own trade union, and the BLMU was the most powerful, influential and financial union in the land. However, it had no idea how to use its muscle or increase its income.

While at Harvard, I did a case study of lobbying groups such as the NRA which enlightened me to what I might do when I owned the BLMU. I could not have found a better example of how to apply pressure and raise and use cash. The NRA made the most militant of trade unions look like choirboys. I would copy and apply its tactics at the BLMU. Sure, the executive and most of the members were morons, but if I played my cards right, they'd soon be my morons.

The meeting of comrades at The Trades Hall finished, and I jumped into the old rattletrap Ford that the union provided and drove to the far older two-story bluestone offices on Turbot Street. Oh, how things were going to change when I took over.

Bill's office was on the ground floor. He didn't like climbing stairs. The peeling gold lettering on his office door spelled out, *Bill Kronk, National General Secretary.* Why the union's head office was in Brisbane rather than in a big city like Melbourne or Sydney was a story in itself. Thirty years ago, Col Decker had transferred it from Melbourne because the Brisbane weather was better for his health. I entered without knocking.

Kronk put his whiskey down and got to his feet. He towered over me at six-four with a huge gut fighting to get out of the shirt, barely keeping it in check and a ruddy alcoholic's complexion that had baked to a crisp in the Queensland sun. He looked down and said, "Thought yarself smart today, didn't ya, Winston? I saw the snide look on yar face while I was speaking. Ya think yar better than I am? Ya think yar better than all of us, don't ya?"

His breath stunk of sausages and booze, and I could feel specks of spittle on my face. I pulled back from him, and said, "You have it wrong, Bill."

An ugly sneer crossed his face. "Scared I'm gonna get yar Armani suit dirty, or is it a Zegna today? Look at ya. Soft hands, manicured nails, capped teeth, and dyed blond hair. It wouldn't surprise me if ya were having facials."

"At least, I'm not having steam baths to clean my skin," I said, knowing by the look on his face that I'd surprised him. I also knew they had nothing to do with his complexion. He was paranoid about being taped when doing one of his dirty deals with the big builders, and the only way he'd meet with them is if they were naked.

"They're not for my skin. They're to help me lose weight."

I dropped my eyes to his gut and said, "I have to tell you they're not working."

"Yar such a smartass," he snarled. "Yar not a worker, and yar not a unionist. Whaddya want with the union?"

"You've asked me that before. I want to help our members have better lives. I want to look after their interests."

"Bullshit. Yar wet behind the ears, and ya'd still be a research assistant if I'd had my way. Don't think I don't know how ya made assistant national secretary. You conned and sucked up to those sitting on the National Executive, and they fell for yar crap. I was fifty-four when I made assistant national secretary. I dunno what yar game is."

"I don't have a game, Bill."

"More bullshit! Ya have the qualifications, and yar still young enough to join a bank, a finance company, or a firm of stockbrokers where ya will be with other pretty boys. Do it before yar thirty because, after that, no one will want ya."

"I have no plans to leave," I said, knowing that my smile would annoy him. I'd made it my business to get to know more about him and his medical history than he knew about himself. He was overweight, had high cholesterol and high blood pressure, drank too much, and had had a heart attack when he was forty. The shock had caused him to undertake a weight reduction and fitness program. Col Decker, his predecessor, had died of a stroke a few years earlier, and Kronk had been appointed national general secretary of the union. He'd fallen back into his slovenly bad habits. He was perfect, and I knew I could push him over the edge anytime I wanted. "If you don't have anything for me, I'll head down the Gold Coast to Progressive Builders' Broadbeach hotel site."

"Have you finished the report on Luke Cramer and CramerBuild?"

"I'm still waiting for some data from one of the private detectives. I'll have it on your desk by Friday," I replied. I knew that he had information about Luke Cramer that I did not. Every time his name was mentioned a mix of fear and anger flicked across Kronk's eyes, but when I questioned him, he was not forthcoming.

"Make sure it is. CramerBuild employs four thousand, nonunion members. You know what that's costing us? Three million. Three million a year! I'm gonna get our members to picket its sites. We'll shut them down."

This was typical of Kronk. He was another small-time thinker. The BLMU was the powerhouse of all unions, owning its own premises and having more than $100 million out on the short-term money market, and here Kronk was focusing on how much CramerBuild was costing us in members' dues. He'd forgotten about the smaller builders and miners who were copying CramerBuild and thumbing their noses at us.

Worse, he'd completely overlooked the increase in kickbacks that we'd get from our preferred subcontractors and suppliers, plus our share of the drug and prostitution profits from the Ferals. Kronk was talking three million when the real figure ran to tens of millions. The faster I was sitting in his chair, the better for all of us, particularly me.

Chapter 46

It was nearly midnight on Thursday as I sat in my office poring over my inch-thick report on Luke Cramer and CramerBuild. Kronk had told me to spare no expense, and I had consulted with accountants, lawyers, engineers, politicians, public servants, other builders, and suppliers in the industry. I had also availed myself of the services of investigators in Chicago, Las Vegas, and Brisbane. I knew far more about the man than I had when I started. He was tough, ambitious and ruthless but so were many others who hadn't come close to achieving his level of success. *What made him different?*

The first twenty pages covered the period from when he was born in Chicago fifty-two years ago, to when had slugged a Las Vegas mobster and gotten out of town in a hurry before heading to the Gold Coast.

A few months after arriving, Cramer had secured the help of influential English financier and Queensland powerbroker Montgomery Beaurepaire. It was incongruous – they had nothing in common, and there was a twenty-year age gap – but Beaurepaire had funded CramerBuild. They remained close friends, and Beaurepaire sat on CramerBuild's board. Without Beaurepaire, Cramer would still be a bum instead of a reputed billionaire. The highly paid professionals I had hired had no idea why the Englishman had helped him and couldn't establish a connection.

Beaurepaire's involvement aside, it was relatively easy to track Cramer's achievements on the Gold Coast. The union had ignored him when CramerBuild was small and that had been a major mistake.

I had reached the appendices which were mainly news clippings. Cramer was a complex character, and there were many photos of him with notorious Brisbane underworld boss Charlie Gorman in the social pages of the dailies. There were also pictures of him with prime ministers, ministers, premiers, and the movers and shakers of Australian business and society.

I wondered whether anyone else had ever compiled a report like this. I asked myself this question because, by setting out the events in chronological order, one aspect of Cramer's life became apparent. He had been in disputes not only with the union but also with councils, the state government, politicians, public servants, utility providers, and landowners. In many instances, in the early years of CramerBuild, his opponents had simply disappeared from the face of the earth. Too many had vanished for it to be a coincidence. There was no doubt in my mind that, if anyone had gotten in Cramer's way in the early years, he'd had them killed. I had discovered what made him different.

As he had grown in status and wealth, he had turned to more conventional means of solving problems – lawyers and lobbyists. I wasn't worried about him. I was where he was thirty years ago. Like Cramer, the difference between me and those who'd gone before me was that, if I had to remove him permanently, I would. I smiled to myself. I had the cart before the horse. Before I started thinking about removing Cramer, I needed to get rid of Bill Kronk.

I put my hands on my forehead and massaged my temples. I was tired, and it was late, but I had to be back in the office at eight o'clock in the morning to go over my report with Kronk. I was torn between going home to my wife and kids or going to my mistress's Brisbane apartment. Avril was everything my wife used to be - slim, desirable, and firm but also sexually demanding. No, I was too exhausted to perform. I'd go home to Francesca and the kids.

Before I left, I dropped a copy of the report on Kronk's desk. He was an early riser, and I knew that he'd finish reading it before I arrived in the morning.

Chapter 47

I walked past our shared PA, Wendy Moore, on the way to Kronk's office. She was one of the many who hated me. Old battle axe. She was fat, frumpy, and fifty-five but looked twenty years older. She reminded me of one of those old, faded, boxy Volvos. "Good morning, Wendy," I said.

She looked up and nodded. I might as well have been the office boy. She'd been with the union since her twenties and was Col Decker's PA before he was consigned to the promised land. She'd shifted saddles easily when Bill Kronk got the big job and was fiercely loyal to him. She also had the ear of the executive members, including the president, Warren Wilson.

Unbeknown to her, I had done a lot of groveling, and Wilson was also one of my supporters and the main reason I was assistant national secretary. Once I had the top job, I'd replace her with the latest-model Lamborghini – sleek lines, well finished, with a nice rear and plenty under the hood. That was my type of PA.

I knew Kronk was already in his office by the stench of the roll-your-own cigarette emanating from it. I'd told him that it was illegal to smoke in the office, and he'd told me to piss off. He was all class. His sleeves were rolled up, he wasn't wearing a tie, and his large nose – which had been broken many times – had a dribble of mucus coming from it. Yeah, all class. "What do you think?" I asked.

"I thought you'd find more." He glared. "We still don't know why the Englishman backed him, and you're just surmising about the deaths."

"I disagree, but even so, it's irrelevant. Our job is to convert CramerBuild's workplaces into closed shops. That's where our focus should lie."

His ruddy face turned purple, and the veins in his temples took on a life of their own. "Irrelevant?" he shouted. "I'll tell you what's irrelevant. You are."

I grinned, knowing the effect it would have and then noticed the open, half-full bottle of bourbon and the glass with about quarter of an inch in it. Surely, he wasn't drinking. No one drank at this time of morning. "I want to go see him," I said. "I'll negotiate. We're on prime land here. I'll tell him that we're going to tear this shithole down and replace it with a thirty-story office block. If he scratches our back, CramerBuild gets to build it."

There was no holding him back now. He gripped the arms of his chair so tightly that I thought his face was going to explode. "Lunatic! New office block? What are you talking about? Is that the type of shit they taught you at Harvard? There's nothing wrong with this building."

"Jesus, settle down," I said, egging him on. "You look like you're going to burst an artery."

He stubbed his cigarette out with such force that I thought he'd smash the ashtray, grabbed the bourbon dregs, and downed them. He was fuming and breathing heavily as he filled the glass. "Here's what you do. We have a legal right to talk to his workers. I want you to go see him and demand to be allowed on his sites."

I was surprised that he was still capable of rational thinking. I needed to push him a little more. "I'm happy to do that," I said, "but you've been here a lot longer than I have, and we've hardly set foot on one of his sites in thirty years. Why?"

"Didn't you read your own report?" he sneered.

"Oh, you mean the part where I surmised about the deaths?" I said, smiling innocently. "Are you telling me that Col Decker, you, and the others have been too scared to confront Cramer for all these years, but you're happy for me to? Gutless bastards!"

He charged around the desk and came straight at me. I slowly got up and flexed my arms. He didn't know it, but I had a fifth dan karate black belt, but the last thing I wanted to do was use those skills. "Don't take your frustration out on me, Bill. It's not my fault that you have no balls."

His face was contorted in rage, his lips had all but disappeared, and the cords in his neck looked like they would burst. He cocked a meaty right fist. Then, suddenly, he seemed to freeze, and the color drained from his face. He tilted over and stumbled toward me. I could have caught him, but I stepped back quickly. He bounced off my chair and slumped to the floor.

I knelt and took his pulse. It was weak. I'd done a CPR course when I'd started my karate training, but I did nothing to help him. More than two minutes had elapsed when I took his pulse again. There was nothing. I flung the door open and screamed for Wendy.

By the time she arrived, I had rolled him onto his back, was massaging his heart, and was making like I was giving him mouth to mouth. His breath was vile, and even though I was only faking it, I had to fight back the urge to puke.

Wendy burst into tears. "First it was Col, and now it's Bill. It's the pressure of this job. They gave too much of themselves."

That was bullshit – they were slobs, didn't exercise, and drank and smoked to excess – but I didn't say anything.

Ten minutes later, two paramedics rushed through the door and checked his vitals. I sat down and hung my head. "I'm sorry, sir," one of the paramedics said, "he's gone."

"God," I said, reaching for a tissue to wipe my eyes. "But-but he-he was fine-fine just a few minutes ago-ago."

"Sometimes it happens without warning, sir. I know you did everything you could to save him. I can tell that you're in shock. You need to go home and rest. It's going to take weeks, maybe months, to get over what you've just experienced."

Wendy fetched me a glass of water, rested her hand on my shoulder, and said, "I saw how hard you tried to save him, Winston. You couldn't have done anything more."

It was the first time the old slug had ever gotten me anything or had a kind word for me. "Thanks, Wendy," I sniffled. "I-I can't hel-help feeling that I let-let him down. I tried, I really tried."

"I know you did. Don't beat yourself up. Why don't you take the paramedic's advice and go home?"

"I-I think I will-will," I replied, teetering as I got to my feet. God, I was good.

As I walked out onto the sidewalk, I thought about going to the gym but quickly dismissed the idea. What if someone saw me working out? I couldn't give a crap about Bill, but that wasn't for others to know.

Chapter 48

Poor Bill's widow, Mary, was too distraught to arrange the funeral, so, despite my own suffering at having to participate in the fool's funeral, I stepped in and filled the breach. After my eulogy, there wasn't a dry eye in the church. It was so passionate and beautifully worded that it even brought a tear to my eye.

Members of the National Executive entered the church in a group and were sitting in the second row. When I praised Bill for passing on his enormous knowledge to me, I was pitching for his job. In four years, I'd learned nothing from the dumbass. Well, that was a lie – I'd learned how to scratch my balls, pick my nose, cuss, and spit. Yeah, Bill had been a wealth of knowledge.

Still, that wasn't the point. I knew the older members on the National Executive, those who revered Lenin and Marx, loved Bill and would be reluctant to give me a shot at the top job. As I expressed my admiration for him, I watched their faces carefully, and in some, there was a distinct softening. They were buying my crap. Why wouldn't they? I was a super salesman, particularly when the product was me.

At the wake, many mourners went out of their way to shake my hand and commend me for the valiant efforts that I'd made to save Bill. I, of course, was a picture of modesty, saying that I had done nothing, and that I felt so bad having been unable to save him. I finally got a break, and Warren Wilson beckoned me over to the corner of the room. "That was a wonderful eulogy," he said.

"Thank you."

"The Executive met before the funeral and–"

"Did they?" I interrupted with what I hoped was the right level of disdain.

"The business of the union has to go on," he said, reaching out and gripping my forearm. It was so touching.

"I understand. Sorry, it was such a shock."

"Yes, it was, but you're holding up well. I know that many on the Executive have already congratulated you for handling the funeral and easing the burden on Mary. I know you didn't do it to seek personal acclaim, but we couldn't help but be impressed by your compassion and organizational skills. It's not an easy mix, but you've handled the funeral with aplomb."

Was he kidding? Everything I did was for personal acclaim. Now all I needed him to tell me was that they wanted to offer me the top job. Christ, I deserved it. "That's very kind, Warren."

"Anyhow, we want you to fill in as national general secretary while a firm of consultants conducts a national search for a suitable replacement."

Fill in? I was stunned, and my face must have reflected it.

"I can see you're disappointed," Warren said. "I supported you, but there were others – a majority – who thought you were too young, brash, and inexperienced."

I was gutted. My job application via the eulogy had been too late. "Yes, I am disappointed," I said. "I've busted my gut for the union, and this is how I'm rewarded? Perhaps I chose the wrong union."

Now it was Wilson's face that dropped. I knew he didn't want to lose me. I also knew that the union would be in deep shit in the short term without me. "Don't do anything hasty," he said. "You may think this strange, but I think that if the vote had been taken after the eulogy, you would have had the numbers."

"That's nice to know, but it doesn't help."

"Don't be so sure. We have our regular monthly executive meeting this Monday. I'm going to be working the phones leading up to it. I'll get you the numbers. Trust me. Can I let them know that you'll fill in in the interim?"

I felt like telling them to piss off, but I'd spent ages maneuvering myself into this position and didn't want to blow it. Besides, there wasn't another union in the country that had close to the power, cash, and revenue that the BLMU enjoyed. "Of course," I said.

Over the weekend, I shifted into Bill's office and got rid of the booze, ashtrays, and cigarettes. I also stripped the walls of his pictures of the Broncos' Premiership teams and the horses that he had raced. I wasn't into rugby or horse racing. I wanted it to look like an office, not a sports bar.

When I arrived on Monday morning, the members of the National Executive were meeting in the upstairs conference room. Brendon Murphy and two of his fellow thugs were sitting in the visitors' chairs opposite my desk. This had been their regular practice with Bill, and he used to spend half his day talking sport, gambling, and women with them. All that was about to end. Murphy didn't dislike me, he hated me. He and Bill used to roar laughing as they ridiculed me about being a pretty boy.

"What can I do for you?" I asked, while cleaning my already perfectly manicured nails with my gold letter opener.

I knew this would incense Murphy. I also knew that he was a creature of habit and that, when making a point, he would stand in front of Bill's desk and put his beefy hands on it. I was counting on him doing the same with me.

"Ya couldn't have jumped into Bill's chair any quicker, could ya? I'm damn sure ya wouldn't have jumped into his grave that fast."

"The business of the union has to go on," I said. "If that's all you have to say, get out. I'll call if I need you."

Murphy was on his feet in an instant, leaning his huge body across the desk at me. "I'm just getting started," he said. He outweighed me by at least fifty pounds, and the two jackals with him were nudging each other and laughing.

I got to my feet and said, "I asked you to leave."

"If I don't, what are you gonna do ab–"

Without hesitation, I drove the letter opener through his right hand and impaled it on the desk, while simultaneously delivering a brutal angled karate chop to his nose. I'd learned that impacting at an angle not only broke the nose but splintered it as well. His nose had been broken many times before, but never like this, and he let out a piercing scream. Before Wendy came running into my office, I deftly removed the letter opener. Murphy was in agony, not knowing whether to hold his hand or his nose. "An accident," I said. "Poor

Brendon tripped when handing in his resignation. That's right, isn't it, fellers?"

The two jackals were no longer laughing. One of them said, "Yeah, that's right. He tripped."

"Take him to first aid, Wendy, and get them to call an ambulance. He won't be coming back. Get the payroll department to mail his final check. Oh, and tell them to add an additional week's wages. I want to be generous with him."

After Wendy left, I said to the larger of the two thugs, "Your name's Ted, isn't it?"

"Yes, Mr. Broderick. Ted Spurway, and this is Mac McKenzie."

I looked at Mac and thought, *It had to be a nickname because if it weren't, he sure had cruel parents.* On the other hand, "Mr. Broderick" had quite the ring to it. It had been a successful morning, and I knew my exploits would be common knowledge and probably grossly exaggerated before the week was out.

"I'll call if I need you," I said and nodded toward the door. They couldn't get out fast enough.

The day got even better when Warren Wilson came into my office just before midday and said, "Congratulations. You're no longer a fill-in. It was close though. Nine-eight in your favor."

I shook his hand and thanked him. Eight of the bastards had voted against me, even after hearing my eulogy. I would soon find out who they were and shorten their tenure on the Executive. Collectively, they had strength, but I would pick them off one at a time and replace them with supporters of mine.

"We heard an almighty scream during our meeting," Wilson said. "What was it?"

"One of the men tripped on the threadbare carpet," I said, pointing to the pool of dried blood. "We have to get out of these offices. They're an accident waiting to happen."

Chapter 49

I'd picked up a heavy cold and was continually wiping my nose as I drove to Avril's apartment. Luckily, I was still clear-headed enough to contemplate the changes I would make.

I was earning a fair salary but nowhere near what I was worth. I had an extravagant lifestyle, and Armani, Zegna, and Brioni didn't come cheap, nor did a mistress like Avril. I'd offered to pay her rent, but she declined saying she didn't want to lose her independence. Funny that. She had no such concerns when it came to jewelry, shoes, and designer clothes.

Supplementing my income was easy though. The large builders lived in fear of industrial disputes and strikes. I merely had to suggest that trouble might be brewing, and, voila, I would be the recipient of a nice, fat, brown envelope. Australia had some of the most draconian, industrial-relations laws in the world where striking was virtually unlawful. Most unions complied with the law, but we at the BLMU danced to our own beat, and the bosses knew it.

If we wanted to strike, we did. If we wanted to physically attack the police, we did. If we wanted to disrupt the courts, we did. Soon, under my rule, we would be in a position to shut the whole country down.

For some crazy reason, Wendy was a joint check signatory and had countersigned every check signed by Kronk. Well, that sure as hell wasn't going to happen with me. I had already resolved to show her the door on Friday. Once she was gone, I'd do what I wanted with the union's millions.

I took a left-hand turn a fraction too quickly, and the suspension shook. God, my car was a bomb. Faded paintwork, frayed seats, a worn-out engine, and more than a hundred thousand miles on the clock. I'd made up my mind to replace it with the biggest and most expensive Mercedes. My thinking was that there'd be screams if I bought a smaller Merc or BMW so, if I were going to bear the criticism, I might as well go whole hog.

Kronk had been earning two hundred thousand a year, and his value was about a tenth of that. In contrast, my value far exceeded two hundred, and I intended to increase my salary to five hundred thousand. I was worth more, but we all must give something.

Unlike those of corporations, union rules were slack. Once I was rid of Wendy, I'd just instruct the payroll department to increase my salary. If the auditors were stupid enough to make an issue of it, I'd get rid of them. The BLMU was unique, and even the audit fees were juicy which, if need be, provided me with additional leverage.

I was about to take the first steps toward becoming very wealthy and the most powerful person in the country.

My thoughts turned to Francesca and my marriage. We were the same age and had met during my first stint at BHP. She was my PA. No, that's an exaggeration. She was the PA – or, perhaps shared secretary is a better description – for half a dozen management trainees that BHP was fast tracking.

There was an attraction, almost electric, from the first time we set eyes on each other. Her features were distinctly European - jet black hair, high pronounced cheekbones, an aquiline nose, beautiful olive skin, and a curvy body that filled me with lust. Perhaps it was her Mediterranean background, but her sexual appetite was nearly as strong as mine, and we couldn't get enough of each other.

Despite her two brothers' disapproval, we married, and she went with me to the U.S. The early months were fantastic, but on reflection, we had little in common other than the sex. The first cracks appeared when she got pregnant with Oliver. I was in shock. I was only twenty-three.

When I asked her to abort, she went crazy. Francesca took her pregnancy very seriously, and I not only found out how Italian she was but how Catholic she was. I had converted before we married, but it had meant three-fifths of seven-eighths of fuck all to me. With the sex we were having, I would have converted to Judaism, Islam, Buddhism, or any other faith because they all meant nothing to me. I apologized and told her that I hadn't been thinking. The tension eased, but it was the beginning of the end. Two years later, Pia was born which was a miracle because by then the sex was as rare as hen's teeth.

I hadn't wanted kids, but I loved Oliver and Pia, and it was impossible to imagine life without them. I didn't want more though – well not with Francesca anyway. She was still curvy – in fact, far too curvy. She had let herself go, and her flabby arms, rapidly descending boobs, and fat ass did nothing for me.

When I suggested she have her tubes tied, she hit the roof and told me what a selfish bastard I was. "Why don't you have a vasectomy?" she screamed.

What could I say? *Nah, I might want more kids in the future, just not with you, fat ass.* "That's not going to happen," I said.

I need not have worried because after Pia's birth, we virtually ceased having sex, but Francesca knew what I was like and let me know in no uncertain terms that she'd castrate me if she caught me playing around - that is, after her brothers had finished beating me to a pulp.

The only threat that had any impact was when she told me that I'd lose the kids too. "You'll never see them again!" she screeched.

Stupid bitch! Surely, she realized that, once I achieved my goal of running the union, my power would be immense. If push came to shove, it would be she who would never see the kids again. I wouldn't be castrated, and if her imitation Mafioso brothers got in my way, they'd find themselves in a world of pain.

As part of my MBA studies, we had studied British tycoon Sir James Goldsmith's takeover bid for British Tobacco. I was more fascinated with his personal life and a quote attributed to him – "When a man marries his secretary/mistress, he creates a vacancy." I thought it sounded perfectly reasonable and would soon put it into practice.

When I returned from the U.S., BHP promoted me, and as part of the deal, I got my own PA. Avril Sinclair was one of those rare, slim, petite women with disproportionately large, firm breasts that couldn't be concealed by the business suits she wore. Blue eyes, dirty blonde hair, a button nose, and long slender legs added to her allure.

When I first laid eyes on Avril, Sir James Goldsmith's quote popped straight into my head. The lust I'd once felt for Francesca now found its way to Avril. She was thirty-two but looked younger than I did. I'd never been with an older woman and was aroused by the thought of what might lie in store. Fortunately, Avril felt the same way, and we were soon engaged in a steamy affair.

She was far more than a casual fuck, and casual sex was something that only had sporadic appeal, usually when I was desperate, which wasn't often. She was savvy, bright, and witty, and when I told her about my plan to join the BLMU, she praised my ingenuity. Yes, she was probably massaging my ego, but I wasn't complaining. She could massage any part of me she wanted.

I rarely called Avril before going to her place - not because I was jealous – rather, because I lived in fear of picking up an STD and found it hard to believe that her life revolved around being screwed by me. Surely. there was someone else, and that's what worried me. It was time for her to answer some hard questions.

Avril had a corner apartment in the exclusive Renaissance Residential Building. I parked on the road at the front and used my card to enter the foyer. I nodded at the concierge as I strode toward the elevators. As I was whooshed to the thirtieth story, I wondered whether he was on the phone tipping Avril off, and she was quickly trying to get rid of a visitor. I was paranoid, but at least I knew it and wasn't self-deluded.

I pressed the buzzer on her door, and a minute later, she had her arms around my neck as she kissed me. She was wearing a sleeveless, lemon-colored cotton dress and sandals. She looked like a carefree, young girl rather than a woman who was on the wrong side of thirty-five. Her two-bedroom apartment was immaculate, and my feet sunk into the deep chocolate carpet. There were no glasses lying around, no strange smells, no sign that anyone else had been there.

"Can I get you a drink?" she asked as she led me to the living area. Floor-to-ceiling tinted glass windows overlooked the Brisbane River and the surrounding parks and gardens.

Not for the first time I asked myself how she could afford it. "I'm fine," I said, enjoying the feel of her firm body.

"You're so strong," she said, pressing herself into me.

I could feel the heat from her loins, and all the questions I was going to ask disappeared. It was true that men had enough blood supply for their penises and their brains, just not both at the same time. I took her arm and led her to the bedroom. Twenty minutes later I lay sated, staring at the ceiling, wondering what she did when I wasn't there. "What did you do today?"

She took out a cigarette and lit it with trembling fingers. Was it passion or guilt? I wondered. She knew I hated smoking but told me when we met that no man was ever going to dictate to her. "I went shopping with my sister. You've been acting strange lately. Why don't you get it off your chest?"

We'd been together four years, and the sex was spectacular. Without her, I doubted whether Francesca and I would still be together. Yes, I had questions but didn't want to say anything that would jeopardize our relationship. "I wonder what you do when I'm not here."

She propped herself up on her elbow and turned to face me. "You mean you're worried that I might be with another man. I've been out with other men, but I haven't taken anyone to bed."

Strangely, I felt a tinge of jealousy. "What men?"

"Prospects," she said, holding my gaze.

"I don't understand."

"Do you think you're the only one with ambitions? I've been searching for a wealthy man for years. Someone who has a grownup family. Someone who doesn't want kids. Someone who appreciates my talents."

"Talents? Is that what you call them?" I snarled. "Where's the talent in lying on your back and spreading your legs?"

She didn't look angry. She looked sorry for me. "They talk about a woman scorned," she said. "Don't be angry. What we've had was convenient for both of us, but surely, you knew it couldn't last."

"I take it you've found someone?"

"Yes, and you probably know him. Ewan Gilchrist. He's–"

"Who doesn't know him? Gilchrist Properties is the largest apartment investor in Victoria," I said. "How long have you been bedding him?"

"You didn't listen to me," she said, pulling the sheet up around her neck. "I haven't been with anyone else, nor will I be until I have a gold band on my finger accompanied by the words - 'I do.'"

"When's the big day?"

"Two months."

"We better make the most of it." I grinned.

Avril got out of bed with the sheet still wrapped around her. "I thought we had an adult relationship," she said, shaking her head. "You've chosen to make it something dirty. Get dressed. Get out and don't come back. I feel sorry for your poor wife."

I felt a surge of anger course through me, and I clenched my fists. She had a look of superiority, disdain written all over her face, and I had to fight the urge to wipe it off with one well-directed punch. "Don't you talk about my wife," I snapped, trying for my own form of moral superiority. I'd spent many hours with Avril telling her what a dog Francesca was, but she was my wife. I could say what I wanted. That didn't mean I had to put up with Avril's shit.

As the elevator descended, I thought about the pain I would inflict on Ewan Gilchrist and Gilchrist Properties, and it brought a smile to my face. Avril might marry a rich man, but by the time I'd finished with him, he'd be a pauper. As the doors opened, my mind turned to Wendy and, more importantly, her replacement. I told myself that I'd been growing tired of Avril and that she was no loss. I was looking forward to interviewing the applicants for my PA's position.

Chapter 50

I lived in a quiet court in Holland Park, a middle-class suburb about five and a half miles from the heart of Brisbane. It was only a fifteen-minute drive to my four-bedroom Queenslander which was forty years old. On stilts and constructed of timber with a corrugated iron roof and a large veranda, it had seen better days. Still, when you're twenty-five and don't have any money, you can't be picky. On the plus side, it had appreciated a lot over the past four years, and when it came time to sell, I would make a tidy little profit. That time was nigh.

I pushed the toys away from the front door, and Pia ran down the hallway and grabbed my leg, saying, "Daddy, Oliver was naughty today. He wouldn't tidy his room. Mommy was very cross."

I picked her up and threw her into the air, and her dark brown eyes twinkled with joy. "What about you?" I said. "Were you naughty too?"

She slithered from my arms, put her hands on her hips and looked up at me. "Daddy! I'm always good. You know that. I help Mommy."

"Little, goody two shoes," Oliver shouted from the kitchen.

"You shut up. Shut your silly mouth, Oliver."

"Hey, don't talk to your brother like that."

If anything, Pia's stance was more defiant. "He started it."

"Did not," Oliver said.

"Enough," I said, barely raising my voice. "Where's Mommy?"

"She said she needed a fifteen-minute nap and asked us to be quiet. I haven't made a sound, but Oliver's been banging around in the kitchen."

Before Oliver could respond, I raised my finger to my lips.

"Can you take me for a swim in the pool?" he whispered.

"Me too," Pia said.

"I'm a bit sniffly, but I'll go and watch you," I said. "First, I'll see how Mommy is."

I walked into the bedroom and sat on the end of the bed. Francesca was lying on her side wide awake. *How did she go from being a fox to a walrus in eight, short years?* I wondered. "Are you okay?"

"I just needed a few minutes by myself. I told Oliver he couldn't go out in the backyard until he tidied his room. He went anyway. When I screamed at him to come inside, he ignored me. He's becoming unruly. He needs a father figure."

"You never let up, do you? I bust my guts to give us a better life, and all I get from you is cheap shots," I said, getting up. "I'll be with the kids."

I rarely snapped at her, and she was taken aback. She was under the misunderstanding that I was scared she would complain to her brothers. Dumb and Dumber was how I thought of them. "Don't take that tone with me," she said.

"Yeah," I replied, as I left to go to the laundry room where I threw my business shirt in the dirty linen basket and changed into a polo. A few minutes later, I was standing next to our crappy above-ground pool watching the kids splash around. When my plans came to fruition, I'd be able to spend more time with them.

I already had my eye on a house in New Farm that had a beautiful in-ground pool. I had chosen New Farm for one reason. It was the priciest suburb in Brisbane with a median house price of two million. However, there were other plusses too. It was only two miles from the city center, and the house I was looking at backed onto the Brisbane River.

Dinner was sausages, mashed potatoes, and peas. I was convinced that there were dogs in Brisbane who ate better than I did. When I'd first met Francesca, she would whip up lasagna, fettuccine, spaghetti carbonara, bruschetta, salmon, barramundi, chicken parmigiana, steak, and huge salads dressed in olive oil, vinegar, and lemon juice. She had been a cook to die for – now you were more likely to die if you ate what she cooked.

The kids were tired from the pool, and we ate in silence. I was annoyed with the shit she was serving me but seething that she was feeding the kids the same. Lazy bitch! I was about to become the most powerful man in the country, and here I was being dictated to by an Italian peasant. It could not go on, but now was not the time to bring it to a head. I bit my tongue.

After dinner, I went to my study and perused my plans for the union. I had never been considered one of the boys or been popular but soon I would be loved. On the darker side, I had connected with notorious Sydney hitman Arthur Barker over the past year, and he would be joining the union on Monday as my bodyguard. It was all part of my grand scheme.

I picked up the file on the Wharf Workers Union and salivated. They had 140,000 members, and, if I could persuade them to merge with the BLMU, we would have more than 300,000. The WWU didn't have our power, cash resources, or assets, and it wasn't anywhere near as militant. What it did have was the ports, and that had me drooling. I had the power to shut down every city in Australia, but I didn't have the power to bring the country to a standstill. I would if I could control the ports.

One stopper was that I knew that the dopey old fossil who ran the WWU would insist on being general secretary of the merged union with me as his assistant. As if I were going to put up with that. After the merger, I would see that he met with a fatal accident.

I was about to examine my file on the Ferals when a shadow crossed my desk, and I looked up to see Francesca holding my shirt and glaring at me.

"What is it?" I asked, as I opened the Ferals file.

"You bastard. You're a cheating bastard!" she screeched, throwing the shirt at me. "Smell it."

I left it lying on the desk. "If you haven't noticed, I have a cold. I can't smell anything. What is it that you think you can smell?" I condescendingly asked.

"Perfume. I know you've been playing around."

I rolled my eyes. "Christ, you should hear yourself. I meet women every day. Some even grab me and do the Italian thing, kissing me on each cheek. The lord mayor's wife did it today. It's probably hers."

"Liar. Liar. It's one of your whores' perfume. I'm leaving you and taking the kids with me."

I had never laid a hand on Francesca, and I rarely retaliated against the plethora of smartass comments that she had made over the years. I pushed my chair back, got up, and was standing only inches from her.

"Don't you touch me," she hissed, her eyes flashing like bullets.

My right hand moved like a snake and wrapped around her throat. The fire in her eyes was replaced with fear, and she tried to pull my hand away. I exerted a little more pressure, and she started to gasp. "You can go whenever you like, but you try to take my kids, and I'll kill you. Capiche?" I snarled, slightly releasing the pressure.

"Si. Si," she croaked. "Let me go."

I tightened my grip. "If you're stupid enough to sic your Guinea brothers on to me, they will die. Remember that before you pick up the phone. You'll be signing their death warrants."

She was in shock. "I-I won't say-say anything to them."

"You might think you can run and hide with the kids. You can't. The police will find you, and when they do, they'll tell me. If that occurs, you'll never be seen again," I hissed, drawing my finger across my throat.

"I-I won't leave. I-I won't take them. Let-let me go."

I dropped my hand to her chest and shoved her out the door. "Look at yourself, you fat sow. Get some weight off. I'll sleep in the spare room from now on."

She was dazed. There had been a changing of the guard in the Broderick household, and if she knew what was good for her, she would never assert herself again. I watched as she slunk down the hallway, and smiled. Like her, many others had also underestimated me. Their turn was coming.

I picked up the file on the Ferals again, and a jolt of excitement coursed through me. The Queensland government had recently introduced the most draconian laws in the world to crush the biker gangs.

It was now a jailable offense for two or more bikers, wearing their biker colors, to be seen together in a public place. Mandatory fifteen-year sentences in addition to normal penalties for serious crimes applied to bikers. Biker club office bearers were subject to being sentenced to an additional ten years in jail, and parole would only be granted if the offenders cooperated with police. There was much more, including the crushing of motorcycles and the establishment of a "bikers only" prison.

Had no one learned from Prohibition in the U.S.? Draconian, unenforceable laws did not curb crime, but they did provide opportunities for people like me. Once the Ferals joined the BLMU, would any government be stupid enough to take them on? If it did, it would be a short-lived government.

I was pleased. Within six months I would add the WWU, the Ferals, and Arthur Barker to the BLMU. I would be omnipotent, but it was all dependent on bringing Luke Cramer and CramerBuild to heel. I had to show the doubters that I could deliver and set an example of what would happen to those who dared defy me.

First thing tomorrow morning, I intended to convene a mass meeting of our members in Brisbane that would be beamed into every capital city on huge screens. I was about to become popular – very popular.

Chapter 51

I was staggered to find the dealer had a 2014 Mercedes-Benz SLS AMG designo Edition in his showroom with a price tag of more than $1 million. I'd resolved to buy the most expensive Merc, but that was crazy. Instead, I leased a silver E63 with a price tag of slightly more than $300,000. I told the dealer to drop it off on Friday afternoon, and I'd give him a check for the first month's lease payment.

On Friday morning, I called Wendy into my office and told her that I was sorry, but I would have to let her go. Understandably, she was stunned. "Why?" she asked. "What have I done to deserve this?"

I had decided not to take the rough route with her because she still had the ear of some on the Executive. Why invite her to badmouth me? I had my own spies on the Executive and had the names of the eight who had failed to support me. They'd all be gone within six months, but in the short term, they could cause me trouble, and I didn't want Wendy to sic them on me.

"Nothing," I lied, "it's not you. I still haven't recovered from the shock of seeing Bill die, and, well, every time I see you, thoughts of that dreadful day come flooding back to me. You were such a great team."

Doubt was written all over her face. "I don't have to stay as your PA," she said. "I used to work in accounts. I could go back there, and since I'd be on the first floor, you'd never see me."

I rested my chin in my hand as if I were giving her suggestion serious consideration. I wasn't. "I'm sorry, Wendy. There'd always be the possibility that I'd bump into you. Great idea, but it wouldn't work."

Doubt was replaced with anger. "What if I take a month's leave? You might be over your problem by then."

"What if I'm not?" I said. "No. It's time to make a clean break."

"You're in his office, sitting in his chair, using his computer, and it doesn't seem to be impacting you," Wendy snarled. "What game are you playing?"

I would have liked to have told her to get lost, but I didn't need an enemy who could hurt me in the short term. "You're right," I said, brushing my eyes with a tissue. "I should have stayed in my office, but then I still would've seen you, and the memory of Bill dying in my arms in the adjoining office would have haunted me. I'm getting out of these offices. It's the only way I can put that dreadful event behind me."

Doubt was still there, but there was also a tinge of sympathy. "Do you think you should be working?"

"No one can fill Bill's shoes," I said, almost puking, "but if I don't try, the union will be in turmoil. Wendy, you've been fantastic, and I'm sorry. I'm adding an extra year's salary to your final payout." It was nothing in the big scheme of things and a small price to pay to keep her from spreading venom.

Her face softened. I exaggerate. A layer of hardness lifted. She came around to my side of the desk and put her hand on my shoulder. "That's very generous. Thank you. Would you like me to work the day out?"

"I'd prefer you didn't," I replied, hanging my head. "It's the memories. Sorry."

"I'll tidy my office and be gone before midday. Good luck, Winston."

"Good luck, Wendy."

I waited until she had left the premises and then called the bank and asked them to email the forms removing her as a signatory and making me a sole signatory. When the bank manager had the audacity to query my authority, I snarled, "I'm the union's national general secretary. Do you know what that means? We have more than a hundred million with you on short-term deposit. Would you like me to pull it this afternoon? How do think your bosses would feel about that?"

He couldn't babble his apologies fast enough. "Are you going to replace Ms. Moore with another signatory?" he asked.

"No," I replied. "We have more than enough joint signatories as it is."

I hung up and immediately buzzed our accounts department and told them to draw a check for the first month's payment on the Merc. I'd already signed the lease documents authorizing future payments by direct debit.

I was on a roll. I quickly knocked out a memo authorizing an increase in my salary from two hundred thousand to five hundred thousand and buzzed our human resources manager to tell him to come to my office immediately. He didn't blink as he read the memo, merely saying, "Yes, Mr. Broderick. Is that all?"

"No. Get me a temporary secretary and draft an advertisement for Wendy's replacement."

"Are there any specific qualifications or experience that you're looking for?"

I wanted to say *less than thirty, attractive, intelligent, and sexy*, but in this PC world, that would be grounds for emasculation. "The union is about to change direction," I said. "We need to become more dynamic, to get involved in social issues, to flex our muscles, and to grow by possibly merging with another union. The successful applicant will have to be prepared to work the same hours that I do, when required, and that could mean sixteen-hour days. A career woman would be ideal."

"It's a difficult ask. It'll have no appeal for women with young families, and older women might not be able to stand the pace."

Good. I have him focused on young single women. I smiled.

"Perhaps, we should be looking for a man?" he said.

Jesus! I racked my brain, hoping my face didn't convey my thoughts. "Great suggestion," I lied, "but are you trying to get me hung? We're a union dominated by males, but we're always preaching equality. How do you think it's going to look when we add another male to the fold at the expense of a female?"

"You're right," he said. "I didn't think. Do you want me to prepare a short list and handle the initial interviews?"

"No. Let me have the applications as they come in. I'll decide who I want to interview."

"There could be hundreds."

"I'm a fast reader," I said, dismissing him.

Later that afternoon, the boss of Progressive Builders called to set up a meeting with me. I knew that he had been paying Kronk plenty under the table, and he probably thought he could screw the new boy. He was in for a big shock.

I had a good idea of what Kronk had been getting, and I wanted double that. He would soon learn that the days of fat, brown envelopes were over, replaced with transfers to an international, untraceable bank account. I agreed to meet him in the steam rooms on Turbot Street.

"Not the steam rooms," he moaned.

"Yes, the steam rooms," I said. It was the only Kronk policy that I would adopt. I had to admit that it was a great way of ensuring that I was never taped.

Chapter 52

When I arrived at the offices on Monday morning, Arthur Barker was waiting for me. The union had its own thugs and could always call on the Ferals for help, but while they were violent, there was a limit to what they would do.

Luke Cramer had been successful in repulsing the union because he had employed Joe Ratsch, and there was nothing that Ratsch wouldn't do. From my research, I estimated that he and his helper, Cas Herrera, had permanently removed more than a dozen impediments to CramerBuild's expansion on the Gold Coast. Arthur Barker would tilt the playing field.

"Good morning, Winston," he said, extending a hand more like a pianist's than a hitman's.

"Welcome aboard. Take a seat," I said, studying him closely.

Arthur was about five feet nine, slim, with dark hair receding at the temples. Dressed in a light gray, linen suit, he could easily pass for a doctor or lawyer. If I had to describe him in one word, it would be "distinguished."

I had spoken to many underworld figures in Melbourne and Sydney, but he was the standout. He was articulate, didn't try to intimidate by facial expression, and was rational – something many of the others I spoke to clearly were not.

After our first meeting, I ran a detailed check on him. Despite his benign appearance, he was respected and feared. I had been concerned that he might be a sociopath, but there was no evidence of this. He had friends and many girlfriends and was far from anti-social. When I quizzed him, he explained that he had the ability to divorce his business life from his personal life. I liked that.

"Is it still the same plan?" he asked. "Every time you meet with a builder, contractor, or subcontractor, you want me to be with you."

"Yes, but as I told you, there will be times when I need privacy.

However, that will never occur when I'm meeting with Luke Cramer and his supposed executives. If I suggest it, you are to ignore me."

"You want me to balance the Ratsy factor."

"No, I want you to more than balance it. That's what you said you could do."

"Don't worry. Ratsy's dangerous and very good, but you hired the best. If I have to take him out, I will."

"Your car's in the parking lot," I said, throwing him a set of keys. "As requested, a black Ford Falcon XR6 capable of one hundred fifty miles an hour with tinted windows and all badges removed. It looks like a conventional Ford. I still don't know why you wanted such a powerful car."

"In my line of work, sometimes a little extra speed comes in handy," he said.

I glanced down at my watch. Red Maguire, the leader of the Ferals, had accepted my invitation to meet and was due in five minutes. "Stay with me, Arthur," I said. "You'll get an idea of where we're heading."

When Maguire entered my office, he looked far too old to be the leader of the Ferals. He had long gray hair and was dressed in full leathers, but he wasn't wearing colors which didn't surprise me. Under the new Queensland legislation, wearing colors in public was a jailable offense.

Maguire seemed equally shocked when he saw me, having probably expected a Bill Kronk clone. He knew Arthur, and they exchanged cursory greetings. I nodded to a chair, and said, "Thanks for coming in. It must be hard for you to make a living under these new laws."

He plonked his large frame down and said, "Yeah, it is. If you want us to terrorize someone with our bikes, I'm going to have to pass. If you want us to rough someone up, providing it's only one or two, we can still accommodate you."

"No, I have my own people. That's not what I want to talk about. What about the drugs, booze, and girls?"

"Finished. They closed our clubhouses down. They even closed our tattoo parlors, and they were almost legit."

"You can still source the drugs, and the girls are still around?"

"Of course."

"I can put you back in business, and I can guarantee you won't be disturbed."

Maguire looked at me with unmasked skepticism. "How do you intend to do that, sonny?"

I glanced over at Arthur. He was impassive. *What is it with these old bastards like Maguire?* I thought. "I take it that you know the police, federal and state, dare not enter a site where our flag is flying."

"Yeah, everyone does. That's not something you invented."

Maguire was starting to test my patience, and I struggled to remain civil. "If the drugs were stored on our sites, they'd be untouchable."

"Yeah, but they still have to be distributed, and we can't move without the cops being up our asses."

"What if I could provide you with safe houses near the building sites where customers would go to you? You could bring the girls and booze back too."

Maguire sat forward and stared at me. "There's no such thing as a safe house for us."

"You're wrong. I intend to buy four or five houses and get permits to renovate them. I will, of course, use union labor."

A veil seemed to lift from his face. "You'll fly the union flag above them. No copper in the land will dare enter them. It's brilliant."

"I know," I said, "and it gets better. I want your men to join the union. If they're on the road and are hassled by the cops, they'll show them their union tickets and tell them that they're interrupting union business. Then we'll see how big the cops' balls are."

"It's foolproof."

"Don't forget, you'll have thousands of builders' laborers and construction workers as customers for the drugs, lap dances, booze, and sex."

"Jesus, you're good," Maguire said, flashing a huge grin before his face clouded over. "What about Cramer? He controls the biggest sites on the coast in the best locations, and he's the largest employer. He has thousands on his payroll, and none of them are in the union. Without them, your whole plan is shit."

"Don't worry about him. All his employees and subcontractors will be members of the union within ninety days. I'll guarantee it."

"You're gonna take him on. I wondered why Arthur was here. Many have tried. All have failed. Do you remember that politician from up north who wanted to set up a parliamentary inquiry into how CramerBuild acquired that property in Broadbeach from the government for a song? He disappeared without a trace."

"I heard that you terrorized his wife thirty years ago, and you're still here."

"I was lucky. You guys hired two idiots to frighten him. His kid had a little puppy. They slashed its throat. He took retribution by killing them. After that, you backed off. That probably saved me."

"You don't know that he killed them."

"They disappeared. That's enough for me."

"Are you scared of him?"

"Scared? Nah, I'm not scared." He looked from me to Arthur. He couldn't back out now. He knew that, if he did, we'd spread the word that the Ferals were pussies, and reputation was everything. "If I do this deal, what do you get out of it?"

"Half your profits," I said, not batting an eyelid.

"Are you mad?" Maguire said, starting to get to his feet.

"Sit down," I snapped, my patience having finally run out with the fool. "I'll provide the building sites. I'll provide the houses. You'll have access to thousands of builders' laborers. Your profits will more than double. Do you still want to walk away?"

"Well, when you put it that way ..."

"Good. You'll transfer twenty-five percent from your Caymans account to an account that I'll nominate in the Virgin Islands. You'll pay me the other twenty-five percent in cash, and I'll bank it in the union's account."

"What account in the Caymans?"

"Don't waste my time, Red."

"You heard him," Arthur added.

Maguire tried to maintain his bravado but couldn't hold Arthur's gaze. When a tough guy faces off against a killer, it's always the tough guy who gives ground. "You can't bank the cash. If it's more than ten thousand, you'll have Austrac all over you, and it's gonna be a lot more than ten thousand."

I sighed loudly. "The union gets cash donations every day. The comrades and the union's supporters are very generous. I don't give a shit about Austrac or the government. If they give me any trouble, I'll unleash mayhem on this country the likes of which has never been seen before. The question you have to ask yourself is: Do you want to be my partner?"

"When I heard you beat that big British guy up, I didn't believe it. Now I do. Let's shake on it, partner," he said, standing up.

I shook his hand and said, "Why do they call you Red?"

"I wasn't always gray," he retorted.

I must have touched a nerve. "Really?" I laughed. "Glad you could come in. I'll be in touch."

Chapter 53

It was 9 A.M., and Brisbane's Palladium Hall with a capacity of five thousand was busting at the seams. I was hidden on the edge of the stage with a document in my right hand while watching Ted Spurway and Mac McKenzie rev up the crowd before I made my grand appearance. They lifted their palms into the air, and the members responded with, "United, united, we'll never be defeated. United, united, we'll never be defeated. United, united, we'll never be defeated."

I waited to hear the theme from Star Wars before bounding on stage to the sound of muted applause. I couldn't lower myself to wearing the standard issue black T-shirt with the BLMU lettering. Instead, I was dressed in a black polo, designer jeans, and Givenchy loafers. I spoke about the loss of our esteemed leader Bill Kronk and the impossibility of anyone filling his huge shoes, let alone a mere mortal like me. After about ten minutes, I sensed boredom accompanied by restlessness in the crowd.

It was time. I held the document above my head and shouted, "Does anyone know what this is?" Of course, they didn't. How could they possibly see it? "It's our current enterprise bargaining agreement, and while it was fine when negotiated, it's now out of date." It was never fine, but I couldn't shit on the dead, could I? "Costs have risen, electricity and power have gone through the roof, rates and taxes have climbed, and food prices are exploding. If you don't believe me, ask your wives."

I now had their full attention, and there were cries of "Yeah," and "He's right."

"The bosses are making super profits, but do you think they're sharing them with you?"

Shouts of "No, no," reverberated around the hall.

"There's a builder on the Gold Coast that poor old Bill Kronk spoke about at our last meeting. Luke Cramer's a billionaire and a union hater. He's making so much money that he's looking to expand into Melbourne and Sydney, and we all know what that means: fewer union jobs and less money," I said, staring directly into the camera. I wanted those in the big cities to think that Cramer was coming.

"Maybe if he shared more of his profits by increasing wages, he wouldn't be so keen on Melbourne and Sydney," I continued. I hadn't heard that CramerBuild was looking to expand, but when I took Cramer on, I wanted every union member in the land behind me.

There were plenty of members from the Gold Coast in the crowd, and insults about Luke Cramer flew thick and fast.

"I know that some of you are concerned about the Mercedes I'm driving, and that you've heard I have had a huge increase in salary. Well, I'm here to set the record straight. It's true!"

There were gasps from around the hall, and when I looked down, I saw a mix of angry and forlorn faces.

"Why shouldn't I be paid what I'm worth? What, because I run a union, I'm a bum? Because you're unionists, you're bums? No way. All I want is what I'm worth, but I want to take you with me and make sure you get paid what you're worth."

Now the faces were quizzical and expectant.

"I'm proposing," I said, holding the EBA up and tearing it in half with great theater, "that we negotiate a new agreement with improved benefits and wages, starting with an increase of $300 a week." It was a huge increase, dwarfing anything that had ever been negotiated before.

When one of the bruvvers in the front row shouted, "Is that an ambit claim?" It was like a gift from above.

"No, comrade, it is not. For those of you who don't know, an ambit claim can best be described as a bullshit claim. You know. We ask for $300 in the hope that we might get $50. Let me assure you, there's no bullshit in this claim."

With that, cheering and clapping erupted, and I felt Spurway and McKenzie patting me on the back.

"That's not all," I continued. "We're going to appoint the health and safety officers on CramerBuild's sites, and those jobs are going to our members. I'm sick of Cramer telling us what to do. We're going to take a stand, and we're not backing down."

I was more than a good speaker – I was great, and I could ignite passion and loathing in the way Hitler once had. I stood there basking in wave after wave of applause. The fervor in the room was palpable. They would run through brick walls for me.

A wiry man near the back of the room held his hand up and shouted, "Can I speak?"

Thinking he was going to throw more fuel on the fire, I said, "Go ahead, comrade."

"I was working on CramerBuild's Burleigh Heads site and was injured in an unavoidable accident. I was off work for two months, and CramerBuild made up my wages shortfall and paid for specialist medical treatment that WorkCover wouldn't authorize. It's not uncommon."

Shit! I had gotten caught up in the moment and let one of the members speak without knowing what he was going to say. An elementary mistake. For the first time, there was no reaction as the workers pondered whether to boo or cheer. "Dopey prick," I cursed under my breath.

Out loud, I said, "I'm pleased for you, comrade, but your experience is not the norm. You were lucky. The only way we can ensure that your rights and safety are protected is if we appoint the health and safety officers."

"Yeah," shouted a man standing on my left. "We have to show Cramer who's boss."

More clapping and cheering erupted, but the wiry man was back on his feet. "CramerBuild was good to my family and me, and it wasn't just me."

"If they were so good, why aren't you still working there?" I shouted, not knowing that I was compounding my first mistake.

"I wish I was. I had an argument with a supervisor, lost my temper, and quit. I was stupid," he said, looking around the room. "I'm telling you, if we go out on strike, we'll never recover our lost wages."

I turned to Ted Spurway and hissed, "Fix it."

I watched as he and one of his lackeys made their way down the aisle to the row immediately behind the wiry man. Everyone in the hall saw them but, knowing what was going to happen, looked away.

The wiry man was on his feet again, saying, "I don't agree with–" when a fist smashed into his kidneys, and he lunged forward, grunting in agony.

"I think he fainted, boss," Spurway shouted. "I'll take him outside for some fresh air."

"Do that." I smirked. "Make sure he's looked after."

The enthusiasm and noise of only a few minutes ago was replaced with silence.

I looked over at McKenzie and whispered, "Get after them. Make sure Ted doesn't kill the poor bast–" I halted midsentence when I heard a man in the front row say, "What a bloody fool! Fancy coming here and speaking up for the bosses. What was he thinking?"

"What he said was right," the man sitting next to him whispered back.

"Of course, it was, but that doesn't mean he had to be stupid enough to say it. What an idiot."

I stared down at them until they hung their heads.

I couldn't finish on a flat note, so I grabbed the microphone and shouted, "I'm sure you're sick of hearing my voice. The first round at the pub is on me. Come on. United, united, we'll never be defeated. United–"

I was drowned out by cheering and chanting. I could play them like a fiddle.

I glanced to my left and saw Arthur watching me from off stage. I was confident I had chosen an astute bodyguard. It was just after eleven o'clock when the meeting finished, and I joined the comrades and headed to the nearest pub.

I hated pubs and hated the taste of beer even more, but I knew that if I were going to be accepted as one of the boys, I had to join them. As I entered the bar, I was greeted with hearty slaps on the back and shouts of, "Good on ya, mate."

I threw $200 on the bar and said, "Keep 'em coming until that's gone." The bruvvers who had seen this broke out into another burst of backslapping and applause.

I held my glass of beer in the air and shouted, "to the union," and downed it in one gulp. It tasted like piss. How could anyone enjoy it?

It defied belief. I wanted to order a glass of fine white wine or champagne but knew that wouldn't gain me entry to the boys' club.

The man standing next to me grabbed my glass, thumped it on the bar, and said, "Another beer for our leader."

After my third beer, I begged off, saying that I had to get back to the office. As I made my way to the door, there was a prolonged burst of applause. Morons. My morons.

Chapter 54

My human resources manager was right. There were more than a hundred applications for the position of my PA. If I'd been able to ask them to disclose their weight or include photos of themselves, I would have saved myself a lot of time.

Those who mentioned the gym, beach, and swimming in their recreational pursuits made the short list. I rationalized that they probably wouldn't be fat. My second filter in determining who made it to the first interview was age. I didn't read any application where the applicant was thirty or older. Still, in a ten-hour Wednesday, I held fifteen preliminary interviews.

My theory about fitness and the beach did not hold up in all instances, and I eliminated those who were unattractive or overweight in less than fifteen minutes. Then I managed to subtly ask those whom I was interested in whether they were in a relationship, on the pretext that they would need to travel and stay with me when I was interstate. I told those who answered in the affirmative that I needed to know whether the pressure of the position might adversely impact their relationships. While I couldn't openly say it, I was looking for someone young, attractive, unattached, sassy, and savvy with whom I also had a hint of chemistry.

By the end of the day, I'd narrowed the list to three. I was a master of the double entendre, and I had dropped one with obvious sexual connotations that resulted in smiles from two unattached applicants. As far as I was concerned, that was chemistry.

I made an exception with the third in that she was attached, but also stunning. Monica Carson had glistening, jet-black hair cascading midway down her back, porcelain skin, long, slender legs, and a face that exuded sexuality. As she sat across from me, I mentally had sex with her while lusting for it to be reality. Unfortunately, she came across as a serious professional, and I didn't try the double entendre.

I would wait until the second interview. If I got an inkling of future action, the position was hers.

Before the second interviews, I had the three short listed applicants checked out extensively. These days many attractive women played on the other side, and I didn't want to employ one of them. In that regard, I had nothing to worry about as they were all straight. I interviewed Monica Carson first, on the basis that if she gave me a hint of coming across, I wouldn't need to interview the others.

She arrived for the interview dressed in a smart black suit and a white blouse that revealed just a tinge of cleavage. When she sat down, the hem of her skirt crept up a few inches accentuating her magnificent legs. She all but took my breath away. Twenty minutes into what had been a very formal interview, I smiled and said, "How would you feel about staying with me?"

"What?" she asked, affront written all over her face. "What do you mean?" The other two applicants had also asked me what I meant, but they had been smiling. Monica was snarling.

"When we're interstate on business," I innocently responded.

That should have closed the matter, but she said, "I know your type. I know what you were hinting at. You were smirking. There's a movement against men like you. I should report you to the equal opportunity commissioner."

"Do what you like," I said, "but bear in mind, you'll never get a PA's position in this town again if you do. Oh, and I'll make sure your dad loses his job as a civil engineer and that no employer hires him in the future."

She stood up, pushing the chair back angrily. "You might have been able to do that in the old days. No one can now," she said. "You haven't heard the last of this."

I got up and strode over to the door, blocking her exit. "You know why the feminists were successful in bringing those other limp-wristed males down, don't you? They were worried about the law. They were worried about what society would think of them. They were worried about being shamed. You might not know it, but I'm the most powerful person in the country. I don't care about the law or society, and if you think you can shame me, think again. I'm shameless!"

I could tell she was taken aback. "You-you don't scare me. Get-get out of my way."

I genuinely didn't care what she did. I had 160,000 members, and 155,000 of them were male, many whose sexual proclivities were undoubtedly no different to mine. If any statutory body were stupid enough to take me on, I'd shut the country down.

"Would you like to see me pick up the phone and have your father fired?" I asked. "Do you want to see me on television tonight, telling the world that you propositioned me to win the job, and when I rejected your advances, you squealed to the authorities?"

"You-you wouldn't."

"Bloody skank, get out of my office," I said. I knew I wouldn't hear another word, but, if I did, Monica Carson would find herself in a world of hurt.

By the end of the day, I had employed Zoe Barbour, an auburn-haired, slim, hot looking, twenty-six-year-old with a provocative smile and an enticing demeanor. She knew exactly what the job entailed and hadn't objected. The position was a big leap upward for Zoe.

I was on a high when I called Luke Cramer and told him that we needed to meet. As expected, he procrastinated, but I insisted on seeing him at 11:15 on Friday morning, and in the end, he said, "We might as well get it over with. How many others will you be bringing with you?"

"Just one."

"That's a first." He laughed. "Have you sacked the thugs?"

"We've never employed thugs," I replied. I was going to enjoy doing Luke Cramer over. I'd do him slowly. "See you on Friday."

Chapter 55

Australia's industrial relations laws were draconian and drafted to favor employers. Both major political parties supported these laws. It was another case of the workers being sold out, but more galling was the fact that we were supporting the Labor Party with huge donations, and they – the supposed workers' party – were shitting on us. What a joke. Within a year I would control it, and it would be my nominees who sat in parliament carrying out my orders. I didn't intend to comply with any laws that attempted to curb union power or, worse, my power.

We were one of the few countries in the world where workers were denied the right to strike, despite it being recognized as a fundamental human right under international law. I had studied the law extensively and understood that the United Nations had declared "strike action to be a right and one of the principal means by which workers and their associations could legitimately promote and defend their economic and social interests."

Obviously, the restrictions Australia placed on that fundamental right put us at odds with international conventions, a point repeatedly made by the International Labour Organisation. Many unions and their leaders were pussies and ceded their human right to the detriment of their members. Not the BLMU, and not me.

In keeping with this stupidity, unions had to give employers twenty-four hours' notice in writing before visiting their workplaces, but even then, we had to have a right-of-entry permit. It was akin to your opponent in the boxing ring telling you that, before you fought him, you had to tie one arm behind your back and wear a twenty-ounce glove on your free fist. It was stupid to say the least.

Worse, though, the laws banned strikes unless they had been previously sanctioned. Fortunately, I knew more about the IR laws than most lawyers and judges. Were the BLMU and I going to obey them? No way!

The meeting room on the first floor was like the rest of the building. Cream paint flaked off the walls, the carpet was threadbare, and frayed chairs surrounded two old tables pushed together. Bare light bulbs hung from the ceiling, and glum-faced portraits of the losers who had been my predecessors hung from the walls. I took the chair at the head of the tables, Spurway was on the right, McKenzie on my left, and Arthur stood directly behind me. There were fourteen organizers seated on both sides of me, all dressed in standard-issue, black BLMU T-shirts. All had beefy arms, and most were covered in tattoos. I didn't need to remind myself that they were here because of their brawn, not their intellect. They were talking and joking among themselves when I thumped the table with my fist. "Shut up. It's not a social gathering."

You could have heard a pin drop. "Ted's briefed you on our plan for tomorrow. I want to go over it again. If you have any questions, now's the time to ask them. Are you all focused?"

Murmured assents went around the table.

"As you know, CramerBuild has eight sites: six on the coast and two in Brisbane. At precisely 11:45 tomorrow morning, you will enter the site allocated to you and demand to address the workers at the lunch-break. You will be armed with plenty of application forms. You will get a good reception because we've planted members at each site. They will ask for application forms and encourage others to join the union."

"What if they won't let us speak at lunchtime?" one of the organizers asked.

I gave Spurway a snaky look. I'd already covered this with him, but he mustn't have told the others. I was about to unleash when he growled, "Don't you listen, meathead. Members of the Ferals will make themselves available here in the morning. They're paid in full members of the union. They can't ride their bikes, or they'll run the risk of being arrested. However, they can travel by car. I suggest you take at least six with you. They won't do anything, but their presence will curtail any objections."

I patted Spurway on the arm. "Well put, Ted. Are there any more questions?

There was silence.

"Then let's give Cramer hell," I shouted, leaping from my chair and punching the air.

"I've been waiting for this day," McKenzie said, shoving back his chair. "Luke Cramer's ruled the roost for too long."

Everyone was on their feet, and loud "hear, hears" and "yeahs" came from both sides of the tables. I crossed my fingers and hoped that none of the idiots would start chanting the mind-numbing *United, united, we'll never be defeated* bullshit.

Chapter 56

I'd never set foot in Luke Cramer's office, but I knew exactly what to expect, right down to the animal heads and the antelope. I didn't mention them as I introduced Arthur Barker, and Cramer introduced Joe Ratsch and his son Carlos. Cramer and his son were big men of similar size, probably about six feet two and two hundred twenty pounds. Ratsch was small with narrow shoulders and a distinct paunch.

"You called the meeting," Cramer said. "The floor is yours."

"Thank you," I responded. "I'd like you to hear me out. I won't take your silence as assent to any of my propositions. After I'm finished, I'd welcome your response."

"Fair enough. Lay your cards on the table."

"I don't know the history of CramerBuild and the union," I lied, "but I want to start with a clean slate. I think we can help each other. I know we can help you."

Ratsch interrupted me by putting his hand to his mouth, and saying, "Bullshit," disguising it as a cough. It was a real smartass gesture.

I was about to continue when Arthur looked at Ratsch with a twinkle in his eye, and said, "Cool it, little feller." I wondered whether anyone had ever called Ratsch "little feller." His eyes narrowed, and his lips all but disappeared as he shot daggers at Arthur who just smiled in response. Arthur had just pissed on Ratsch's lamppost, and the tension in the room went up tenfold.

"Go on," Cramer said.

"We can help you with health and safety. We have expertise and experience that we're prepared to make available. Oh, and we'd like to avail ourselves of your expertise. You've made an awful lot of money. We'd like you to sit on the board of the corporate trustee of our members' pension fund."

"You weren't worried about Adam Lasik's health."

"Adam Lasik?"

"The guy who you had beaten up at your last meeting because he had the audacity to say CramerBuild was a good employer."

"I don't know where you heard that. I've never had anyone beaten up."

"That's not what he told me," Cramer said.

"He's a liar," I responded.

Cramer was about to argue, but I held my hand up. "You agreed to let me present without interruption. There's more than fifty billion dollars in our pension fund, and, with all due respect, it dwarfs CramerBuild. Directors are generously rewarded for their input."

"I bet they are," Cramer said, under his breath, but loud enough for all to hear. The meeting was going exactly as I'd expected.

"You may not have heard, but we're moving into leased offices while the old building is demolished. We're going to replace it with a thirty-story office block that's being designed as we speak. I'll let you have the contract to build it for us," I said, watching Cramer intently. For the first time his eyes lit up, and he showed interest.

"How do you know I'd have the best quote?"

"I'd let you have copies of your competitors' quotes. Providing yours is one dollar less than the lowest, the contract is yours."

"Why would you do that? You have cozy arrangements with them. If they found out, you'd be in trouble."

"Why would I do it?" I mused. "Because you have something I want, and they don't. Oh, and they won't make trouble. They wouldn't dare."

"What is it that I have that you want?"

"Don't play games. It doesn't become you. I want you to bury the hatchet, to come into the fold, and to make your sites closed shops."

"I'd like to bury the hatchet," Ratsch snarled.

Cramer pushed himself back in his chair, shook his head, and looked at me like I was a piece of shit. "Thanks for coming in, but the business is running just fine as it is. We're not going to be making any changes." As he was speaking, his PA came in and dropped a message in front of him. He glared at me, jumped up, and followed her out the door.

"Trouble?" I said, glancing innocently at Carlos.

"I dunno," he replied.

I glanced at Ratsch. He was simmering. When I looked at Arthur, I knew why. He was grinning, and his eyes were filled with mirth.

Five minutes later, Cramer stormed back in the room. "You bushwhacked us!" he shouted. "You have thugs on every site. You can't do it. You have to give us twenty-four hours' notice in writing."

"Report me to the Fair Work Commission," I said. "Better still, sue me. Hundreds of your workers are going to sign up with us today. Your days of only employing non-union labor are over."

Ratsch started to get up, but Arthur was already on his feet, and he put a hand on the hitman's head, and pushed him back down. "Just stay there, little feller," he said.

"I think we're all done here," Cramer snarled.

"Your days of dictating to us are over," I said. "I'll give you seven days to change your policies, to go on site and tell your men that you're only employing union labor and subcontractors."

"If I don't?"

Cramer's PA interrupted again with another message. Cramer read it and pushed it over to Carlos. "You know what to do. Handle it. I'll be with you in a few minutes," he said.

"You don't want to know what I'll do. Your days of dealing with limp dicks are over, Cramer." I smirked, staring at Ratsch who was now standing and obviously fuming. "I know what he is - a hired killer from Chicago. He has quite the reputation, but he's yesterday's man. Isn't that right, Arthur?"

"Little Ratsy." Arthur laughed. "You'd be wise to get on a plane back to Chicago while you still can."

They were shocked. No one had treated them with such contempt. I reached the door and abruptly turned around. "I saw your daughter, Madison, on the *Young Talent Show*. She's a real looker with a great voice. How old is she? Fifteen?" Cramer's face dropped. I knew he'd got the message. "Seven days," I said. "Do what I told you, or you'll live to regret it."

Book 7

LUKE 2017

Chapter 57

"I'll kill that prick," Ratsy seethed.

"He was baiting you," Luke replied. "Charlie Gorman said he'd kill his own mother if the money were right. I haven't seen Charlie wary of anyone before, but he has more than respect for Arthur Barker. He told me that the difference between Barker and the others is that he's whip-smart."

"And I'm not?"

"Settle down, Ratsy. I know how clever you are. You're my right arm."

"I'll call Cas, and we'll take the pair of bastards out. I haven't visited the foundry for years."

"It's not as easy as that. Twenty-five years ago, CCTV was virtually nonexistent, there were no tollway cameras, computers were in their infancy, and forensics was limited to taking fingerprints and blood samples. The foundry is now surrounded by other factories, many operating around the clock. Besides, after today, if Broderick were to suddenly disappear, who do you think would be the prime suspect? No, hitting them is not an option."

"I never thought I'd see the day when Luke Cramer had cold feet."

"Do you remember when I told Rapidmix's CEO that I'd kill his kids if he didn't supply?"

"Yeah, but you were bluffing. Frightening the shit out of the poor bastard. You never would have done it. Why are you bringing it up now?"

"If you hadn't been so obsessed with Barker, you would have heard Broderick threaten Madison. The difference is that my gut tells me that he'll carry out his threat."

"Jesus! That's why you're on edge."

"Yes. What do you think he's going to do in seven days when I don't meet his demands?" Luke sighed, his hand tapping nervously on the table.

"I dunno. What can he do? I think he's bluffing, like you were."

"I don't. I'm going to get Sally and the kids out of the country. She's always wanted to see Italy's artworks. They can spend a month touring the cathedrals and galleries."

"What about Carlos?"

"He won't go. He's like his old man - too stubborn. Can you get one of your security guys to keep a discreet eye on him?"

"I'll do better than that. I'll get Cas, but I'm telling ya, yar making a big mistake. We should strike first. Once I take out that prick from Sydney, Broderick will shit his pants."

"Ratsy, he's waiting for you. He wants you to make a move. He'll have some of those bikers watching his back. You won't even get close to him. Maybe in a month or so, he'll let his guard down."

"Yeah, but by then, it'll be too late."

"I need to talk to Monty."

As Broderick climbed into the car, he said, "That couldn't have gone better. I thought Ratsch's face was going to burst when you put your hand on his head and shoved him back down."

"Yes, he surprised me. He's not the professional that I thought he was."

"I'm not with you."

"When you do what I do, you have to eliminate emotion. I don't hate anyone, and I never get angry. If I did, it would adversely impact my objectivity and lead to mistakes. It's just a job."

"You're a cold fish."

"I have to be."

"Do you think Ratsch will come after you?"

"Yes. If not now, in seven days when we send them our message."

"You're not worried?"

"Why would I be? He'll make a mistake, probably more than one. He's been out of action for at least ten years. His emotions will cloud his judgment. Think of him as the antelope on Cramer's wall and think of me as a lion, not one of those hyenas."

"I want to send a second message," Broderick said, gripping the steering wheel a little tighter. "There's never been a fatality on a CramerBuild site. Cramer always raises it as the main reason he doesn't need union appointed health and safety officers. That smart-ass Lasik must have run straight to Cramer after Ted beat him up. I'll bet you he got his job back at CramerBuild. Find out whether he did and what site he's working on."

Chapter 58

Seven days had elapsed, and the world hadn't caved in. Luke asked his PA to hold all calls while he pondered his next move. All CramerBuild's sites had been infiltrated, but he was confident that in time he could weed out the unionists, just as he had in the past. There was a sharp knock on his door, and when it opened, his PA was standing next to a courier holding a box. "Sorry, Luke," she said, "the courier says that he has to have your signature."

Luke signed and shook the box. It was weighty, but there was no movement. "It's not a bomb, is it?" He grinned.

"I hope not," the courier said, backing out the door.

"Do you want me to open it, boss?"

"No, it's marked 'personal and confidential.' I'll open it. Shut the door and no more interruptions please. I have to do some serious thinking."

Luke cut through the tape with a pair of scissors and slowly opened the box. He had only been half joking about a bomb. The contents were tightly packed with foam. When he removed the foam, he was staring at a Beretta Cheetah, a shoulder holster, an ankle holster, and an envelope. He tore it open and read, You were warned. He felt sick. He knew whose gun it was. He had gone to so much trouble to get the Beretta after Cas had complained about the Smith & Wesson. He flung the door open and shouted, "Jill, get me Joe on his cellphone."

"Will do, Luke," she said, "but Mr. Beaurepaire's holding for you. He said it's urgent."

Monty fought back the tears as he told Luke that a police insider had called him to say that they'd found Cas's body on the side of a well-used road. No attempt had been made to hide it or make it look like he had been robbed. His wallet, cash, and credit cards were still in his jacket pocket. Strangely, Monty's business card was in his shirt pocket. His fingernails had been torn out. He had a bullet in each kneecap and two in the chest. It had been an agonizing death. The message was clear.

Two hours later, Ratsy sat across the desk from Luke, tears streaming down his cheeks while he slapped the Beretta from hand to hand. "His bed wasn't slept in. He-his car's still in-in the parking garage. The owner of the adjoining penthouse said he saw Cas and two men get into a black Ford. One of them was dressed in biker gear. You should have let me kill that bastard from Sydney. It-it's your fault."

"It's too late for should-haves," Luke said, wiping his eyes. "I knew Broderick was dangerous, but I never thought he'd go this far. I underestimated him."

Jill knocked at the door and asked whether she could get them coffee, but Luke shooed her away saying that they weren't to be disturbed.

"Yeah, and it cost Cas his life. Carlos was home by just after nine last night. Cas would have waited until he was sure Carlos was settled in before heading for his apartment. That asshole must have been waiting for him."

"Don't do anything stupid, Ratsy. They'll be prepared for you."

Ratsy's gun was clearly visible under his tight-fitting suit coat. He hadn't worn the shoulder holster in years, and it pinched his chest. "Stupid? I tell you what was stupid. Letting those bastards live."

"I'm hurting too."

"I loved him," Ratsy said, kneading his hands together with such force that they turned red. "He never did anyone a bad turn and made the world a better place to live in by ridding it of vermin."

"I know he did. Promise me that you won't do anything for forty-eight hours, and that you'll talk to me first. Don't forget you have a wife and two young sons to look after."

"I won't."

"I think you should move Ginger and the boys to a safe location, and Ratsy, I want someone with you at all times. Get your security guards to watch your house around the clock. Position one permanently near the garage roller door."

"I'll think about it. What about you?"

"They're not going to try to hit me, and Sally and the kids are safe in Italy."

"Why are you so sure?"

"I'm too high profile - too big time. There'd be too much media attention, and Broderick doesn't want that."

Chapter 59

On Thursday morning, Luke was at home getting ready to go to Cas's funeral when his cellphone rang. He looked down at the screen, annoyed at seeing it was the Burleigh Heads site office. He had told his project managers to direct their queries to Max Tilson while he was grieving. "Yes. What is it?"

The voice of the site's project manager, Clem Norton, blurted out, "We've had an accident, Mr. Cramer. A death."

"What? What?"

"Adam Lasik fell from the sixteenth floor. He's dead."

Luke felt his chest compress. After he had heard that Adam had been beaten up for defending CramerBuild, he had asked his human relations manager to offer him a job. This was no accident. "I'll be there in thirty minutes. Find out where he lives and if he has a wife and children. I'll need to go see them."

As he sped south along the highway, he called Ratsy and related what had occurred.

"But you're delivering the eulogy," Ratsy protested. "You have to come."

"I can't. You're going to have to do it. Jill's on her way to see you. She has a copy of what I was going to say. If you want to make changes, do so. Alternatively, use your own words. Don't be ashamed to let your passion show, Ratsy."

"I-I-I've never spoken in pub-public before. I-I hope I do-do him justice."

"You will. I wish I could be there. You'll be fine. Good luck," Luke said, finishing the call. *Ratsy's killed at least ten men and is fearless,* he thought, *but he's panicking about speaking to a funeral gathering. Sometimes life is strange.*

Adam Lasik had a wife and three young children. Luke spent three hours with her, offering words of comfort and assuring her that she and the kids would never want for anything. While devastated, she was gracious enough to tell Luke that Adam had said that he was the best employer he'd ever worked for. It gave him no comfort because he knew her husband, an innocent, had been murdered because of him.

Talkback radio jocks milked Lasik's death for all it was worth, attacking corporations who put profits before workers' safety. Enraged listeners called citing their experiences at the hands of unscrupulous, uncaring employers. CramerBuild was pilloried, and callers demanded tougher health and safety laws.

The minister for housing and public works said that his department would conduct an investigation, independent of WorkCover, and that, if there had been breaches of Queensland's laws, the responsible parties would be held to account.

That night Channel 12 televised an interview with a glum-faced Winston Broderick. Dressed in a charcoal gray suit and a black tie, he expressed his sorrow for the widow and what he described as her orphan children. When asked whether CramerBuild was to blame, he looked into the camera and said, "Today is for mourning, not for retribution. Before laying blame, we will have to wait for the investigations to be completed."

"Will the union be investigating?"

"Definitely."

"Have you spoken to the union's on-site health and safety officer?"

"I'm afraid that's not possible."

"Why?"

"The union is not involved in the appointment of CramerBuild's health and safety officers," Broderick said, slowly shaking his head. "The company has refused our offers of help."

The journalist's face clouded over, and she rolled her eyes. "Why is that?"

"The company doesn't like dealing with the union."

"Is that because you enforce stricter safety standards?"

"Perhaps. I honestly can't say. Sorry," he said, wiping his eyes with a tissue. "It's really hit me hard."

"I can see that. Just a few more questions. Had there been a union appointed health and safety officer, could this tragedy have been avoided?"

"I don't know. I can say that we would have insisted that Mr. Lasik wear a safety harness."

The journalist gasped. "He wasn't wearing a safety harness?"

"I've been informed that he was not."

Luke seethed as he watched. Broderick was a master of innuendo. Why would it be necessary for Adam Lasik to wear a safety harness? He was a floor tiler. Luke turned the television off, called Monty, and arranged to meet with him.

Chapter 60

Monty was in his early seventies and had retired but still sat on several boards. He opened the front door of his Hamilton mansion and led Luke along the corridor to the study. "Bourbon?" he asked.

"Thanks."

"I knew you'd call. Winston Broderick is a formidable opponent. He's nothing like the jailbirds who've headed the BLMU in the past, even though he's more ruthless."

"He's employed a Sydney hitman. They murdered Cas, and they killed one of my workers. - dressed it up as an accident, but it was murder."

"I thought the foundry might come back to haunt you one day."

Luke couldn't hide his surprise. "You knew?"

"Of course."

"But you never said anything."

"No matter what you did, I owed you. I didn't want to know the specifics. I knew you were a good man, and that was enough for me to look the other way. Nonetheless, you shouldn't have taken the law into your own hands. Now the wheel has turned a full circle, and you're under it."

"That's not true. There's a huge difference between what I did and what they're doing. I've never taken an innocent life."

"Cas was an innocent?" Monty said, shaking his head. "Would you say the same if something happened to Ratsy?"

"You're no help."

"Oh, but I am. I had a long talk with Ratsy at the wake today. He was raging, but I managed to calm him down. I–"

"Sorry, I didn't mean what I said. Thanks," Luke interrupted.

"Let me finish. I managed to slow him down because I came up with a plan that, hopefully, might restore order without anyone else being killed. He's not totally convinced and is still full of murderous intent. If you talk to him, he might come onboard."

"Let's hear it, Monty."

More than twenty percent of the workers on CramerBuild's Creek Street Brisbane site had joined the BLMU. Luke drove onto the site and parked. Ratsy was waiting for him at the door to the site office. They exchanged greetings, and then Ratsy shouted, "You cheapskate. Pay me what you owe me, and I'll go."

"I'll pay you what you're entitled to. If you want to go back to Chicago, that's your business."

"You're a piece of work. You make sure your family's safe overseas, but Melbourne's good enough for mine. You try to cheat me, and you'll regret it. Write me a check for half a million, and you'll not see me again."

"Half a million?" Luke laughed scornfully. "Half a million? Why? You're not entitled to anywhere near that."

"You're a greedy bastard with a short memory. Do you think you'd be a billionaire without me? I made you."

"You can't be serious. When I went back to Chicago, I had my choice of the best men. I chose you because I felt sorry for you. What did that guy call you? Little Ratsy. He sure got that right."

"You asshole," Ratsy snarled, grabbing Luke by the shirt.

In one swift movement, Luke grasped Ratsy's shoulders, spun him around, and hurled him into the side of the site office. "I can smell the booze on your breath!" he shouted. "Go home and sleep it off. You can apologize to me in the morning and consider yourself lucky to still have a job."

Most of the men within hearing distance had stopped working and were watching and listening in astonishment. "It's not a holiday!" Luke yelled at them as he watched Ratsy storm off the site.

Winston Broderick had some huge deals on his plate, but he didn't overlook the smaller matters. He made sure that Zoe, his new PA, sent a large wreath to Cas Herrera's funeral, and the union published a small bereavement notice. She would send an even larger wreath to Adam Lasik's funeral. Neither had been union members, but Broderick wanted to send a message in the case of Herrera while showing his supposed caring side in respect for Lasik.

He had already ticked the box next to CramerBuild, but he knew that it would probably take a few more months and many more site visits before he had closed shops across the board. The next major project was the merger with – make that the takeover of – the WWU. He knew that no conservative government would endorse a 300,000-strong union; after all, it was four times the size of the Australian Defence Force.

Nor would the Labor Party be clapping and cheering him on. The difference was that the BLMU was, by far, the Labor Party's and the Greens' biggest donor, and if the tap were turned off, both socialist parties would struggle. On the other hand, the BLMU had the capacity to increase its donations by fivefold which would allow the left-aligned parties to far outspend the NewsCorp backed conservatives.

The first move that Broderick made was to draft an email to the president of the Labor Party to advise him that the BLMU was going to immediately cease making political donations. He knew that those heading the party would be outraged and bluff and bluster, but in the end, they would come begging to him. He smiled as he hit send. It was a play straight from the NRA playbook, and unless the Labor Party consented to the merger, he would not only withhold donations, he would also threaten to redirect them to the conservatives.

It would be an idle threat because he could achieve his goals only if a socialist government were elected, but he knew they wouldn't dare call his bluff. Within three years, he intended to control political nominations and the Labor Party. He would be more powerful than any king. He would be the king maker and, if necessary, the king breaker.

Chapter 61

Ratsy didn't like doctors and disliked hypodermics even more. He looked at the doctor, gritted his teeth, and said, "Let's get it over with, Doc."

Thirty minutes later, he entered Brisbane Firearms, produced the license Monty had obtained online, took out his credit card, and said, "I'm Joe Ratsch, I ordered the 10-shot Ruger pistol."

It was midday when he got back to Southport. He entered CramerBuild's offices, caught the elevator to the fourth floor, and, without knocking, entered Luke's office. Within minutes, angry voices could be heard, and then Ratsy flung the door open and shouted, "All I want is what's fair."

"You're not in Chicago now. They call what you want extortion here. I haven't backed down from the unions. I'm not going to back down from you."

"I should put a bullet in your worthless head."

"That's it." Luke said, "You're fired. You have thirty minutes to pack your personal stuff and get off the premises. Jill, get someone from HR to go to Mr. Ratsch's office. Tell them to make sure that he just takes personal stuff."

"You low dog - after all I've done for you."

"And Jill, tell HR to add a month's pay to his final entitlement. Maybe that'll stop his whining," Luke said, slamming his door.

Ratsy took two steps forward and kicked it, leaving a large dent in the bottom.

"Come on, Joe," Jill said, "before you get yourself in trouble."

Arthur Barker came out from the Fortitude Valley hairdresser's having just had a trim. He jumped into his car and pushed the starter. There was no sound. The car had run perfectly up until now.

Suspicious of anything outside the norm, he climbed gingerly out and looked under the chassis.

He breathed a sigh of relief when he saw there were no packages or attachments. He had heard the stories about Ratsy going completely mental and knew it wasn't beyond the mad bastard to put a bomb under his car.

When he called the union, he was told to stay with the car until a tow truck came to return it to the dealer and then to grab a cab. It was a typical, beautiful Queensland day and only a twenty-five-minute walk to the offices. When he got back, there was a message waiting for him. The dealer's service department had called to apologize and say the problem was a loose wire, and the car was already on the way back to him.

On Friday night, Luke took Max Tilson and the other project managers to dinner at Harry's. It had been a tough week for everyone, particularly those who had known Cas and Adam. Unfortunately, the private dining room was already booked, but there was nothing private to talk about so Luke wasn't worried.

The restaurant was doing a raging business, and they could hardly hear themselves talk over the din. Within about thirty minutes, the alcohol kicked in, and some of the managers started to lose their inhibitions. "What's the story with Ratsy?" Max asked.

"Simple," Luke replied. "Sadly, the company outgrew him. The job got too big. Let that be a lesson to all of you. It is better not to promote than to over promote."

"But you were so close for so long," another manager said.

Luke was about to respond when there was a commotion at the front, and a drunken, angry Ratsy staggered toward them. "You bastard," he shouted, and the restaurant went quiet.

Luke got to his feet and said, "You're drunk, Ratsy. Don't do anything that you'll regret."

"Oh, I won't regret anything," Ratsy said, drawing the Ruger with a trembling hand and placing the barrel on Luke's forehead. "Goodbye, you penny-pinching asshole."

Tables and chairs went everywhere as patrons rushed to get out. "Don't do it, Ratsy. Don't do it," Max Tilson begged.

"Ratsy, I've called the police!" Harry shouted. "You better get out while you still can."

"Yeah," one of the managers said.

The wail of sirens could be heard in the distance, and Ratsy glanced out to the street.

"You got lucky this time, asshole. Next time you won't be," Ratsy said, staggering toward the door. "Pay me what you owe me or die."

"He needs to be locked up and the key thrown away," Max said.

"Yeah," Harry agreed.

"He's been a loyal friend of mine. He's going through some rough times. We need to cut him some slack."

"Jesus, he would've killed you if he hadn't heard the cops' sirens," Max said, as two policemen entered the restaurant. "Don't tell me you're not going to lay charges."

"I'm not," Luke said, "and I don't want you to say anything."

"Others saw it," Max replied. "They're going to tell the cops."

Chapter 62

Ratsy had overstepped the mark, and he knew the cops would come looking for him. There was one place where he was confident they wouldn't think of looking. He drove straight to Cas's apartment building, parked around the corner, put on a pair of sunglasses, and pulled his collar up around his face before entering the foyer. There was an eeriness to being in his friend's penthouse. Memories of the good times flooded back, and he was struck with an overwhelming sadness.

News of the fallout between Luke and Ratsy was common knowledge in the building industry, and Winston Broderick had been following every fracas. He shoved the clutter on his desk to one side and shouted at Zoe to bring him a cup of coffee. Sitting opposite him, Arthur said, "You're driving yourself into the ground. Why don't you slow down?"

"Slow down? You just don't get it, do you? Time is of the essence. If we're going to take over the WWU, we need to prove we can deliver. That means getting our members a three-hundred-dollar-a-week pay increase and, more importantly, bringing Luke Cramer to heel. It also means getting it done pronto. If Cramer weren't around, I could lean on the other builders to agree to the wage increase."

"You want me to hit Cramer?"

Broderick sighed. He had been told that Arthur was smart. He'd obviously been lied to. "Of course not. That would lead straight to me, even though the thought of doing it and framing Ratsy crossed my mind. It's too hard. We'd have to make sure he didn't have an alibi. It's messy. I still think we might be able to use Ratsy and kill two birds with one stone."

"Go on."

"From all we've heard, Ratsy is desperate for cash, desperate to

274

return to Chicago, and hates Cramer. What if I offered Ratsy half a million to take him out?"

"I don't like it."

"Why? You told me that Ratsy's a lunatic, a loose cannon. His recent stunts confirm your opinion."

"What if it's all an act? What if they're trying to set you up? If Ratsy says yes, he'll demand half the money in advance and once you make the transfer, they'll be able to prove you ordered the hit."

"Arthur, you have a lot to learn about international banking. The transfer will be made from one numbered account that I have no connection with to another numbered account."

"What if Ratsy's wearing a wire when you make your proposition?"

"You can't wear a wire in a steam bath." Broderick laughed. "Ratsy will kill Cramer. The murder will point right to him. The cops will nail him, and he'll be sent away for life. We save two hundred and fifty thousand and then make sure CramerBuild is split up and sold to builders friendly to us. It's perfect, and what a message it'll send to the WWU. Get Ratsy's number. I want to call him."

Chapter 63

It was midday on Saturday, and Creek Street was surprisingly quiet. Broderick easily parked in front of the steam rooms. Fifteen minutes later, Arthur Barker parked in the space in front of the Mercedes. He paid no attention to the old white van parked three vehicles behind him. Turning to Maguire, he said, "I don't like it, Red. Something stinks."

"What can possibly go wrong? We'll make sure Ratsy's clean, and we'll be right out the front. You worry too much, Arthur."

A few minutes later, a man who looked like a deadbeat staggered toward them. "That's him."

Ratsy was unshaven, his eyes were red, and he looked like he'd slept in his clothes.

"And to think he was once feared," Maguire said, getting out of the car. "Hey, Ratsy, we gotta frisk you before you go inside."

Maguire patted him down and said, "He's clean."

Barker was far more thorough. "You're clean, but you stink, Ratsy. You're a disgrace to our profession. Get inside," he said, shoving Ratsy toward the door.

The attendant behind the counter saw what had happened on the sidewalk, and when Ratsy entered, he handed him a towel and a locker key, saying, "The changing rooms are along the corridor. Mr. Broderick is in steam room number two. You won't be disturbed."

Ratsy was immediately hit by the heat. "Bloody hell," he said.

There were three rows of wooden benches, and Broderick was sitting on the top one stark naked. He wasn't carrying an ounce of extra weight, and the perspiration accentuated his rippling stomach muscles. "Not quite," he said. "Drop the towel, Ratsy. There's no room for modesty in here, and I want to make sure there's nothing hidden underneath. Then you can come up here."

Ratsy did as he was told. Over the years his shoulders had never widened, but his stomach had, and his body was triangular. "What's this about?" he asked. "You said you might have some money for me. Why?"

"First things first," Broderick said, turning up the steam. "How's your relationship with Luke Cramer these days?"

"That cheating bastard. After all I've done for him, he still screwed me."

"Do you hate him?"

"What do you think? If someone you trusted screwed you out of half a million, wouldn't you hate him? Yeah, I hate him to the point where I feel sick in the gut," Ratsy said, wiping the sweat from his eyes. "Can you turn that thing down?"

"It'll do you good. You look like you've been doing it hard."

"I've been sleeping rough. The cops are chasing me. The heat will die down in a few weeks."

"I heard you want to go back to Chicago."

"Yeah. Look, can you get to the point? I'm not gonna be able to stay in here much longer."

"Do you hate Cramer enough to kill him?"

"I go to sleep every night thinking about it."

"Good. If I were to offer you half a million dollars to eliminate him, would you be interested?"

"I can't get near him."

"Oh, Ratsy, you're not thinking. You've known him for nigh on forty years. Are you telling me that he wouldn't meet you if you called and said you wanted to apologize for the turmoil you've put him through?"

"You're right. I didn't think, but why me? You had Cas killed and got that poor bastard shoved off the sixteenth floor of the Burleigh Heads Towers. Why don't you use the same people for Cramer?"

"Arthur and Red could never get close enough to him."

"They killed Cas and the other guy?"

"Yeah, they killed Herrera, but someone else pushed Adam Lasik. You understand it wasn't personal. It was just business."

"Yeah, but you were the brains behind the killings."

"Yes." Broderick smiled. "Nothing happens without my

imprimatur. Since we're talking about killings, how did you get rid of those two thugs' bodies all those years ago? Ace Cordy, and I can't remember the other guy's name. Did you dump them in the ocean?"

"I dunno what you're talking about."

"Oh, is that how you want to play it? Tell me you didn't kill Councilor John Wiese."

"I don't recollect the name," Ratsy replied.

"Have it your way. Are you interested in my proposition?"

"Yes. How are you going to pay me?"

"Half up front, and the balance as soon as it's confirmed that Cramer is dead. Do you have an offshore bank account?"

"Is the pope a Catholic?"

"Good. Let's meet here again tomorrow. Same time. Bring your bank account details," Broderick said, holding out his hand.

"I gotta get out of here," Ratsy said, ignoring the extended hand. "I'm melting."

"That's what happens when you get old and soft. Take a cold shower, and you'll feel fine."

Ratsy skipped the shower and made his way quickly out to the street. The black Ford and its occupants were still there. The white van had gone.

Chapter 64

Broderick lay naked in the steam room pondering the meeting. It was hard to believe that the small rotund man was a professional hitman. There was something about the conversation that disturbed him, but he couldn't put his finger on it.

He slowly replayed it, and then it struck him. He had admitted to having Herrera and Lasik killed and had offered Ratsy half a million to kill Cramer, but Ratsy had not admitted to killing anyone. Broderick realized that it was the type of conversation you'd have when you were wearing a wire but didn't want to incriminate yourself. But how? It was impossible.

Nonetheless, he ran from the steam room to the changing room, took his cellphone from the locker, and called Arthur. There were half a dozen men in various stages of undress. "Arthur," he said quietly, "pick up our friend. I don't know how, but I think I might have been taped. Find out what you can."

There was a long pause as he listened to Arthur's response.

"Good. There's no time to waste. Yes, the same treatment as Herrera."

When Arthur told his boss that Ratsy was still in sight, he had understandably sounded relieved. There was no hurry. Arthur pulled out slowly, anxious to avoid drawing any attention to himself. A few minutes later, he pulled up next to Ratsy; Maguire jumped out of the car, trying to conceal the gun in his hand, and said, "Get in the car. Front seat."

"What th–"

"Now," Maguire said, shoving the gun into Ratsy's ribs.

As Ratsy climbed into the car, Arthur leveled his pistol at him. "Don't do anything stupid. Red is sitting behind you with a gun pressed into the seat. Try anything, and you're dead."

"What is this?"

"Boss's orders. He thinks you set him up."

"He's mad. What are you going to do? Where are we going?"

"To the hinterland," Barker replied. "You have ninety minutes left to live. If you tell us what we want to know, we'll make it quick. If you don't, you'll go the same way as your friend."

"Yeah," Red said, "when we pulled his fingernails out, he cried like a little girl."

"But he never told us how you got rid of the bodies," Barker said, with a tone of begrudging respect. "Not even after we shot him in the kneecaps. You will, and you'll tell us if you were taping the boss."

"Are you mad? How could I tape him? I was naked. Jesus, Arthur, give me a break. We're in the same business."

"Boss's orders, Ratsy. It's nothing personal. Do you have a last wish?" Barker asked.

"Can I have a cigarette?"

"I don't see why not. No funny business. Red's itching to pull the trigger."

Ratsy took two deep drags and lunged forward in a violent coughing fit.

Barker smirked. "Camels a bit too strong for you, Ratsy? What do you smoke? Menthols?"

Ratsy sat upright, his eyes watering, and took another drag. "Very funny. It went down the wrong way. That's all."

"Look out the window," Maguire said. "This really is God's country. Make the most of your last few minutes."

Ratsy sucked hard on the cigarette and again broke out coughing, this time a little longer than before.

"Weak as piss," Maguire said.

The traffic thinned as they turned off the highway and started up into the hinterland. "Can I have another cigarette?" Ratsy asked.

"It's worth it to see you cough and splutter everywhere," Barker said. "You have fifteen minutes to finish it."

"I won't cough this time."

Two minutes later, Ratsy lurched forward, only restrained by his seat belt, and coughed intensely. Nearly a minute elapsed before he raised his head.

Barker slowed the car, and it was obvious that he was looking for a side track. "Not long now, Ratsy," he said, swinging off the road before coming to a stop, half a mile along a dirt track. "Are you going to talk, or do I need the pliers? Were you taping the boss?"

"Your friend squealed, but he was tough." Maguire laughed. "Made us change our methods. If ya don't talk, we'll burn your eyes out."

"I'll talk, but before I die, let me have one last puff," Ratsy said, taking an enormous drag on the last inch of his cigarette.

As the coughing and spluttering started, Barker said, "Bad move."

"Not really," Ratsy said, sitting up, his Smith & Wesson in hand. The first bullet killed Barker, and in one lightning move, Ratsy released three rounds through the seat at Maguire. When he opened the rear door, Maguire had a bullet in the thigh and two in the stomach. He was still moaning. Ratsy flicked the trunk open, removed the first aid kit, and started bandaging Maguire's wounds.

"What-what are you doing?" Maguire moaned.

"I don't want you to bleed out," Ratsy snarled. "I'm gonna torch the car and you're gonna burn alive. You can think about what you did to Cas as you fry, you lowlife bastard."

"No, no."

Ratsy reached under the seat and found the spare magazine and the burner phone. He flicked it on and punched 666. There was only one saved number.

"Are you all right?" Luke answered on his burner.

"Yeah, it's done, but it's messy. Evidence everywhere. I'm going to torch the car."

"Replace the magazine. Then leave the gun in the car. Hang on to the burner phone and the other magazine. We'll get rid of them on the way to the airport."

"I know what to do, Luke."

"Where are you?"

"According to the SatNav, I'm on Boggy Creek Road, but it's no road. It's a dirt track. I doubt there's another living soul within a five-mile radius."

"Drive the car as deeply into the bush as you can and stay out of sight. Don't torch it until I'm there."

"Shit! Can you get a move on then?"

"Why? It doesn't matter when you set it alight."

"Yes, it does," Ratsy said, as he watched the color draining from Maguire's face.

There was no sign of the car or Ratsy when Luke drove one of the company's SUVs along the track. Then the little man came out from the bushes and waved. "The tank is full, and I've stuffed a shirt in it," he shouted. "Are you ready to go?" He didn't mention that Maguire was still alive.

"I want to make sure it explodes before we leave, Ratsy. Light the shirt, and then I'll pull over under that old gum tree a hundred yards down the track."

Two minutes later, there was a bloodcurdling scream, a whoosh, and flames shot high into the sky.

"They were still alive?" Luke gasped.

"Just the bastard who tortured Cas," Ratsy snarled. "I wish we had have had more time. I would've made him really suffer."

"I can't think of a worse way to die. You did good, Ratsy. Let's go," Luke said. When he reached the junction, he turned right and headed higher into the hinterland.

"Where are you going?"

"I don't want to backtrack. I didn't see anyone, but why run the risk? We don't have to worry about how long it takes to get to the airport. Monty has the pilot on standby, and the Lear's fueled and ready to go. You'll be with your family in Melbourne in time for dinner. You were magnificent, Ratsy."

"If it hadn't been for Monty, I'd be where those two suckers are. He missed his calling in life. He would have made a great master criminal." Ratsy grinned.

"I wouldn't tell him that. He never let on that he knew what we were doing over the years. I think he can live with that. Being part of it is something altogether different."

"How did the recording go?"

"Clear as a bell."

Chapter 65

Winston Broderick paced his office nervously. He was a control freak and hated not knowing what had happened. He knew something had gone wrong when he called Barker and Maguire on their cellphones after he left the steam baths, and his calls went straight through to voicemail.

The day after the police woke him at six in the morning to say that two hikers had found Barker's burned out car and two bodies, one of whom they suspected was Barker. It wasn't long before forensics confirmed that Arthur Barker and Red Maguire had been shot. Three pistols, all with full magazines, were found, but they were too badly melted to be of any forensic use.

Broderick knew what had happened but didn't understand how. How could Ratsch have gotten the better of Arthur and Red? He had even tried to call Ratsch, but the service was disconnected. What had happened that Saturday afternoon?

When police interrogated him, he denied having any knowledge of what had occurred, saying that the last time he had seen them was at the union's office on Saturday morning.

Eight days had elapsed since the bodies were found, and Luke Cramer was being interviewed on Channel 8's *Australian Week*, hosted by probing journalist Ellen Langton. The focus of the one-hour program was the success of a prominent member of the community. The subject could be a doctor, politician, social worker, lawyer, businessperson, or other pillar of society.

It was soft journalism that allowed the interviewees to boast about their achievements and the interviewer to fawn over them. Broderick would watch it but didn't expect to learn anything.

Luke heard the producer counting down from ten, and Ellen

Langton say, "I'm pleased to introduce one of Queensland's and Australia's greatest success stories. Give it up for Luke Cramer."

"Thank you, Ellen."

"Let's go back to the start. Why did you leave Chicago to come to the Gold Coast?" Langton asked, her spectacles midway down her pointed nose.

Wearing jeans and an open-necked shirt, Luke stretched his long legs and ran his hand through a full mop of gray hair. Then he picked up the jug of water on the table between them and poured himself a glass. "I was young and vacationing with my wife and son. We spent a few weeks here and fell in love with the place."

"And?"

"I saw an opportunity to make some money, so I arranged a two-year visa, and I'm still here thirty years later." Luke smiled, accentuating the furrows in his weather-beaten brow. "I've had a lot of luck, and Australia's been good to me."

"You've also had your share of bad luck. You lost your high school sweetheart, Kiara to bone cancer shortly after you arrived here."

Luke's relaxed demeanor abruptly changed, and his steely blue eyes stared straight through Langton. Through tightly compressed lips, he said, "I thought we agreed not to go there. I don't like getting bushwhacked."

"I-I-I'm sorry," Langton replied without sincerity. "Carlos was only eight. It must have been difficult bringing him up as a sole parent."

"Next question," Luke growled, peering over the top of his glasses and shaking his head.

"You married Carlos's teacher Sally, in 1996, and have another three children. Have they shown any interest in the company?"

"They're still young. Lloyd wants to be a pilot. Trent wants to study psychiatry. I think he sees me as his main client. Oh, and just in case you didn't get it, that's a joke."

"I've heard that Madison is your favorite. Has she shown any interest in the business?"

"I don't have favorites, but yes, I'm proud of Madison. She's a straight A student, and I'm pleased to say she loves the business. It's still early days though."

"How does Carlos get on with your other children?"

"He loves them of course, but there's a huge age gap. He's only eighteen years younger than I am, and I sometimes look at him as a brother rather than a son. Ellen. I think that's enough about my family."

"All right. You've been very successful - a mansion in Surfers Paradise, another in Hawaii, a super yacht, and a Gulfstream. Are you a billionaire?"

"I have no idea, Ellen, but I want to correct you." Luke laughed. "The yacht and plane are owned by the company and used by its executives and staff. They're tools to promote the business, not personal toys."

Langton shook her head and smirked. "I suppose I should be grateful that you didn't tell me your twenty-million-dollar mansion is owned by the company. Some say it's the most expensive house in Queensland."

"No, I own it, but let me assure you, I didn't pay twenty million for it."

"I'm sure you didn't. You run and own one of the country's largest private companies, and I know you've had countless offers from merchant bankers to take it public. Have you been tempted?"

"Not in the slightest. I like keeping my cards close to my chest. As the CEO of a private company, I don't have to make announcements to the stock exchange or talk to the media or stockbrokers, nor do I have to appoint new directors at the insistence of institutional shareholders who'd add nothing to the bottom line and waste my executives' time. CramerBuild will remain private during my lifetime."

"When you retire, or, if, God forbid, something happens to you, will Carlos take the reins?"

"Probably. He knows the business backwards, but if I last another twenty years, it might be something he doesn't want. If that's the case, perhaps Madison will take over, or it might be one of my executives. There's nothing in my playbook that says the next CEO has to have the surname Cramer."

"You have the reputation of being a hard man. You've always had an acrimonious relationship with the unions. Why is that? Your competitors don't seem to have your problems."

A scowl crossed Luke's face, and he bit his lip. "One union, and it would take far too long to explain why my competitors don't have problems. Let's just say I don't do sweetheart deals."

"You're fighting the BLMU over the appointment of health and safety officers on your sites. Aren't you concerned about the safety of your workers? After all, one of your employees was killed in a terrible accident. Don't you support the recent changes to the health and safety legislation?"

"Of course, I'm concerned, and I support the legislation. However, the unions were dying before it was introduced, membership was declining rapidly, and the unions saw an opportunity to use the legislation to control and disrupt construction sites. Their members would create false safety breaches to allow the unions to come onto sites and stir up trouble."

Langton raised her eyebrows and said, "Aren't you exaggerating? It's a fundamental duty of unions to look after the health and safety of their members. As I said, your competitors don't have a problem with it."

A broad grin crossed Luke's face. "Ah, Ellen, that's union propaganda," he said, taking a piece of paper from his pocket and reading from it. "Federal court judges and a royal commissioner have described the BLMU's conduct as disgraceful, illegal, and criminal, so no, I'm not exaggerating. This union makes Jimmy Hoffa and the Teamsters look like choirboys."

Langton's thin face was bright red, and she crossed and uncrossed her legs. She wasn't accustomed to being talked down to. "Your father supported the Democrats and was an active member of the United Steelworkers. You're a supporter of the Liberal Party, Australia's equivalent of the Republicans, and you've been a fierce critic of the Labor Party. Do you think he'd be proud of you?"

"We introduced the pension for our workers long before it was legislated, and we have no limit on the payment of sick leave where the illness is genuine. Dad was all about workers being paid a fair day's wage for a fair day's work, and, if he were alive today, God bless his soul, there's no way he'd support the Labor Party which thinks the path to equality is paved by handouts. Yes, I think my father would be proud, and if he were working for me, I'm fairly sure he'd see there was no need to join a union."

"Up until very recently, there had never been a fatal accident or life-threatening injury on any CramerBuild site. Did you let your standards slip with the death of Adam Lasik?"

Luke pushed himself back in his chair and pursed his lips. "Adam's death was no accident, Ellen. He was murdered on the orders of the secretary of the BLMU."

Gasps permeated the auditorium. "You can't make wild statements like that," Langton said, totally blindsided by the response.

"I have proof," Luke said, pulling out his smartphone. "You're about to hear the voice of BLMU secretary Winston Broderick confessing to the murders of Adam Lasik and Cas Herrera. You'll also hear him offer to pay half a million dollars to have me killed."

Cries of "no" and "that's terrible" came from the audience. Ellen Langton should have gone to a break, but like the audience, she was caught up in the moment. For the next five minutes, you could have heard a pin drop as the voices of Broderick and Ratsy echoed around the auditorium.

"I don't understand. It's common knowledge that you and Mr. Ratsch had a terrible falling out."

"An act, Ellen. Mr. Ratsch has broken no laws, and he and I remain as close as ever. He risked his life to get that recording. He's a brave man."

"Why didn't you take it to the police? Why play it on national television?"

"There's more than one way to skin a snake. Since Mr. Broderick was appointed secretary of the BLMU, he has met and courted senior officers of the police force. I didn't take the tape to the police because I didn't know who I could trust. My lawyers are delivering a copy to the chief commissioner in the morning."

"I think you meant cat."

"No, I meant snake."

"Are you suggesting that police corruption in Queensland has risen to the levels experienced before the Fitzjohn Royal Commission?"

"No, but there are some rotten eggs who need to be weeded out."

"Do your revelations have anything to do with the murders of Arthur Barker and Red Maguire?

"Not that I know of," Luke said, resting his chin in his hand. "Perhaps, they were also on Winston Broderick's hit list."

"I'm sure you have much more to tell us, but we've already run ten minutes overtime. I don't know about you folks in the audience, but I'm spent. Thank you for a sensational *Australian Week*, Luke Cramer. Next week my guest is Father Michael O'Brien, and we'll be discussing the magnificent contribution he has made to alleviating starvation in Sudan."

Broderick sat in the study of his New Farm home and stared out at the in-ground pool. He silently cursed. The incompetents, Arthur and Red had let him down. Why had he trusted them? He didn't know how he had been tricked and didn't care. His life was over. He would be imprisoned and never get to see Pia and Oliver grow up. Anger surged through him as he imagined seeing Cramer's smirking face as he was hauled off to prison. Well, he'd not let Cramer have that satisfaction. He marched down the hallway to the bathroom, took a huge handful of sleeping tablets from the cabinet, and strode back to his study where a bottle of Johnnie Walker and a glass awaited him. Even in the face of death his arrogance was greater than his fear.

Chapter 66

When Ratsy returned from Melbourne, the police interrogated him at his home and took possession of the Ruger. It had never been fired. "Why did you buy the pistol, Mr. Ratsch?" the detective asked.

"It was all part of the act to create the impression that Mr. Cramer and I had become mortal enemies."

"To flush Mr. Broderick out?"

"Yes."

"Do you feel any guilt about his suicide?"

"Why would I?"

"He shot himself because of your recording."

"Don't try to hang that on me. He took his own life because he murdered two innocent men."

"You've never murdered anyone?" the detective smirked.

"Never."

"He had two small children."

"I feel sorry for them."

"When was the last time you saw Arthur Barker and Red Maguire?"

"I honestly can't remember - a long time ago."

"Can you account for your movements on the afternoon of Saturday, July 16?"

"I thought you might ask." Ratsy grinned. "I was at the steam baths with Mr. Broderick until 1:30. The attendant will confirm that. I then went to Mr. Beaurepaire's apartment in The Meridien where we had a few drinks and watched the Gold Coast Suns play the Richmond Tigers. It was a great game. The last quarter had just started when Mr. Cramer picked me up and drove me to the airport. I boarded Mr. Beaurepaire's Lear jet which immediately took off for Melbourne. I can tell you every play in the Gold Coast game for the first three quarters."

"As if that proves anything," the detective said. "You could have watched the replay."

"Very astute, Detective, but I couldn't create the steam bath attendant, Mr. Beaurepaire, Mr. Cramer, or the pilot."

"The whole business is just a little too pat for my liking."

Ratsy frowned. "I hope you're not one of the policemen who Mr. Cramer was talking about on *Australian Week*."

"No, I'm not," the detective said, getting abruptly to his feet. "Thank you for your time, Mr. Ratsch. We'll be in touch if anything else arises."

"Always pleased to help," Ratsy said.

Luke and Monty were sitting on Luke's veranda sipping whiskeys when Ratsy joined them. He hugged Monty tightly and said, "I owe you my life. Why did you think Broderick might see through me? If that gun hadn't been planted under the seat of Barker's car, I wouldn't be here."

"I didn't," Monty said, "it was just insurance."

"Why do you think he suspected me?"

"He was very smart, and if you listen carefully to the recording, it's obvious. He admits everything, and you don't even fess up to so much as a parking ticket." Monty laughed. "Your acting and deception skills need work."

"Oh, I wouldn't say that, Monty," Luke butted in. "Max Tilson still can't believe Ratsy's performance at Harry's was an act. He wants to nominate him for an Oscar."

"Ah, but that was a role far more suited to his talents."

"Are you two quite finished?" Ratsy said. "When can I get this thing out of my arm, Monty?"

"The transmitter? It's tiny, and it's harmless. My doctor friend said it will dissolve in time."

"Yeah, that's what he told me too. In the meantime, you can listen to all my conversations. No thanks. I want it removed."

"Ratsy, Ratsy," Monty said, "don't you understand anything about wireless technology?"

"No, and I don't want to. Call him, Monty, and set up another appointment. I want it gone."

"Okay, will do. Luke, where do you think Broderick fell over?"

"We were lucky," Luke said. "Overconfidence killed him. He was charismatic, smart, cunning, and lusted for power. He was like another fanatic who started the Second World War. Thank God, they only come along once in a generation."

"What do you think the BLMU will do now, Luke?" Monty asked.

"They'll revert to the norm. They'll appoint a tough guy as secretary whose muscles will be far bigger than his brain. I think the executive members were overwhelmed by Broderick and all but lost the influence they once had. They're not going to let that happen again. I've instructed our HR department to let the unionists know that they can stay in the union, but they can't work for CramerBuild."

"Won't they cause trouble?"

"They might have, but everyone on the street knows what my industrial relations and security manager did. They're petrified. No, they won't cause trouble. Here's to Ratsy," Luke said, clinking glasses.

"You've never told me why you hate the unions," Monty said.

"I don't. I think there are some great unions that are good for their members, good for their industry, and good for the economy. I think Bob Hawke was a great prime minister, maybe Australia's greatest. It's just that I've never run across a decent union in the building industry. Kiara used to tell me that it was an industry, no matter where it was, which was run by criminals. She was right."

"Do you see yourself as a criminal?"

"Yes, but I'm more like Robin Hood than Al Capone." Luke laughed.

"Monty, with your brains you could have been a master criminal," Ratsy said. "I can see you as the Godfather."

"I'm too old for this." Monty replied. "I've never condoned violence, never will. Luke, it's thirty years since you saved my life. Can we call the debt square?"

"There was never a debt, but if there were, you repaid it twentyfold."

Sally came onto the veranda and said, "What are you talking about?"

"Just business, honey."

"You're always talking business."

The End

FREE DOWNLOAD

FOG CITY FRAUD

Why is an irate investor holding his advisor's receptionist hostage on the 16th level of a high-rise building?

Sign up for Peter Ralph's reader's group and get your FREE copy of the eBook Fog City Fraud: a financial suspense thriller.

Visit here to get started:
http://www.peterralphbooks.com/

Other Books By Peter Ralph

More white-collar crime suspense thrillers
by Peter Ralph are on the drawing board.

For updates about new releases, as well as exclusive
promotions, visit the author's website and sign up for the
VIP mailing list at http://www.peterralphbooks.com/